THE QUEST

VICTOR ATYAS

ISBN 978-1-957220-06-2 (paperback)
ISBN 978-1-957220-07-9 (digital)

Rushmore Press LLC
1 800 460 9188
www.rushmorepress.com

Printed in the United States of America

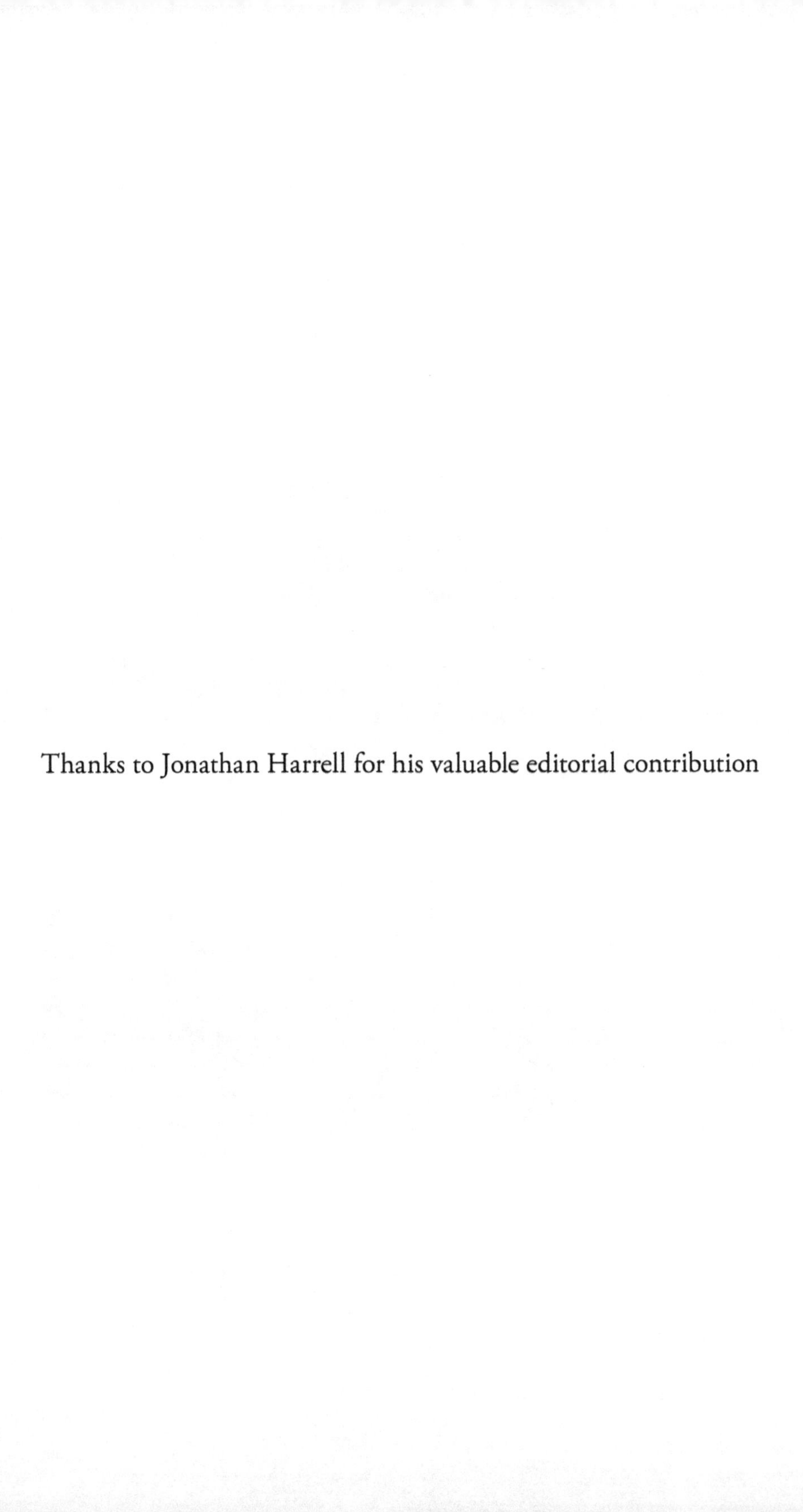

Thanks to Jonathan Harrell for his valuable editorial contribution

PROLOGUE

This sunny August afternoon, Paul Theroux lay on a recliner under a Chestnut tree, a book in his hand. He wore faded jeans, felt sandals, and a corduroy long-sleeved shirt. A swarm of bees hovered over a nearby bush of Bougainville. In the far distance, Mt. Olympus' craggy peaks shone above a cover of thick clouds.

Standing some fifteen feet in front of him, I prayed to the gods that my unannounced visit wouldn't sour his mood. A dog barked. Mr. Theroux let go of the book, stared at me, and grumbled, "Who are you? What do you want?"

"I am Adam, from Santa Fe, New Mexico. Three months ago, I mailed you a letter in care of your publisher. Not having received a reply, I decided to come in person to—"

"A letter about what?" he interrupted.

"About my enjoyment reading your *My Secret History* and *Milroy the Magician.*"

"Hm . . . no one is supposed to know I am here. How did you find me?"

"Moses, an old friend, told me that you come here to heal your soul and body, and to consort with living and dead writers and philosophers."

Frowning, he continued, "You appeared out of thin air."

"Indeed, I did. I hitched a ride on that gray cloud heading west toward Turkey."

"A cloud?"

"Moses arranged my journey."

To my relief, he didn't accuse me of speaking nonsense. "You went through a lot of trouble finding me." Pointing at a chair, he continued, "Might as well sit down. Did you bring a copy of your letter?"

I pulled the missive out of my pocket, passed it to him and, noticing De Saint-Exupery's *A Sense of Life* on his lap, said, "The book you're reading lightened my days in college,"

"Perhaps you would enjoy hearing my favorite passage." He flipped through the pages, stopped at a marker, and read, *'It is impossible to survive on refrigerators, politics, balance sheets, and cross-word puzzles, you see! It is impossible! It is impossible to live without poetry and color and love.'"*

"Yes, yes, those words have inspired me more than once."

"In the Second World War, at the age of forty-four, he flew over the Mediterranean in a reconnaissance plane and disappeared. It was a great loss to mankind. But you didn't come here to talk about De Saint-Exupery."

He lifted my letter, read it for a few minutes, and yelled, "What's this gibberish about the protagonist of *My Secret History* periodically being self-indulgent and narcissistic?"

"Please, continue reading. You'll find complimentary comments significantly outnumbering the negative ones."

"I'll resume reading after you retract your offensive statement."

"The part you object to is minor."

"It may be minor but it is intolerably offensive."

"But the book is fictional."

"Hardly. It is a memoir."

"True to life?" I cried, "The protagonist boasts about having nonstop sexual escapades while a Peace Corps volunteer in Africa. His addiction is so deep that he goes on screwing native women even after catching gonorrhea."

"My good fellow," Mr. Theroux said condescendingly. "In this day and age, a young man is entitled to having some fun."

"You call that fun? Milroy, the character in *Milroy the Magician,* also has fun, but his fun ennobles him and the people he comes in contact with."

"You're mixing apples with oranges. The two books refer to different universes, each universe offering a valid commentary on life."

I felt as if in a boxing ring exchanging intellectual punches. Respecting Mr. Theroux too much to appease him, I felt determined to hold my ground. "In contrast to *My Secret History, Milroy the Magician* upholds the virtues of integrity, honor, and respect for oneself and others. The two books indeed belong to different universes, but only Milroy's is on the side of life."

"You're taking things too personally. You're imposing your values and biases onto my characters."

"Reading IS a personal experience," I exclaimed. "You are writing for the public. I am that public. I embrace your characters. I make them part of my universe. They matter to me. I rejoice at their successes and I suffer at their failures."

"And to think you accused me of being narcissistic."

Accusing him of being narcissistc? Was he losing his mind? The clouds had departed, and Mt. Olympus' peaks glowed brightly in the sunshine. I shut my eyes and inhaled deeply the aroma of the nearby flowers. Two years earlier I had hiked to a refuge halfway to the top of the mountain. Gazing at the mighty peaks, I finally understood why the ancient Greeks made Mt. Olympus the residence for their gods.

And now, so close and so remote from the mountain, I was being castigated by my favorite contemporary American writer for responding honestly to his literary output. Defeated, I rose, "I think I'll be leaving now."

"What's the hurry? Relax. Have a cup of tea."

My jaw dropped. "You treat me as if were a pain in the ass and then invite me to have tea."

"You are a pain in the ass, but for better or worse, you're captivated by my writing."

"Ever since I've—"

"Hush. Look at the thicket."

At the edge of the lawn stood a stately red deer, its almond eyes directed at us. One of the largest free-roaming animals in Greece, it was a favorite of the goddess Artemis. The significance of Mr. Theroux's writing, his arguments, and my counterarguments vanished as if by magic. I longed to join the deer in its pursuit of freedom and adventure.

"Now and then he shows up." Mr. Theroux said. "I feel blessed having him as a friend."

Mr. Theroux had displayed narrowmindedness since my arrival and now, suddenly, he showed a soul. Could he be trusted? The change came too abruptly. As I stood there pondering on my next move, an elderly man dressed in white stockings, pink pantaloons, a frilly blue shirt, a blue-velvet vest, and a luxurious white wig stepped out of the resort's door.

Mr. Theroux rose, offered his hand, and said, "Glad to see you back on your feet, Monsieur Voltaire. Does that mean that your knees are getting better?"

"Good enough to leave the building for some fresh air. Pointing at me, he said, "I see you have a visitor."

"Yes, the gentleman came to discuss my writing."

"Monsieur Voltaire," I said, "Your Candide inspired me greatly during my college years."

"Ah, Candide. It took him decades of traveling around the world before finding his garden. Have you found your garden yet?"

"Not quite, but I am getting close."

"Well, I'll leave now so you two can complete your conversation. Au revoir."

"Au revoir, Monsieur Voltaire. It was a pleasure meeting you."

Watching him shuffle toward a recliner adjacent to a bed of roses, I said, "He is a great thinker. I imagine the two of you have provocative talks."

"He's hard of hearing, but we manage. But getting back to us, you do like Jasmine tea?"

I nodded with a sigh.

"Perk up. I've been obstinate. Milroy is indeed a more exemplary human being than the protagonist of *My Secret History*."

Leaves rustled in the wind. Bees flew above Mr. Theroux. Monsieur Voltaire appeared deeply absorbed with his book. The waiter deposited our drinks. Lifting my cup, I said, "Milroy periodically failed to live up to his human potential but after every fall he rose taller. He redeemed himself again and again."

"Indeed, he did," Mr. Theroux nodded. "I wanted him to be inspiring. It puzzles me why in talking with you I depicted him as ordinary as the protagonist of *My Secret History*. But we have discussed my writing long enough. Is there anything else on your mind that you would like to talk about?"

"Indeed, there is. But I don't want to impose on you."

"You put up with my cantankerousness. The least I can do is listen to your concerns."

I cleared my throat and began, "I am at a critical junction in my life. For close to a decade, I had been earning my living as a psychologist in a mid-high school. To wean the kids from drugs and alcohol, and to introduce them to a healthier high, I had taken them skiing, hiking, and camping. On a recent camping outing, one eighth-grader threw stones at my tent. When I asked him if I had done something to upset him, he shook his head. Did he do it to impress his buddies?

He scratched his belly and answered, "I don't know why I did it."

"Mindless violence is the scariest one, even when carried out by a child." Mr. Theroux frowned.

"Two days later, still smarting from the experience, I stepped into the classroom with a head cold and a slight fever. Liza, an obese girl with a severe case of acne, pointed her hand at me and grinned, 'Here comes the Old Fart.' She eyed the class like an actress might do after delivering a particularly catchy line. The kids rewarded her with laughter. The kids that I had treated as if they were my own, the kids I had taken to more fun places than their combined parents had taken them since the days of their births, laughed at me."

"'Liza, is something bothering you?'" I asked. She shook her head. 'Please, watch your tongue then. I don't like being called names.' She nodded, stared at her shoes, and said, 'I meant no harm. My grandpa is also an old fart.' My mind went blank. My vision blurred. I grabbed her by the shoulders, shook her, and yelled at her face, 'Shut up, you swine!' It was horrible. I had manhandled a student, a cause for dismissal. The next day I called in sick. There were two more weeks left to the end of the semester. I never returned."

"It must have been a deeply demoralizing experience for you. Can you think of another way of earning a living?"

"I am a professional jeweler as well but jewelry making, unless you're well known in the field, doesn't provide financial security."

"Assuming you didn't have to worry about generating an income, what would you do?"

"I would go to France and make jewelry in the shadows of Modigliani, Matisse, and Chagall."

"France has wonderful food, museums, architecture, medieval villages, and natural scenery, but the French people are insufferable."

"They feel superior, and for good reasons. Their literature, philosophy, art, and music have enriched mankind for centuries." Smiling, I went on, "In my next life hope to be one of them."

"God Forbid," Mr. Theroux laughed, "What else, besides jewelry making, would you do in France?"

"Enjoy the cuisine. Travel, camp, write, and look for my soulmate. French women are graceful and self-confidant. Men treat them as if they were royalty."

What will you do if your soulmate doesn't cross your path?"

"I'll make jewelry, write, travel, camp, and so on. Creativity makes a lonely existence tolerable. Love is great but not essential."

We stopped talking. The setting sun cast deep shadows on the lawn. Monsieur Voltaire got up and headed toward the resort, his feet scraping the ground. I waved. Either because he was short-sighted or because he didn't see me, he failed to respond. I wished him well.

Mr. Theroux leaned closer, stared at me with sparkling eyes and exclaimed, "De Saint-Exupéry covered the Spanish civil war battlefields for a newspaper. He volunteered for reconnaissance flights during WWII. He sacrificed much for his ideals. Follow in his example. Don't hold back. Live passionately. This may well be your last chance."

His words resonated at my core. The shackles that had held me back throughout my life melted away. I felt free, confident, and determined to be fully myself. I imagined roaming the forest with a red deer. I imagined sailing off the Cote d'Azur coast with my soulmate. I imagined sipping wine with fellow artists and intellectuals in a French medieval village.

Mr. Theroux must have sensed my euphoria, for he said, "So, it's settled?"

"There is residual anxiety but my will is stronger. I'll go to France. I'll live on my Santa Fe house rental and my retirement income. Modigliani almost starved while creating glorious art. I'll emulate him. I'll be a modern-day Bohemian. I will sacrifice comfort for my artistic aspirations."

Mr. Theroux embraced me and patted me vigorously on the back. "I'm glad you found your answers. Come back at the end of your quest to tell me the outcome."

"I will. I owe you a great deal. Thanks."

I walked away, hitched a ride on a wind current, and landed on a plump white cloud headed for New Mexico. Mount Olympus' rugged snow-covered crown grew smaller, then vanished. The Bay of Corinth, the columns of the temple of Apollo in Delphi, and the Meteora monasteries, rising out of brown earth like so many gigantic beehives, appeared and disappeared in rapid succession. Sometime later, the Sangre de Cristo's white peaks appeared above a cover of clouds. Below them, Santa Fe glowed in the sunset. Eagerly, I arrived home. I couldn't wait to start preparing myself for my journey to France.

S anta Fe lay under a blanket of sunshine this late day in July. The Sangre de Cristo peaks shone above the clouds. Birds sang outside the Downtown Coffee House. I was waiting for Deborah. We both worked in the Paseo mid-school, she as an academic counselor and I as consultant psychologist in the special-ed department. Caught in the tumultuous world of children gone astray we held our places on the front lines of a chaotic, insane world, strengthening each other with an iron friendship.

Appearing breathlessly, she exclaimed, "I had to park far from here. It seems that everyone is downtown today."

"So, how have you been?" I asked.

"Getting ready for the new school year. And you?"

"Getting ready for France."

"Isn't it kind of late to go on a vacation?"

"It's not a vacation. I gave my resignation and am packing for my move overseas."

"You what?"

"A couple of weeks ago I had my 62nd birthday, and decided to relocate to France. I am drained. I need an emotional and spiritual remake."

"But the kids need you. You can't just abandon them."

"I gave them nine years of my life. That is long enough. I hardly sleep. The walls of my house are closing in on me. If I stay, I'll become as dysfunctional as they are. Think of me as a wounded bird. Birds have instincts that tell them where to fly. My instincts tell me to go to France."

"You love fancy talk, don't you?"

"It's the artist in me," I smiled. "In France, I will practice my art, regain my emotional and spiritual equilibrium, and be my natural self again."

"Sure, just like that. For all you know, you might get lonely and depressed. Paseo did offer you deeply gratifying moments. Remember how you felt at the graduation of kids you thought hopeless, and at their eventual marriages and parenthood."

"Yes, some did make a new start in life and I am happy for them but now I must think what's best for me."

"Poor Adam," Deborah said, taking my hand in hers.

"Please, don't pity me," I said, freeing myself "I willingly worked with them as long as I did."

"Nothing I say will change your mind?"

"I am afraid not."

"I hope you won't regret your decision. Let's get together before you take off."

We hugged. I watched her leave with a lump in my throat, for there was no telling when if ever I would see her again.

A blackbird landed by the feet of a little boy in a faux sailor suit at the next table. He jumped, scaring the bird away. "I want more ice cream," he yelled.

"It's too close to lunchtime," the woman he was with replied.

He banged on the table. She grabbed his hand and dragged him away. The boy was a brat, yet I admired him. I never challenged my mother. I endured her emotional outbursts without complaint. *Going to France should do more than revitalize me. It should also free me of the shackles that have held me in their grip throughout my life.*

The next day I called a car shipping firm and the French embassy and arranged with my real estate agent to deposit my house rental into my checking account, and to forward my mail to the American Express office in Nice.

Deborah called in the evening. "We found you a place to stay," she said breathlessly.

"You found what?"

"A place for you to stay in France. I can't talk now. I'll call you in the morning." I was stunned. Deborah wasn't one to joke about serious matters. Perplexed, I waited to hear from her. She rang the next morning, moments after I finished my breakfast.

"Carl stumbled upon a French scientist's video game website. He sent him a message and, one thing led to another, and they became friends. When I learned about it, I asked my son to tell the man, his name is Roberto, that a friend of ours is heading for France and that he needs a place to stay. Roberto replied that he lives in Biot, a medieval hill village between Antibes and Nice, and that he has a room for rent."

"What's Roberto doing in the States?"

"He just completed a Ph.D. in computer science at Carnegie Mellon University. On the Internet, he looks like a musician, with long hair and everything."

I sent Roberto an email introducing myself. "You'll love Biot," he wrote back. "It's an art center perched on a promontory three kilometers from the sea. We're a friendly bunch of people. Make sure to bring your own bedding."

On my past travels I never made arrangements for an overnight stay. I welcomed the unknown and the adventure. Roberto's offer amounted to booking a room in a bed and breakfast. But, upon deeper reflection, I concluded that this journey would be different. It would lead to relocation, to a lasting change of residence. Living with a local family would provide valuable insights into the cultural and commercial amenities in the area. I wrote to Roberto that I welcomed his offer.

The first week of September, I drove to a large adobe on the outskirts of Santa Fe to meet a representative of the French embassy.

Wearing a dark suit and checkered blue tie, the young man led me to a room with a clear view of the Sangre de Cristo mountains. He pointed at a chair opposite a mahogany desk, inserted a cigarette into an ivory holder, lit it, and asked why I wanted to live in France.

"To savor the culinary delicacies, impressive architecture, magnificent art, and last but not least, to marvel at the beauty and charm of your women."

To my consternation, he began talking in French. I raised my arms in a gesture of helplessness.

"Hm . . . I thought for sure you were fluent. Have you brought proof of your financial independence?"

I passed him my most recent checking and savings bank statements. Nodding, he said, "Everything is in order. We'll mail you a long-residency visa in a week."

The next two days I packed camping equipment, clothing, shoes, books, and bedding into my Acura Legend's interior, and hid silver to make jewelry with inside the spare tire compartment. The morning after, under a light rain, I departed for Los Angeles, where I left the car with a shipping agency.

Flying home, I reflected that I had passed the point of no return, the point where one leaves one's past and embarks on a hopefully fulfilling future. On my last day in Santa Fe, I visited Deborah and her husband, Evan. We drank wine, shared the sadness at our pending separation, reviewed some of my experiences with the Paseo kids, and discussed my plans in France.

On the way out, Deborah said, "Watch out for Roberto."

"But it was you and Carl who introduced him to me," I said.

"I am sure he'll be alright. Still, keep your guard up."

Leaves fluttered in the wind like so many crazed birds the morning of my departure for the Albuquerque airport. The Sangre de Cristo peaks shone above white clouds. When the shuttle bus reached Interstate 25, I waved goodbye to Santa Fe and sang a silent hallelujah to my new life in France.

Inside the plane for Atlanta, I welcomed with a smile an elderly woman easing down by my side. Women don't seek total control of the armrest. As if by an unspoken agreement, the lady took the front of the divider and left the remainder to me. A stewardess served drinks. After finishing my orange juice, I fell asleep and didn't awake until our arrival in Atlanta.

Two hours later from the window seat of a much larger plane destined for Paris, I watched with some trepidation a muscular man in his thirties place his backpack in the bin above my head, then taking the seat to my right. He unbuttoned his shirt at the collar and rested his elbow on the front of the divider. I placed mine on the back. When the plane reached the cruising speed, he suddenly pushed my elbow off. Shocked, I gazed at him. Motionless, he made the light sounds of a sleeping man. But I knew better than to believe him. No sleeping man would have kicked my elbow. Half my age and twice as strong, he was a formidable opponent. Believing that I had no chance recapturing my half of the divider, I resigned myself to defeat.

An inner voice protested. It reminded me of the Muslim kids in Sarajevo, the city of my birth, calling me a "dirty Jew," throwing me into pools of mud, and I doing nothing to defend myself. It reminded me of the day in college when a student threw a cream pie at my face, and I smiling as if it were a joke.

Disturbed by the humiliating memories, I resolved to recapture my part of the armrest. I pushed my elbow against his. I pushed and pushed and felt as if trying to dislodge a brick wall. Sweating, my heart beating fast, exhausted, out of breath, I gave up. The inner voice called me a shrimp, a quitter, and a loser. It displayed on the screen of my mind Jews in a concentration camp walking passively toward the gas chamber.

Outrage exploding at the core of my being, I took another look at my tormenter, then pressed my feet against the metal holding the seat in front of me in place, straightened myself and, using my whole body as a weapon, pushed my elbow against his. His elbow slipped, lost ground, and fell off. Turning toward the woman to his right, he said, "There are bullies on the plane. It's going to be a long, tedious flight." A pacifist, I didn't thrill in my victory. *But even a pacifist, I mused, must teach an asshole a lesson in human dignity and honor.*

I let him have the back of the divider but he ignored my offer. A stewardess passed me a tasty omelet with apple sauce, a whole wheat bun, and salad. The lights dimmed. After half an hour of listening to Strauss waltzes, I closed my eyes, then fell asleep. I woke up to the sight of the plane entering a thick mass of white clouds. The engines hummed. All sense of motion vanished. I felt as if journeying to infinity. The thumping sound of dropping wheels and the wail of a boy in the back brought me back to reality.

When we reached the gate in Charles De Gaulle Airport, I grabbed my one bag from the overhead bin, jostled for position in the aisle and, like a sprinter, waited for my turn. Customs formalities over, I headed for the subway going to the Opera Train Station, bought a second-class ticket for Le Havre, and stepped into a compartment worthy of Queen Elizabeth. A waiter in black pants, white shirt and black tie served drinks to elegantly dressed men and women at the bar. *The French trains have certainly come a long way since my last ride,* I mused, easing down on a leather window seat.

"Le billet, s'il vous plait," a husky male voice called from behind me.

I handed him my ticket. "Thiz iz first class. You pay one hundred more francs."

"But, the sign by the entrance said—" I protested.

"One hundred francs or change compartment, yes?" he interrupted.

Tired from the long flights, I gave him the money. Cornfields stretched into the horizon. A little girl with a bonnet waved from the porch of a weathered farmhouse. I waved back. Cars raced the train. One was an Acura. At the Los Angeles shipping company, I had asked the agent, "Can I have your assurance that my car will be waiting for me in Le Havre?"

"Absolutely, if there are no complications."

"What kind of complications are you referring to?" I asked.

"Pirates hijacking the ship, mutiny aboard, you name it."

"Your wife may enjoy your sense of humor," I said, "But, I don't."

"You're well insured. Why worry?"

"Why worry? Because I don't speak French. Because, should anything go wrong, I'll have a hell of a time getting things straightened out."

And yet, like a fool, I left Santa Fe without calling the shipping company to ascertain that my car had arrived.

Moments after disembarking in Le Havre, I rushed to a taxi. All my thoughts were on my car. At a hangar-like building in the harbor, I presented my papers to a young man in jeans and a flannel shirt, "Your car is ready," he said, in fluent English.

The French, oh the wonderful, marvelous French! My instincts had been right to lead me to them. I wanted to hug the man. I wanted to invite him to a dinner of escargots and wine.

"But first, you must give me one thousand five hundred francs," he continued.

"The shipping agent in Los Angeles assured me it wouldn't be more than 750," I protested.

"Do you wish to pick up your car today?"

"But of course. Why do you ask?"

"Because the customs office closes in one hour."

Feeling as if I was being robbed, I handed him the money. and ran to a nearby building with corridors fanning out like spokes of a wheel. Seeing no customs signs, I started opening every door in sight. At quarter to five, my shirt drenched in perspiration, I showed my papers to a tall, gaunt man. He pointed at a chair and asked something in a sonorous voice.

"*Oui,*" I responded, without any idea what I was agreeing to.

He continued emitting sentences ending with a rising inflection. Thinking that he wanted to know if the belongings in my car were for my personal use, I said, "For my utiliza*tion,*" stressing "*tion,*" and

"For my disposi*tion,*" stressing "*tion.*" The clock on the wall pointed at three minutes to five. He glanced at a woman at a nearby table. She shrugged. He stamped my forms and passed them to me. I suspected he did that so he wouldn't have to deal with me again the following morning. I offered him my hand. He ignored my gesture and put his jacket on.

Back at the warehouse, the young man led me through a dark passageway to a large garage. Had I been alone, I would have kissed my Acura Legend's hood. I threw my luggage in the back seat and took off. Le Havre had been totally destroyed during the Second World War. I longed to see how it was rebuilt, but my yearning for Biot prevailed, and I kept my eyes focused straight ahead and my foot pressed on the accelerator.

2

At a filling station on the outskirts of town, the price of gas shocked me. I knew that petrol was much more expensive in France than in the States, but I hardly expected the equivalent of sixty dollars for a fill-up. To save on gas, I resolved to drive at no more than 55 miles per hour, even as I knew that the French handled their cars with the enthusiasm of Formula One drivers and that my slow driving would drive them insane.

The second day at sunset, I arrived at a village with tight, twisting lanes, weathered stone houses, and a slow-running stream cutting through its center. Wooden balconies hanging over water created the effect of an outdoor theater. In one balcony an elderly woman in a chair leaned over a sweater with a needle and thread in her hand. In another, a young man balanced himself on his head in a yoga position. At the parapet skirting the river, an overweight, middle-aged woman and two teenage girls pointed their hands at the appearing and disappearing fish and laughed. A couple on a bench held hands and gazed seemingly in awe at the spectacle, now and then bringing their lips together. Their display of affection filled me with nostalgia. Booking a room in a nearby hotel, I vowed to return one day with my soulmate.

After a tasty dinner of shrimps, white rice, salad, and half a liter of Sauvignon Blanc in the hotel's restaurant, I returned to the river, watched the fish darting in floodlight for a few minutes, then returned to my room, brushed my teeth, and dropped on the bed

9

with my clothes on. Ten hours later, filled with flaky croissants, butter, strawberry jam, and tea, I resumed my journey. Uneven fields, tall bales of hay, rolling dark hills, rushing streams, church spires reaching out for an azure sky, offered endless visual entertainment.

The third morning, the scenery grew increasingly urban. Luxurious villas, with swimming pools and front yards with lemon and palm trees, announced the arrival of the Côte d'Azur. The traffic grew thicker and menacing. The drivers clearly annoyed by my slow speed, blew their horns, cut sharply in front of me, and gave me the finger. Stressed, my heart beating fast, I turned into a rest stop.

Eyeing the faraway Mediterranean sparkling like a tapestry of crushed diamonds, I ate a couple of croissants, took a long drink of water, and rejoined the maddening traffic, determined not to let the crazy drivers intimidate me again. Leaving the expressway for Antibes, I got lost. The half a dozen pedestrians I asked for direction to "Bio," gave me puzzling stares. I left out the "t" because in French the last consonant is typically not pronounced.

At a loss what to do next, I parked illegally in front of a telephone booth intending to call Roberto. The phone required a calling card, which I didn't have. A police car stopped. The officer waved at me. Apologizing profusely for parking illegally, I pointed at my map, and said "Bio."

"Ah, Biot." Pronouncing the "t," the constable motioned for me to follow him. Past several residential streets, a hospital, and a train station, we arrived at a large ceramic manufacturing plant. He pointed at the parapets on top of a hill and left. Roberto's words came to me, "Biot is a medieval village perched on a big rock, three kilometers from the sea."

Minutes later, at wooden barriers controlling motor traffic in and out of the village, a young female gendarme, raised her hand. "Streets small. No room for cars."

Offering my friendliest smile, I said, "I'm on a very important business."

"Sorry, only commercial vehicles."

A small pickup blew its horn. The gendarme waved the vehicle on. "Please," I pleaded. "I must deliver precious items. Just a little time."

"Okay, five minutes but no more."

Relieved, I entered a narrow cobblestone street. Past a bakery, a flower shop, an arts and crafts store, and an obelisk commemorating soldiers who perished in the First World War, I arrived at the tourist information office, a small brick building with an ancient spinning wheel behind a glass panel. Inside, I asked a short, dark-haired woman to please dial Roberto's number. She obliged and handed me the receiver.

"Go back to the building with a kiosk in front. We are on the second floor, the first door on the left," he said, without as much as offering a word of welcome.

In one of his emails, Roberto had described Biot as the prettiest medieval village on the Riviera. It was scrupulously clean, as most French villages are, but hardly medieval. Puzzling over his description, I stepped into a dark foyer, switched on the lights, and climbed up, my heart pounding with anticipation. *Will Roberto be glad to see me? The French are notoriously suspicious of foreigners. A stay in a motel would have provided a more relaxed introduction to my new life. But shared accommodations with a local family were bound to offer a more seamless entry into the daily village life.*

A hefty young man with a long ponytail and a shadow of a beard opened the door. "Come," he said. "I'll show you your room."

No preambles. No introduction. Not even a handshake. He led me through a kitchen smelling of onions, garlic, and cabbage to a living room furnished with a discolored sofa, an armchair with sagging springs, a low table stacked with dirty dishes, a small cabinet with three books, and a large television on the floor by the window.

He opened a door to the left of the television, and said, "This is it."

Shocked, I gazed at a bare mattress on the floor and at a wheeled, metallic rack holding assorted clothing. My shock changed to hope after I reminded myself that I had come to France to live the life of a struggling artist. A mattress on the floor, a kitchen that smelled like a vegetable market, and tattered furniture provided ideal accommodations for a Bohemian life.

"Great!" I cried.

"There are three of us, William, a graduate student, Marie, my girlfriend, and I. I teach at the Sophia Antipolis campus of the University of Nice. Our finances are a bit shaky right now, so, you will be responsible for your share of the rent, electricity, gas, food, et cetera," Roberto announced.

Was it my imagination, or was Roberto's tone apologetic? "I thought you recently got a Ph.D. in computer sciences," I said.

"I did, but I have been teaching only a couple of weeks."

"I see. Would you like now to learn something about me?"

"Such as what?"

"Well, I don't know, my age, my ethnic background, my profession, my—"

He shrugged. "People come, and people go. Now, if you will excuse me, I must leave to do some errands. Make yourself at home."

I wouldn't have welcomed a total stranger into my home. Yet Roberto had displayed no interest in knowing me. And he looked more like a musician than an academic. Deborah had said to be on guard. *Did I make a mistake agreeing to stay in his apartment?* I wondered.

Curious about my new residence, I ventured to the bathroom on the other side of the living room. Brassieres, panties, and nylon stockings hung over the bathtub. They had to belong to Marie. But where did she, Roberto, and William sleep? Recalling a door at the far end of my room, I walked to it and knocked. Receiving no response, I opened it ever so slowly and saw an unmade single bed, a chest of drawers, a pair of shoes, and clothes on the floor. That had to be William's room. What about Roberto's and Marie's? At the end of William's room stood another door. I knocked. Receiving no reply, I stepped inside and was greeted by long yellow curtains cascading softly from the ceiling. A double bed with a blue satin cover, an old wooden dresser with a mirror, a hairbrush, and several small bottles indicated Alberto's and Marie's room.

Oh, my God, I thought, *all the rooms are connected. For Roberto, Marie, and William to leave the apartment, they have to pass by my mattress. I could ask them to knock on my door, but if I was asleep, knocking would wake me up.* With terror, I imagined standing naked as Marie suddenly stepped in. Their friend, who had occupied the room and who was now on a world-sailing journey, must have found the arrangement acceptable. Not wanting to complicate matters, I decided to let things be and hope for the best.

Roberto and a rubicund young man stood by my Legend when I descended to collect my belongings. "Meet William," Roberto said.

"Pleased to meet you," I said. "Where are you from?"

Instead of answering my question, William glanced inquisitively at Roberto.

"He grew up on a farm," Roberto explained.

Farm life awoke in my mind images of clear air, healthy activities, cheese, and wine-making. "Is the farm near Biot?" I asked.

"We'll talk about it later," Roberto replied. "Now you have to take your car to the municipal garage outside the village."

After receiving directions, I carried a suitcase, toilet articles, bed sheets, and a woolen blanket to my room, dumped them on the mattress, got in the car, waved a greeting at the lady constable at the entrance to the village, turned right at the first street, and came to a musty garage. My Legend, the largest of all the cars, screamed for attention with its New Mexico license plate.

But I wasn't worried. Having read in the *New York Times* that crime rates on the Riviera had skyrocketed, I had installed chains in the trunk which, when padlocked, allowed only two-and-a-half inches of clearance for hands to get in. Another padlock controlled the opening of the hood. Alarm speakers in the engine and in the passenger's compartments triggered a hair-rising racket. A metal bar kept the steering wheel locked in place.

As I stood there, admiring my handiwork, I imagined the author of the New York Times' article appearing, taking a picture, and congratulating me on having the most theft-proof car in all of France.

Upon my return, Roberto was stretched on the floor in front of the television. On the screen, a strange little critter darted this way and that way in a brick maze.

"It's Nintendo," he said, "Do you want to join me in the game?"

"I know nothing about it. Thanks anyway."

A young blond woman appeared at the door. Tall, wearing a flowing skirt that came to her ankle and a blouse buttoned up to her neck, she looked as chaste as she was beautiful. *"Bon jour, mademoiselle,"* I said. "You must be Marie. I am Adam."

"So, I see," she said in an indifferent voice.

Roberto had made it clear in his emails that she mattered a great deal to him. Her seeming coldness troubled me. I knew that I had to win Roberto's friendship. Now, I realized that I had to conquer hers as well.

William walked in, eased down by Roberto's side, and picked up a remote. They consulted on the progress of the little critter with utmost seriousness. They acted as if the fate of France depended on the outcome of the game.

The television cast a pale light in the darkening room. A dog barked. A male voice said something and the barking stopped. Marie, wearing a long blue gown, passed us on the way to the kitchen. *Will I be invited for dinner?* I wondered. I had written to Roberto that I was vegetarian, except for seafood. Should I excuse myself and go out to a restaurant? Marie's announcement, "Dinner is ready," ended my uncertainty.

Roberto, William, and I joined her at the kitchen table, laid out with cheese, salad, bread, wine, and fruit. That puzzled me, as I was under the impression that the French enjoyed substantial evening meals. As if reading my mind, Roberto announced that there would be more food after their friends came.

Imagining the friends to be a bunch of artists, writers, and philosophers, the moment I finished my dinner, I picked up my best clothes, and walked to the bathroom. I was finishing drying myself from a refreshing, hot shower, when faint voices told me the guests had arrived.

Opening the door, a scene from the movie, *My Dinner with Andre*, multiplied several times over, greeted me to my immense delight. In the movie, two male protagonists discuss literature, ethics, philosophy, and other weighty topics over food and drinks. I couldn't tell what the folks in the room were talking about but my instincts told me that the conversations focused on very relevant matters. The young guests sat on chairs, sofa, floor, and anywhere their derrieres managed to fit. The women wore miniskirts, black stockings, and silk or angora blouses. The men wore designer jeans, checkered shirts, and light sweaters. I had expected a gathering of Bohemians. The guests looked like fashion models from glamourous magazines.

On the wobbly sofa, on the other side of the room, a blonde with a narrow waist, lovely broad shoulders, and gold-framed glasses was filing her nails. She was half my age but this was France, the land of romance and all-encompassing love. After she put her file away, I eased down by her side, as Marie placed a dish full of nuts on the table in front of us. I took a handful, glanced around, and pretended to be interested in my surroundings.

Suddenly, she said in lovely accented English, "You're a friend of Roberto's, aren't you?"

"I hope to become one soon."

"Did you meet him in America?"

"Sort of. Your English is faultless."

"Everyone here works or studies at Sophia Antipolis, the high-tech park. English is the dominant language there."

Glancing at her well-toned thighs, made extra appealing by black stockings, I asked, "Are you a hiker?"

"God no. What gave you the idea?"

Your sexy legs, I wanted to say, but blurted out instead, "Your healthy appearance."

"Thanks for the compliment," she said and yawned. Thinking that her yawning was in response to my superficial chatter, I cleared my throat and said, "An article in the *New York Times* commented that your government is deeply concerned about Anglo-Saxon words bastardizing the French language. Do you share in this concern?"

"What concern?"

"The French love their language, don't they? The article—"

"The English love English; the Bulgarians love Bulgarian; the Greeks love Greek. Nothing unusual about that."

"But the French are particularly attached to theirs."

"They certainly are. Well, I must be going. It was nice chatting with you. Good luck to you."

"I can do without your 'good luck,'" I snapped.

"I beg your pardon?"

"Life is not a game of chance, you know."

She shrugged and walked away.

Annoyed to have been dismissed, I turned toward the portly, bald man sitting to my left, and said, "I'd like to talk with you but first I want assurance that you won't wish me good luck and leave me."

"I'm sorry. What was that?"

"After I asked the woman who sat to my right if she was concerned that English was corrupting the French language, she wished me good luck and left."

"Not very polite of her, I must say."

"It would be different had I been a Buddhist. Buddhists have no expectations."

"I've been reading in the papers that New Age is spreading like wildfire in America. Can you tell me about it?"

"Different people have different definitions. To me, it's a mélange of metaphysics, astrology, black magic, and Tarot cards. Santa Fe, my hometown, is the New Age mecca. New Agers don't walk; they levitate."

"Hm . . . I'm not sure I follow you."

"New Age is damn simple, yet as complex as a well-spun fable. Allow me to introduce myself. I am Adam."

"I am Roger, a librarian at Sophia Antipolis."

"Ah, a man living in a universe of books, enamored with ideas."

"Just a job, I'm afraid."

Roberto refilled our glasses with wine. The mini-skirted woman who had wished me good luck talked animatedly with a thin, pale man by the balcony's door. She smoked. He smoked. Everyone in the room smoked.

"I can hardly breathe. I feel sorry for your countrymen," I said.

"It's an addiction. Nothing can be done about it. *C'est la vie.*"

"For the sake of the public good, I'd put every smoker in a rehabilitation center until he or she outgrows the smoking habit."

"Is that what they do in America?"

I laughed. "Hardly. America is the home of the free and the brave. People do what they damn well please, like gorging on high cholesterol fast food. The country's Constitution gives all a God-given right to indulge themselves to death."

"I buy a hamburger at McDonald's often. My favorite is 'Big Mac.'"

"And I buy, now and then, a seafood sandwich with French fries flavored with animal fat. *C'est la vie!*"

Our conversation was all small talk. A librarian had to have more on his mind than french-fries and hamburgers. "I bet you read a lot," I ventured.

"Actually, a couple of days ago, I started a book of short stories by Hemingway. I didn't get very far—too complex for my taste."

"Hemingway too complex?" I asked incredulously.

"He uses a language all of his own, doesn't he?"

"Don't we all?" I sighed.

The entire time I was talking with Roger, I was eyeing a woman with an upturned nose, a thin mouth, and large blue eyes on the floor with her back against the wall. Her high forehead conveyed impressive intelligence.

I nudged Roger's arm. "That woman on the floor, do you know her?"

"Her name is Suzanne. She works as a secretary at Sophia Antipolis."

"She's reading a book while everyone else is talking. She must be an intellectual."

"No one in this room is. Money and professional advancement are all everyone is thinking about."

Could he be right? I wondered, as I left him to join Suzanne on the floor. When she closed her book, I said, "Roger told me you are Suzanne. I am Adam. May I ask what you're reading?"

"A guidebook to the Côte d'Azur. Some friends are coming to visit, and I want to entertain them well. You're an American, aren't you? What brings you to France?"

"I came to make jewelry and to indulge my passion for intellectual pursuits."

"The foreigners I know come to the Cote d'Azur to enjoy food, scenery, and glamour."

"Glamour has no appeal for me. Food and scenery do but the French mind fascinates me the most. Take your philosopher Albert Camus. In *The Stranger,* he explores human alienation. In *The Myth of Sisyphus*, he explores the morality of suicide. In *The Rebel,* he explores the morality of murder. I can't think of anyone but a Frenchman writing about such formidable topics."

"You are very kind," she said and lit a cigarette.

After the smoke cleared up, I asked, "Do you enjoy the outdoors?"

"But of course, especially a day at the beach."

"You go with your boyfriend, I presume."

"Do you really expect me to answer? We just met."

A strange woman, I thought. *It wasn't as if I had asked her if she indulged in a one-night stan*d. We stopped talking. The silence grew heavier by the second. I was about to leave when she dropped ashes on my pants. Dusting them off, she said, "I am sorry I snapped at you. I don't have a boyfriend."

Suddenly, all the people in the room turned into shadows. My eyes were only for Suzanne.

"Voltaire is another writer I admire greatly," I exclaimed. "Poor Candide. He pursued Cunegonda to the end of the earth, and when he found her, she was old and decrepit."

"The fate awaiting each one of us. Now, if you'll excuse me, I would like to stretch my legs. Good luck to you."

Oh God, not again. As I debated whether to tell her that I could do without her good luck, Roberto came, pointed at a tall man in red pants, and said, "That's Maurice. He is rich. He has invited everyone for dinner in his apartment down the hall."

My mind turned to Marie. Where could she be? The moment I stepped inside Maurice's apartment; I got my answer. She stood bent over a huge pot exuding wafts of cooked meat.

The guests set up wooden crates in the large living room, covered them with planks, and then layered colorful plastic tablecloths over them. Suzanne went around depositing paper plates and plastic eating utensils. The arrangements completed, I leaned against the wall, imagining being inside a fabulous Mongolian yurt. Marie, carrying a large pot, started filling the plates with the stew. My dish remained empty. When Maurice arrived to fill my glass with wine, he said, "You'll have fish." Roberto must have told him my eating preference. Moments later he returned with a plate filled with steaming salmon and potatoes. "Here it is. I microwaved it."

Ah, the marvelous French. The frozen fish, dipping in an olive oil garlic sauce, crisp on the outside and tender on the inside, tasted much superior to the fresh fish served in the finest Santa Fe restaurants.

The festivities began in earnest after Maurice and Marie joined the sitting crowd. The guests broke chunks of bread and dipped them into the stew. Wines glasses were filled. Animated conversations floated in the air. In Roberto's living room, the guests near me spoke English. Here, they gibbered happily in their native tongue. I didn't mind. There was so much to look at. Chinese and Japanese tapestries and prints hung on walls; green, yellow, and red candles stood on top of twisted terra cotta columns; dolls in kimonos posed on a bamboo shelf; a golden silk partition partially hid a miniature lemon tree. Maurice's taste was as original as his wallet was full. On my first day in Biot, I felt as if in paradise.

A tall woman in her late thirties, elegantly dressed in a suit, silk blouse, and silk tie, appeared at the door. She waved, threw kisses, then eased down across from me. Marie brought her the stew. Maurice filled her glass with wine.

She was a bit older than the other women and that suited me just fine. But in view of my debacles with members of the fair sex in Roberto's apartment, I took my time befriending her.

"The fish is wonderful but ordinarily I prefer a vegetarian meal," I said halfway into our meal.

She gave me a bewildered look. "*Fish? Qu'est-ce que _fish_?*"

"You don't speak English?"

"*Non, seulement français,*" she said and lifted her wine glass.

I lifted mine, emptied it, and refilled it. After finishing it my head began to swim. The people in the room grew indistinct, their words reaching me from the other side of a thick fog. I leaned against the wall and closed my eyes, opening them now and then out of politeness. But I shouldn't have bothered, as no one seemed to notice or care that my consciousness had taken a flight into never-never land. Shuffling feet woke me up. I glanced at my watch. It was past midnight. All the guests had departed.

Marie began to collect the dishes. I wanted to help her but felt immobilized by wine and smoke. Roberto, William, and Maurice, sitting at the end of the makeshift table, conversed in French. Maurice suddenly rose, walked to a corner table, and crawled under, twisting his six-foot frame into a fetal position.

"What's he up to?" I asked Roberto.

He shrugged, "That's Maurice for you."

I found the sight of Maurice curled up like a sleeping baby amusing and disturbing. *Could he be mentally unbalanced?* Eyeing Roberto and Maurice, I said, "Next he will suck his thumb."

Roberto and William frowned, sighed, and raised their eyebrows.

Oh, my God! I had made a faux pax. Maurice had wined and dined us. He had prepared a special meal for me. And here I was ridiculing him. Filled with remorse, I rose and on wobbly legs walked to a table at the other end of the room and crawled under. To my surprise, lying on the floor in a fetal position felt relaxing. Roberto and William nodded, smiled, and gave me the thumbs up.

The next two nights the revelries flowed with the regularity of the river *Var* discharging into the Mediterranean. No sooner had Roberto, Marie, William, and I finished our dinners than guests began to arrive, bringing with them scents of cologne and cigarette smoke. Melodious French words flew overhead like so many colorful butterflies, stirring images of Follies Bergères, of couples strolling in the Luxembourg Gardens, of Bohemians in crumpled suits arguing pros and cons about ethics, artistic and literary trends in Left Bank cafes.

Walking from the television where Roberto and William played Nintendo to the tattered sofa on which two women in miniskirts and net stockings smoked, drank wine, and chatted, I felt if there ever was a Shangri-La, this had to be it.

I stretched on the floor by the women's feet, took the *Nice Matin* from the round table, and pretended to read the paper. One woman had a run in her stockings. They chatted animatedly, their hands swaying as if conducting an orchestra, their voices rising and falling like those of an inspired chorus. "*Livre, film noir* and *auteur* reached my ears. I strained to hear more, but everyone in the room seemed to be talking at the same time. Marie deposited a plateful of nuts and an open bottle of wine on the table by my side. As I grabbed a handful, the woman with a run in her stocking bent over and asked, "You are an American, aren't you?"

"Yes, but I wish I were French."

"Is there something wrong with being an American?" she asked.

Her breath exuded wine and smoke. She smelled of perfume. I imagined us as characters in the movie *Cabaret*. I imagined a tete-a-tete in a Paris nightclub with the orchestra playing a waltz under twirling ceiling lights.

I took a long swallow of wine and said dreamily, "The French know all there is to know about *joie de vivre*."

She turned to her companion, then back at me. "My friend agrees with you. She thinks Americans are too materialistic to appreciate the good life."

"You can say that again!"

Leaning closer, she asked, "What do you plan to do in France?"

"When in France, do as the French do."

"Hm . . . interesting, but that doesn't answer my question."

We didn't talk about anything mind-boggling, but we talked. She was curious. She wanted to know me. "What does it mean? It means . . . it means . . . romance, songs, and champagne, you know, the French way, like *'Vive la différence.'"*

She pulled down at her skirt, said, "Good luck to you," and gave her attention to her friend again.

I had blown it. Me and my big mouth. Dispirited, I left for the bathroom. When I returned, I saw an obese, bald, and middle-aged young man nibbling the ear of the woman with a run in the stockings. Okay, maybe he was just whispering sweet nothings. I took a better look at the guy. He had luminous and intelligent eyes and a high forehead. No book can be judged by its cover. For all I knew, he might have been a poet, a painter, or a philosopher.

On the fifth evening of the festivity, Marie distributed tastier cheeses and crackers. Maurice refilled glasses with higher quality Sauvignon Blanc. Russians manage binges with castor oil. I hated castor oil. Milk? I hated milk, too. My mother had warned me to avoid excesses of all kinds. She was right. I couldn't handle wine any better than cigarette smoke. This evening, though, for reasons beyond my grasp, the smoke suited the occasion. It fused the furniture and the people into a seamless whole. I, though, felt like an outsider. No one addressed a word to me. No one asked what I was doing in France. No one spoke in English. I interpreted my sudden inconspicuousness as an outcome of having become, after five days, as familiar a sight as the rumpled sofa and the armchair with broken springs. Being ignored didn't trouble me. The show was entertaining and there was an abundance of wine.

At our Saturday dinner, Roberto announced that this was the last evening his friends would join us. In response to my question why, he said, "People's priorities change. *C'est la vie.*"

Afterword, I joined Roger, the librarian, on the wobbly sofa, and asked him what the visitors were talking about. "Jobs, studies, families, weddings, apartments for rent, and so on," he responded.

Having come to France to indulge my passion for intellectual exchanges, and hardly able to understand a word, I shrugged my shoulders. The conversations may have had the appeal of an overcast sky but the manner in which they were rendered suggested sunshine. The women held their cigarettes with the tip of two fingers, while their pinkies extended like messengers of goodwill. They laughed temperately. They sipped their wine with polished grace. They pleasantly nodded to what the men said. The men nodded pleasantly to what the women said. Not a voice was raised. It was all grace and harmony, very much the way Dostoevsky had described the French through the eyes of Alexei, the protagonist of his novel, *The Gambler*:

"The French traditional form had begun to acquire elegance at a time when we were still bears. Then the Revolution took over from the aristocracy, and now the most miserable little Frenchie has nice manners, knows how to express himself, and even thinks in elegant forms, without having to engage either his brain or his heart in his way of thinking and expressing himself—all that he has acquired by inheritance; while underneath he may be the most empty-headed creature and thoroughly vulgar at heart."

Alexei's description was clearly prejudicial. True, the elaborate greeting rituals, the well-orchestrated social pantomimes, the effusive pleasantries were too polished to be genuine. But in France, a country that values manners above all else, it is not the sincerity with which the lines are delivered that most matters. It is the skill with which the lines are delivered.

The woman with the run in her stocking was on the sofa cuddled next to the bald fellow. With her hourglass figure, large blue eyes, long neck, and cascading blond hair, she could have passed for a model. But did she have a soul?

My question unsettled me, for ever since my arrival in Biot, I had been mostly ogling women. If I were to be brought before a God-appointed judge, I would plead that I was in the land where men consider women a national treasure, the land where a painter named Delacroix had depicted a gorgeous, bare-breasted female leading soldiers to their heroic deaths, the land where women took pride at being women.

But there was more to it. All the women were at least half my age. Nabokov in *Lolita* and Theroux in *Milroy the Magician* had written of romances between older men and much younger women. Would the fact that at sixty-two, I considered myself as fit, youthful, and energetic as any man in the room, expunge my guilt? What would I do if the woman with the run in her stockings were to invite me to her home? Would I follow her with my chest thrust out, my eyes dazzled with romance, my heart palpitating with anticipation? And would I try to ascertain if she had a soul before taking her into my arms? To my shame, I felt obliged to answer, "No." I came to France to find my soulmate and here I was fantasizing about having a one-night stand.

I met Julie midway into the soiree. She was British and a few years older than the majority of the women in the room. Like the rest of the folks, she worked at Sophia Antipolis. Her looks were classic Anglo-Saxon: fair skin, blonde, tall, narrow waist, broad shoulders, and strong arms and legs. Beautiful as she was, her behavior left much to be desired. She did not sip her wine. She drank it like a drunk sailor. She didn't put a few nuts into her mouth. She thrust a handful. She slapped me on the thigh to stress a point. Her harsh manners unsettled me but, longing for female companionship, I held back my distaste.

We decided to visit the Cannes' flea market. When I phoned her a few days later to make the arrangements, a man answered. Thinking that I had dialed the wrong number, I apologized and put the receiver down. On the next trial, the same male voice asked if I wanted to talk with Julie. He didn't sound old enough to be her father. Perhaps, he was her brother or, God forbid, her lover! I hesitated.

"Yes," I said. "Please, put Julie on the phone."

"Who's this?" she asked.

"Adam," I mumbled.

"Oh, it's you," she responded in an indifferent tone. Taken aback, I said, "Perhaps, this isn't a good time to talk."

"It's okay. What's on your mind?"

"I'm calling about our visit to the Cannes' flee market. Are you still interested in going?"

"I am. What day did you have in mind?"

"This Saturday. By the way, a man answered your phone twice."

"So what?"

"Is he a relative of yours?"

"What difference does it make to you who he is?"

"We are planning to go on a date, and I was wondering if you were free."

"Free for what?"

Is she playing games? I wondered. "Free to form a friendship."

"I belong to myself. No one owns me."

"So, you are not emotionally involved with anyone?"

"You're tiring me with your questions. Call me when you're in a better mood."

"Julie, wait!"

"Up yours," she barked, and hung up.

I felt like a fool. I had barely met her and was already succumbing to jealousy. Still, I didn't deserve to be treated like a dog. *Sure as hell she won't hear from me again.*

5

My housemates left in the morning before I got up. William usually came home about one o'clock for lunch. Friendly and spontaneous, he was my favorite. We practiced languages.

"I'm known as William," he would say.

"No, no," I would correct him. "In English, you want to say, 'I'm William.'"

William would comb his unruly hair with his rough fingers and ask, "*Et ton nom?*"

"*Je suis Adam.*"

"*Non, tu veux dire, 'Je m'appelle Adam,'*" he would correct, then continue, "I've warm."

Laughing, I would say, "I'm warm."

"*En français,*" he would persist, "*On dit, J'ai chaud.*"

"I know English better than you do. *Je suis raison.*"

His turn to laugh, he would correct, "*J'ai raison.*"

And so, we practiced languages and built a friendship.

Two weeks after my arrival in France, William invited me to go mushroom hunting with his brother, Alphonse. I liked Alphonse. Tall, with a mustache and a friendly smile, he came to Biot whenever he was free from his studies at the university in Nice to ogle the barmaid in the café across from the park. The barmaid's boyfriend found out about Alphonse's intentions and dared him to a fistfight. Alphonse agreed with the condition that the woman be the trophy. William informed his brother that the barmaid's boyfriend was an amateur boxer. Alphonse shrugged his shoulders, arguing that he was bigger. Bigger or not, he wouldn't have a chance, William persisted. In the end, with my regret, Alphonse capitulated. I was glad he did, yet my romantic side wanted to see him get bloodied.

We left for the hills of Grass, the perfume-making capital of France, under a turquoise sky and with a refreshing wind blowing from the Mediterranean. I followed Alphonse and William in my own car, so I could come earlier if tired from picking mushrooms. As I approached Grass, distracted by scented air, I hit a curb and blew a tire. I reassured William that I would be alright, and encouraged him to proceed without me.

My spare being in the trunk, I removed books, shoes, pants, shirts, and jackets stored there and deposited them on a tarp on the sidewalk. I carried the items in my car because I had no place for them in my room. A red BMW with German license plates suddenly stopped nearby, awakening memories of armed German soldiers marching in Sarajevo, the city of my birth, in 1941.

Much had changed since then, of course. The German government had established educational programs that expunged the notion of Teutonic racial superiority and held the country accountable for the Nazis' atrocities. Thinking that he was the new, emancipated German, I greeted him with a friendly wave.

Of average height, wearing a checkered red-green flannel shirt and yellow cotton pants, he walked to my clothes, bent over, and lifted my leather jacket.

Perplexed, I asked, "What are you doing?"

"You American?"

"Yeah, please, leave my jacket alone."

"I pay well," he said, putting the jacket on. After tugging at the sleeves a few times, he shook his head and removed it. "Too small."

"Nothing here is for sale. I had to place my clothing on the sidewalk to retrieve my spare tire," I said.

Ignoring my comment, he picked up my blue Ralph Lauren blazer and rubbed his fingers over its brass buttons.

"Haven't you heard me?" I said. "Please, leave my things alone, and go away."

"Blazer fine," he said. "How much?"

My stomach tightened. My knees went soft. I began to sweat. I had to get rid of him, but how? In desperation, I picked up the tire-changing tool and took a step toward him.

"Okay, okay," he said, and dropped the blazer.

Relieved, I got down on my knees, removed the damaged tire, and was about to grab my spare when I noticed him holding my British-made Gore-Tex jacket. It was the jacket that had shielded me from rain, snow, and bone-chilling cold. It was my second skin.

I rose, took hold of the spare, and yelled, "If you aren't gone by the time I finish counting to three, you'll spend your francs on medical emergency care."

He put the jacket on. Perhaps he didn't hear me because of the traffic noise. More likely, he just didn't give a shit.

"One . . . two . . ."

At "three," I threw the spare at him. The tire brushed his thigh and ambled toward the grassy hillside behind him. I ran after it. It stopped at a tree. Breathlessly, I grabbed it and held it as if it were my own child.

Letting go of my Gore-Tex jacket, he snickered, "You're a fucking ugly American."

"And you're a fucking ugly Nazi," I responded, my whole body shaking.

He mumbled something, walked to his car, and drove away. I sat down on my Legend's bumper and took a long drink of water. Fifteen minutes later, restored, I replaced the tire, put my clothes back in the trunk, and drove away.

Past green meadows and villas with palm trees and beds of flowers behind wooden fences, I reached a village. At the traffic stop, while waiting for the light to turn green, my eyes fell upon a basket filled with mushrooms by the entrance of a grocery store. Imagining

Alphonse, distracted by the loss of the barmaid, picking poisonous mushrooms, I decided to have pizza that evening.

A small, hangar-like structure with used tires leaning against its wall, and an old vehicle without wheels resting on cement blocks close to the entrance alerted me to the presence of a car repair shop. I stopped, got out, and—gesticulating and speaking in Italian—pointed at the damaged tire in the back seat. The young, grizzly attendant jotted down the necessary information on a pad, said, "*Sans problème*," stepped inside a small Fiat, and drove away.

Sans problème had foretold trouble in the past. Some years back in Sofia, Bulgaria, I asked the clerk of a hotel if I could pay with my VISA. He said, "*Sans problème*." Three days later, I handed him my card. He demanded cash. Failing to persuade him that his request was unjustified, I gave him my American Express traveler's checks, which he promptly converted into Leva, thus providing me with a generous supply of Monopoly money. On a vacation in Dubrovnik, I explained to the waiter that I was a vegetarian. He said, "*Sans problem*," then brought me a soup with the comment, "I removed all the meat."

A sound of grinding gears told me that the attendant had returned. He pointed at the Goodyear tire in his hand. "Okay?"

"Okay," I responded.

He installed the tire, walked to his office, and returned with a pad and pencil. He licked the pencil and wrote eight hundred francs or a hundred sixty dollars. Stunned by the high cost I shook my head. He frowned and said something that sounded like "*Merde.*"

Fearing that the misunderstanding might escalate into a physical confrontation, I pulled out my VISA card hoping he would say he only accepted cash. As I didn't carry cash, he would then be compelled to remove the tire and install my spare. But fate decreed otherwise. He went to his office and returned with a crumbled piece of paper which I, fuming, signed.

I was about to leave, but realizing I didn't receive the warranty, asked for it in Italian. *"La garantie est dans vos mains,"* ("The warranty is in your hand.") he replied.

No Goodyear tire dealer would honor the crumbled piece of paper, I reflected.

"Merci bien, monsieur," the man said, turned around, and walked away.

I drove away, vowing never again to do business with a Frenchman without first agreeing on the cost of the job. To calm down, immediately upon arriving in Biot, I bought a double-cone of chocolate ice cream and the *International Herald Tribune* and sat down on the sunny bench by the obelisk commemorating the WWI fallen soldiers. Two elders walked in, sat on the opposite bench, and began playing dominoes. Roberto played Nintendo. Did anyone ever play chess? Did anyone ever read a book in Biot? I hadn't done either since my arrival.

I finished reading the paper as the village began awakening from its noon siesta. Women in flowing skirts appeared with canvas and plastic bags in hand. One young lady in tight jeans, with heels that looked at least four inches tall, approached the pudgy constable regulating the motor traffic. She lowered her head. He stood on tiptoes and planted a kiss on each of her cheeks. The ceremony over, she stepped into the bakery. He returned to his duties. In the park across the street children chased each other around the fountain. Trucks blew their horns seeking an opening in the thick crowd. The woman with high heels emerged from the bakery with two baguettes in her hand. A sweet scent of freshly baked bread and pastry wafted my way.

I closed my eyes. Awakening at sunset, I went shopping for a bottle of Cabernet Sauvignon and six carnations. Stepping into the apartment, an acrid odor assaulted my nostrils. William, his thick black hair entangled with bits of twigs and decaying leaves, stood over kilos of mushrooms spread on newspapers on the kitchen floor. Marie, at the stove, stirred a large pot with a wooden spoon. She accepted my flowers with a smile, put them in a vase, and placed the vase at the center of the dining table. The setup was a pleasure to the eye: a red and green checkered tablecloth, two sets of glasses, one for wine and one for water, a basketful of two loaves of white bread, a stick of butter, the necessary eating utensils and plates, and a lit candle at the center.

William explained that the mushrooms not used for the stew would dry on the floor throughout the night. I expected Roberto to invoke a prayer. But he broke a chunk of the loaf and buttered it. Marie served the mushroom stew. I filled the glasses with my wine bottle and we toasted to the health of William and Alphonse, the mushroom hunters. Overcoming my fear of getting poisoned, I swallowed a spoonful of the stew and exclaimed "It's the tastiest mushroom dish I ever had."

"It ought to be," Marie said. "I flavored it with red wine."

Turning toward me, Roberto said, "We're planning to spend next weekend in the country with my father. Would you like to join us?"

"I would be delighted," I replied.

Marie shook her head. "Your father's place is small. It will be crowded. I don't think it's a good idea."

The day I had met her she had stared past me. In my two weeks as a guest in her home, she hadn't initiated one conversation. She responded to my questions in monosyllables. Roberto had described her in one of his emails as sweet. I found her as sweet as a marble statue, though admittedly a well-carved one.

"Did you have a good day at school?" I ventured after Roberto and William settled down on the floor in front of the television.

"Fine," she said, collecting the glasses.

I passed her mine, then picked up the dishes.

"That won't be necessary."

"But you've done the cooking. It's only fair that I should help out."

"I do best alone."

I ignored her comment and followed her with the plates, which I deposited to one side of the sink. When I picked up a cloth to dry the dishes, she snapped, "I've told you I don't need your help."

Hurt, I returned to the living room table, sat down, watched Roberto and William manipulating the silly little critter in the brick maze, and asked myself why had Roberto invited me to stay in his apartment. It couldn't have been out of a desire for friendship, as he treated me rather formally. Why was Marie so cold and disdainful? Why was I so enamored with the idea of staying with them? Could it be because I valued William? But if I moved elsewhere, William and I could still study the languages in an outdoor cafe or park.

That night in bed, staring at the white-washed ceiling, I vowed that if Marie treated me as an unwelcome stranger for one more week, I would start looking for new accommodations.

The next day, the first Monday of October, I woke up to the sound of a jetliner. The jetliner was in fact a mighty storm. Wind rattled the windows. The trees in the park below moaned. The walls shook. I glanced at my watch. It was time for Roberto, Marie, and William to pass alongside my mattress. Would the threatening weather keep them indoors? A noise from William's room announced their coming. They passed by quietly and stepped into the living room. Clicking silverware indicated they were having breakfast.

Cold air rushed in through a crevice in the window. I pulled the blanket over my head and thought that the most reasonable thing would be to stay home with a good book in my hands.

But storms excited me. For years I had been fantasizing about staying in a lighthouse during a tempest and watching waves hitting the lighthouse ramparts while listening to Beethoven's *Ode to Joy*. The chances of this ever happening were nil. But a consoling experience was within my reach: a visit to the shore, three kilometers away. I put on my long-johns, jeans, turtle neck shirt, woolen sweater, water-proof hiking boots, and my Gore-Tex jacket, ate a nourishing breakfast, and ventured outside.

A gust threw me against the closed newspaper kiosk. *You'll get yourself killed,* my father whispered into my ear. *Go back to the apartment. You're too delicate for this kind of weather,* my mother echoed. *I would rather die than be the shrimp you raised me to be,* I answered, and pushed on.

There were no cars. There were no children with their small backpacks on the way to school. Two elderly women walked slowly, pressing their shoulders against house walls. A young man in overalls held onto his beret with his hand. The flower shop and the boutiques selling local crafts were closed. Only the bakery and the post office were open for business. Past the wooden barriers controlling motor traffic to the village, I slipped and fell. Getting up on shaky legs, I questioned my decision to venture on. It was the type of weather that any reasonable sixty-two year-old would want to endure with a blanket over his knees and a book in his hand. But I wasn't an ordinary sixty-two-year-old oldster. I was the man who at the age of twenty immigrated to the United States with seventy-five dollars in his pocket, no knowledge of English, and no education; I was the man who left behind his familiar Santa Fe home to start a new and unpredictable life in France. A gust of wind kicked me. Taking that to be a message from fate to keep going, I pressed on.

Two kilometers from Biot, at the dreadful, narrow, 90-degree tight turn without sidewalks, I paused with my senses on full alert. Here cars passed within a foot or two of hapless pedestrians. Pressing my shoulder against the brick wall scarred by myriad encounters with car fenders, I proceeded cautiously one small step at the time. The sound of a mighty vehicle's exhaust suddenly overpowered the rain. It was the Antibes bus. I closed my eyes and held my breath. Moments later I watched the bus' taillights disappear in the downpour.

At a small shopping plaza, my favorite pizzeria and all the other enterprises were boarded. The rain grew fiercer. By the time I reached the tree-lined boulevard leading to the Biot railroad station, I could barely see the ground in front of my feet. The large amusement park to my right was cordoned off, its tall rides looking like monstrous apparitions. Following the traffic circle at the end of the boulevard, I came to wooden barriers blocking motor traffic to the littoral highway. I entered the underpass leading to the ocean, brushed my shoulder against the wet wall, and came to a nightmarish sight.

Huge waves landed on cabins, boarded restaurants, and concession stands. The road skirting the ocean was a running stream. A gigantic swell exploded out of the sea and headed toward me. I ran for the underpass. A wall of water kicked me in the back a I ran for safety.

Refrains from T. S. Eliot's poem *The Hollow Man* played in my mind:

> This is the way the world ends
> This is the way the world ends
> This is the way the world ends
> Not with a bang but a whimper

This was not a whimpering world. This was a world with a bang! This was the place to sing hallelujah to life and to tremble in fear. Driven by curiosity I returned to the shore. The gap between the earth and the sky grew smaller. A mantle of grayness lay over the land and the sea. From above the cloud cover strains of a chorus sang *Te Deum,* from Berlioz' *Requiem.* With closed eyes, I followed the dead rising toward the heaven. Cold rain droplets dripping down my back brought me back to reality. On my first entry to the underpass, I had kept my feet dry by walking on the raised edge. The edge was now covered with water, which passed through my shoes.

At the traffic circle, I fell into a muddy pool. Drained of will, I lay motionless on the ground while a hand pulled me up by the collar of my jacket. *"Crétin,"* a man in a green plastic poncho yelled. He sounded angry. Thinking heartfelt gratitude would soothe his feelings, I said *"Merci beaucoup"* twice. He released me, called me *Crétin* again, and rushed to a yellow utility track.

Wondering what *Crétin* meant, I started for the village. The flat road was easy to navigate. The steep one was akin to a match with a Sumo wrestler. I arrived in Biot with my knees shaking, and my jeans thoroughly wet.

After a long hot shower, I changed into dry clothes, made hot tea, and opened Paul Theroux's *Mosquito Coast*.

Later, at the dinner table, Roberto discussed the weather from a scientific perspective: masses of air colliding, jet streams going off their customary paths, and so on. William shared with us the damage high winds cause to crops on his farm. My mind went back to the shore, to the gigantic waves, to the awe and dread I felt before nature gone wild.

At a lull in the conversation, I turned to Roberto, "Would you tell me what *crétin* means?"

"Idiot. Why are you asking?"

"Outside in the storm, a man called a boy that. Would you take offense if someone referred to you as a *crétin*?"

"Of course, wouldn't you?"

"It depends on whether the man who said it pushed me into mud or rescued me."

Roberto, William, and Marie stared at each other. William combed his unruly hair with his thick fingers. Marie sighed. Roberto rolled his eyes. "Has someone called you a *Crétin*?" he finally asked.

"Sort of, but he didn't mean it."

That night loneliness engulfed me in a tight grip. Berating myself for not being able to endure solitude, I dialed Julie first thing in the morning.

"How are you?" I asked.

"Reasonably well, thanks. What's on your mind?"

"I was thinking of our plan to visit the Cannes flee market."

"When did you think of going?"

"This Saturday. Would that work out for you?"

"Sure. That would be fine."

"You hurt my feelings when I called you last time. Why did you say, 'Up yours,' and hang up on me?"

"Because you deserved it."

"All I did was ask who was the man who answered your phone."

"And I told you it was none of your business, and you persisted. What was I supposed to do?"

"You still think it's none of my business?"

"I do. You won't start that again, will you?"

"It's just that I would be more relaxed knowing where I stand with you."

"You just can't get it in your head that you don't own me."

"Julie, take it easy, for God's sake."

"You don't give up, do you?"

"Julie, wait!" I cried.

"Up your ass!" She hung up.

I blew it again. She had made it clear the last time we talked that she didn't intend to be held accountable to me. I persisted and received a slap on my face.

Demoralized, I bought two chocolate-filled croissants. collected brochures on Biot at the tourist information office, and headed for the medieval quarter, minutes away from the commercial hub. A small, old plaza containing a long bed of yellow, red, and blue flowers welcomed me. Porticoes fronting two-story stone houses offered an oasis of tranquility. Under one portico a waiter dressed in black pants and shirt set plates, eating utensils, and glasses on tables covered with red and white checkerboard cloths. Under another two young boys in shorts kicked a ball in front of a butcher shop. A pungent smell of sausages and other meats wafted out of the open door.

Next to an arch leading to a smaller, adjacent square, a store window displayed dolls. Standing uncertainly in the center, a three-foot tall Pinocchio sported red britches, green socks, a loose white blouse, and a nose the length of a banana. He looked sad. I glanced at my reflection in the glass, then at Pinocchio, then at myself again, and had the crazy thought that I belonged by his side. Unsettled by the association, I left the window, stepped into the arch, and came to a smaller plaza hosting a sixteenth-century church and a campanile with a frozen clock.

A matronly woman in a fur coat held a rat-like dog on a leash. The poor-excuse-for-a-dog squatted, stared vacantly ahead, and lifted its tail. The woman watched her pet's performance with the utmost interest, now and then uttering words of encouragement. After the dog finished its business, she patted it, said, *"Mon bon, bon chien,"* ("My good, good, dog."), and headed toward an alleyway adjacent to the church. I followed them.

The steep, narrow passage, barely wide enough for two men to walk abreast, exuded humidity. It was bone chilly, the air musty, and the cobblestones slippery. Zipping up my jacket, I caught a glimpse of the blue sky, but not of the sun. *Who in his right mind would want to live in such claustrophobic surroundings?* I wondered.

Algerian, Moroccan, and Tunisian immigrants, the ten percent of the French population, would, I reflected as I observed the woman and her pet step into a left alleyway darkened by suspended laundry. I turned right, lured by roses, tulips, and other flowers in urns on the sidewalk and in pots on balconies and the window sills.

Moments later fingers of sunshine kissed the cobblestones. Vines grew over the shutters of a one-story house. Watermarks stained the brick walls. Weeds grew in the tiled driveway. A statue of a fawn covered with bird droppings rose desolately midway to the house entrance. The absence of life, alternating channels of light and shadows, and an anguished mood awoke images of a painting by De Chirico.

Thinking that a bit of work would make the residence an inspiring home for an artist, I began walking up and down the waist-high wooden fence looking for a rental sign. Finding none, I pushed open the rusted iron gate. The leaf-covered path felt as soft as a woolen carpet. After brushing the dust and leaves off a stone bench, I sat down and thought of Modigliani. Of below average height, sickly, he was a dashing prince in the bohemian Paris of the last century. Even when hungry, he wore his vest and cravat with the flare of an aristocrat. Women found him irresistible. The day after he died of tuberculosis at thirty-five, his pregnant lover threw herself down from a balcony.

Modigliani painted and loved women to the very end. To the very end, he stood apart from established art schools, loyal to his muse and to his calling for artistic excellence. He was a giant of a man. I idealized him.

Back in the alleyway, a smell of garlic and grilled lamb drifted from somewhere. Tambourines, castanets, and strings broke the silence. On the alleyway, from behind a ground-floor beaded curtain, a large shadowy figure seemed to observe my every move.

A door suddenly opened behind me. "Slow down, buddy," a husky male voice called in perfect English.

I pretended not to hear.

"Stop, will you?"

Turning slowly, I gazed at an unshaven, stocky man in a nylon gym suit, with his bare feet ensconced in plastic, green, flip-flops.

"What . . . what do you want?" I mumbled.

"A cigarette, but why are you staring at me?"

"I . . . I . . . don't smoke. I thought you were an Arab."

"I'm from Wichita. Came here to paint. And what made you think I was an Arab?"

"Arabs live in the old town, don't they?"

"And French, Spanish, and God knows who else."

"Yeah, you are right. I shouldn't have suspected you being an Arab. But, how did you figure out that I was—"

"Only an American or a Japanese would go sightseeing with a water bottle and camera dangling from his shoulders. Why the questions? Is there a French law that says you can't ask a stranger for a cigarette? But tell me what did the Arabs do to you that you fear them?"

"I don't fear the Arabs."

"You suspected I was one, didn't you?"

"I support the Palestinian aspirations for statehood," I snapped.

"Next, you'll tell me that your sister is married to an Afro-American."

The man is made of Teflon but he is an artist, so I said, "Listen, I am an artist too. Let's go to a café, have a beer, and chat about our work."

Giving me the once-over, he said, "You a homo or something?"

I shrugged and said, "Have it your way. Good luck to you."

"Don't give me the good luck shit. It's the talent, skill, and inspiration that counts."

The asshole was right. I was acting like an ordinary bourgeois. Turning now and then to ascertain that I wasn't being followed, I arrived at a small plaza with a glorious view of the faraway Mediterranean. On three sides rose renovated one and two-storied pastel homes with large French windows, small gardens with terra-cotta ornaments, and verandas dotted with flower pots. Out of an open window rose strains of a Chopin sonata. With my eyes closed, I imagined a young woman with flowing blond hair and a long white gown bent over the keys of a Steinway. Moments after the music stopped, a gray-haired woman leaned outside the window. I clapped. She smiled, bowed, and returned inside.

A desire to give the woman her lost youth in exchange for more piano playing descended upon me. But why did I fantasize about her being a beautiful young woman? Why did her age matter? The answer came to me promptly: My mother's indoctrination still controlled me.

I was six years old, licking ice cream on the shore of Dubrovnik, on the Adriatic, when an elderly woman dropped her handkerchief. My mother picked it up and handed it to her.

"Thank you, my dear," the woman said. "You have been brought up to be a fine young lady. What's your name?"

"Anna," my mother said.

"And your sister and brother, what are their names?"

"She isn't my sister," I said. She is—"

"Hush," my mother cried. "My sister's name is Carla, and my brother's Adam."

"I'm sure your mother is proud of all of you. You're so well behaved, and so nicely dressed."

After the woman left, my mother said, "No ice cream for you tomorrow."

"But, why? What did I do?"

"As usual, you tried to spoil the little fun I get out of life."

Perplexed, I dropped my ice cream.

"It serves you right," she said, taking Carla by the hand and moving on.

Okay, so I was raised by a mother deeply preoccupied with youth and physical attractiveness. But most men, even those who grew up with normal mothers, are drawn to women in their prime. Rubens, Renoir, and other classic painters used beautiful young women as models. The Greeks and Romans sculpted ideal human forms. True, true, but my preoccupation with female physical attractiveness went beyond aesthetic appreciation. I still had a way to go to attain full emancipation from my mother's fixations.

I walked to the old church, sat down on an outside step, took a bite of a croissant, and noticed a weathered sign above a nearby shop saying "Tonio." Inside a glass case by the entrance, silver bracelets, rings, and pendants shone in the sun. My heart sped up. I had been looking for a workshop to make jewelry in. Could this be my lucky day?

Taking a closer look at the pieces inside the glass case I noticed an object looking like a tie clip holding another clip with a prophylactic! A prophylactic on a tie clip?

Withhold judgment, an inner voice warned. *He is French, and the French invented the French kiss. They know all there is to know about sexual ethics.*

Inside, a dark-skinned man with an aquiline nose, map of gray hair, luxurious gray beard, beady brown eyes, and muscular arms sat at a workbench surrounded by pliers, mallets, files, sandpaper, and other jewelry-making tools. On one wall half a dozen pictures of Arab teenagers throwing stones at Israeli soldiers and burning Israeli flags. On another stood a large map of ancient Babylonia. I resolved to keep to myself my Jewish origins.

"*Bonjour, monsieur,*" I said.

"Where in America do you come from?" the man asked, without lifting his eyes from the silver wire he was working on.

"How did you figure out that I come from the States?"

"Some things I just know, my friend." Pointing at a stool, he said, "Sit down."

"In the very heart of the medieval Biot, what a great place to sell jewelry," I said.

"Thank you, my friend. Los Angeles isn't bad either. I tended bar there for three years. My name is Tonio."

"I am Adam from Santa Fe, New Mexico."

"Ah, the city of art."

"I stretched out my arm holding a large silver bracelet and said, "I'm a jeweler too. I made this."

He shrugged, lifted a silver band from the bench, and said, "I made this in nine minutes."

"All by yourself?"

"But of course."

"No assistant?"

"I am a one-man operation."

"Ever since coming to France, three weeks ago, I have been idle. I would be willing to give you a hand without compensation."

"Thanks, my friend, but I do best alone."

A tall, slim woman in her early forties and a younger, full-figured companion, stepped in.

"Welcome, ladies," Tonio said, bowing slightly. "Feel at home. Ask questions. I am at your service."

"Where do you come from?" I asked.

"From the Border region, not too far from Glasgow."

"Ah, Glasgow, a city of majestic squares, Victorian buildings, and opulent museums."

"And you, where are you from?" she asked.

"Santa Fe." I removed my bracelet and handed it to her. "I made this."

"Very nice, but it's a bit too big for me. Here, Muriel, you try it."

"Hm . . . looks like a small sculpture," Muriel said.

"That's nothing," Tonio said. "Wait till you see what I made."

Annoyed by his dismissal, I took back my bracelet from Muriel, and watched him step into a small storage room. Returning with a strange silver contraption, he said, "I had in mind a lady with regal bearing while making this."

"Donna, I think he means for you to try it on," Muriel said.

Tonio pushed a curl away from Donna's left cheek, then slipped two wires over her ears. The wires held an immense silver pendant in the shape of a mouth with pointed teeth. "Just a small adjustment," he said.

"It looks great on you," Muriel said.

Tonio picked up a mirror from his bench and held it in front of Donna, like a page attending to his royal mistress.

Blushing, Donna said, "It must cost more than I can afford. Still, I would—"

"It's not for sale," Tonio said. "I made it for a gallery exhibit. He removed the necklace, straightened the curls over her face, and said, "Now, if you will excuse me, I must place the necklace back in its box."

When he returned, Donna pointed at a bracelet in the display case by the entrance.

"I'll have one too," Muriel chirped.

Both bought the bracelets without first asking for the price, curtsied slightly, and left without as much as throwing a glance at me.

Watching Tonio placing the money inside his billfold, I barely restrained myself from asking, "Having fun, you asshole?"

By a gentleman's agreement, my housemates used the bathroom in the morning before I did. Friday, awakened by a painfully full bladder, I waited with much urgency for them to pass through. William came first. Roberto appeared minutes later. Half an hour passed and Marie still had to arrive. She had looked pale at the dinner the evening before. Could she be ill? Was the day a school holiday? Unable to postpone the call of nature, I jumped out of the bed, when the door handle to William's room turned. Terrified, I covered my genitals with my hands as Marie, pale as a ghost, stepped in. Wearing a green silk nightgown, she walked slowly, passed in front of me, opened the door to the living room, and disappeared.

Have I been dreaming? I wondered. A scent of sweat and perfume put that notion to rest. My heartbeat was so loud that I thought my heart was going to break loose. Perspiration drenched my forehead. The bladder discomfort growing intolerable, I rushed to the window, opened it, and let a stream out.

I dressed fast, skipped breakfast, and run out. At the park with the fountain, I eased down on a bench and went over my encounter with Marie.

Asking her for forgiveness might be the way out. But forgiveness for what? Like the protagonist in Kafka's *The Trial,* I felt guilty for crimes I hadn't committed. To be on the safe side, I decided to make amends by preparing an extraordinary dinner. The rest of the day I spent meandering in the medieval part of the town. Shortly before sunset I went shopping. I bought juicy shrimps, brown rice, tomatoes, onions, garlic, and herbs de Provence. Timidly, I opened the door to the apartment. Marie stood at the kitchen sink.

"*Bon soir, mademoiselle,*" I said with a forced simile. "It's my turn to prepare the dinner."

"You can have the kitchen to yourself in a couple of minutes."

I deposited the groceries on the counter and headed for my room. Roberto and William sat on the floor in front of the television.

"Did you have a good day?" Roberto asked.

I studied his expression. Nothing, not a line seemed out of place. He was his usual self, friendly in a formal way. Either Marie didn't tell him about seeing me in the nude or, if she did, he decided that it had been an unavoidable accident. Somewhat reassured, I dropped my jacket on my mattress, rolled up my shirt sleeves, and returned to the kitchen. Marie was gone.

The dinner ready, I uncorked a bottle of Sauvignon Blanc, filled the glasses, and called my housemates. Chatting in English for my benefit, they complimented me on my cooking. Not a word or a gesture on anyone's part alluded to the morning incident It was all pleasantries and gracefulness in typical French manner. At the end of the dinner, over a chocolate dessert and ice cream, Roberto announced that for the next several evenings he and William wouldn't be coming home for dinner. They and some friends were planning to cut a CD of their music in a studio in Nice. I had known that Roberto, besides being a scientist was a competent musician, so I wasn't surprised.

"Will Marie be joining you?" I asked, wondering if I should request a key to the apartment. But, then, remembering that the day of my arrival he had said the apartment never gets locked, I let the thought pass.

"If she wants to," he answered, patting her hand.

The next evening, Marie and I ate dinner alone. As usual, she hardly uttered a word. She looked at peace with herself. I felt as tight as a sling. I asked how Roberto's recording was coming alone.

"I believe he is pleased," she answered.

"Do you play any musical instruments?"

"I wish I knew how."

"Would you like to take lessons?"

She shrugged. "Do you like to fuck?" I wanted to ask, but of course, kept the thought to myself. I couldn't wait for Roberto's and William's recording sessions to be over.

The third evening of Roberto's and William's absence, I returned home with six roses. It occurred to me that I had been overly preoccupied with myself, and shamelessly insensitive to Marie's concerns. She had surrendered her privacy to accommodate me in her apartment. She had been cooking more vegetarian dishes than was her habit. And what did she get in return? My phony interest in her life. My flowers would convey long overdue admiration for her dedication to Roberto and to the pupils in the school she taught.

I rushed up the stairs, turned the door handle, turned it and turned it but the door remained locked. I knocked. I banged. I hastened to Maurice's pad down the hall. I rang the bell. I waited seemingly for an eternity, then returned to Roberto's apartment. I knocked and banged again. Did Marie have an accident? Was she in Nice attending Roberto's and William's recording session? Did she and Roberto go to the country to visit Roberto's father? My stomach grew as tight as a balloon. I wiped the perspiration on my forehead with the back of my hand, sat on the floor, and rested my head on my knees. The click of the light switch on the ground floor, followed by a sudden illumination of the staircase, sent adrenalin into my veins. My excitement died fast, though, after I realized that the walk was too heavy to be Marie's. An unknown man glanced curiously at my flowers, nodded, and continued up the stairs. I rose and, on shaky legs, stepped outside.

Leaves swirled in the wind. The full moon stood suspended above the chimneys. I threw the flowers into a trash can, slapped my chest, and stamped my feet. A dog barked somewhere. Quiet returned. I glanced at the balcony. The apartment was as dark as the night.

At the restaurant where Alphonse's barmaid served drinks, I took a window table and over spaghetti and red wine, kept a restless vigil for my roommates. Afterward, I walked to the one-star hotel in the old town. The clerk demanded three hundred fifty francs or seventy dollars for a room. Unwilling to spend that much money for the privilege of spending one night amidst ancient stones, I declined the offer and ventured back to the park. The apartment was still dark, Chilled, I stepped into the enclosed telephone booth close to the fountain and dialed my sister in Rome.

"Are you all right?" my sister asked.

"You seem to think that I only call you when I'm in trouble."

"Well, are you or aren't you okay?"

"Biot is not the paradise I thought it would be," I mumbled.

"Only dreamers and fools believe in an earthly paradise."

"Better to be an alive dreamer than a burnt-out realist," I said with feigned bravado.

"That's dumb talk. You are like Pinocchio, staring at the sky and tripping all over yourself."

"There is an emaciated dog outside the telephone booth. I wish I had some food to give him."

"Forget the dog. How is Marie?"

"Cold as marble, as usual."

"Tell her you like her cooking. Compliment her on her appearance. Express gratitude for her hospitality, and she will warm up to you."

"Any other suggestion?"

"Listen to her. Pretend that you're enthralled by the workings of her mind."

"That's like asking me to toss my standards into a garbage bin, a hell of a price to pay for obtaining someone's acceptance," I said, a bit self-consciously.

"Men are such fools. They make wars and break marriages because of their pride."

I called my sister to unburden myself and was getting additional burden. Eyeing the full moon, I reflected how similar it was to Carla's face: round, placid, and lacking in strong distinguishing features. Window shutters in a house closed noisily. *"Bonne nuit,"* a male voice said from somewhere.

"Biot is settling for the night," I said. "I wish I had a place to settle down too."

"Have you been locked out? Don't you have a key to the apartment?"

"How is the Eternal City? Is your blood pressure under control?" I asked.

"You're changing the subject. Do as I say. Treat Marie like a queen and she will treat you like a king."

"The bitch can go and fuck herself."

"I would appreciate it if you didn't use that kind of language with me. I've got to go. Do as I say. Bye."

Demoralized by Carla's lecturing, I sought the dog to soothe my nerves with but he was nowhere to be found. Slapped mercilessly by the wind, I buttoned my jacket to the collar and began pacing back and forth like the polar bear I had seen doing at the San Diego zoo a few years back. At eleven, shaking with cold, I headed for the hotel in the old town to book a room, when the light in the apartment suddenly lit. I ran into the building, turned on the light switch, and hastened up the stairs. At the door, hearing Marie's squeaky voice, I stopped. The staircase turned dark. After her voice vanished, I cautiously stepped in. She was gone. Roberto and William squatted by the television in the living room, each one holding a remote control in his hand.

When I came to a few feet from them, Roberto asked how my day was.

"You locked me out," I said, barely controlling myself.

"I did?" Robert glanced at William.

William's eyes opened wide.

"I thought you had gone to visit your father."

"We're going next weekend."

Dumbfounded, I asked, "Why did you do it?"

"Do what? Would you like to join us?"

"Join you for what?" I asked stupidly.

"To play Nintendo, what else?"

I stared at him. Was he toying with me? I barely restrained myself from telling him that I thought he was the ultimate piece of French *merde*. But I held back. I hadn't established yet that he had deliberately locked me out. I left for my room, undressed, crawled under the covers, and imagined subjecting Roberto to waterboarding. I almost drowned him and still failed to obtain the answer.

In the morning, exhausted from tossing and turning, I watched Roberto and Marie passing by my mattress. William followed them. Dishes clattering told me that they had started eating their breakfasts. Desperate for answers, I dressed and joined them.

"Did you guys sleep well?" I asked, scrutinizing their faces for signs of guilt.

"I slept like a baby," William said. "How about you?"

Before I had a chance to answer, Roberto said, "You look pale as if you had a rough night,"

The fucker knew darn well that there were plenty of reasons for me to be pale.

"How's your recording coming along?" I asked with an effort.

He lifted his cup of coffee, took a swallow, and nodded. "Quite well, thank you."

Eyeing Marie, I asked, "You joined Roberto last night in Nice, didn't you?"

"She did," Roberto said. "After the session, we all went out for a beer. You should have come along."

"But how was I supposed to do that when you hadn't invited me."

Roberto looked at Marie. She shrugged. He wiped his mouth with a paper napkin, rose, and patted me on the back, "I guess we failed to communicate. We'll do better next time."

If he was acting, he was a mighty good actor. Reluctantly, I concluded that the door to the apartment had been locked accidentally. "Perhaps, I could go to Nice and listen to your session some evening," I said.

"We'll work something out, I'm sure."

After spending the better part of the day visiting the Leger Museum, a couple of miles from Biot, I returned home. Marie, holding a cupful of rice over a pot of water, acknowledged me with a nod.

"You know, Marie," I said, "It doesn't seem right that you should do all the cleaning and all the cooking after a long day at school. No American woman would put up with that."

She shrugged and poured the rice into the boiling water.

"William leaves his breakfast dishes on the living room table. He drops crumbs on the floor. Why not ask him to clean after himself?"

"It doesn't matter. He's a friend!"

And who the hell am I? A passing beggar? The phone rang. She brought it to her ear and left. When the rice absorbed the water, I went looking for her. Unable to find her in the living room, and not wanting to disturb her in her bedroom, I shut the gas off. Moments later, she returned, eyed the pot with the rice, and screamed, "*Merde!*" Then, with her fists pressing against her hips, barked, "I would appreciate it if in the future you minded your own business. Now we'll have to eat HARD rice." Hard rice with all the water absorbed? Has she lost her mind? More likely she was using the rice to justify her notion that I am an idiot. Whatever doubts I had about her negative feelings about me vanished. I grabbed my jacket and left, convinced that I had outworn my welcome.

My first inquiry for an apartment produced no result. The bakery owner shook his head. At the flower shop, the proprietor suggested I put an ad in *Nice Matin*. The young woman managing the clothing boutique proved to be more helpful. "Papa knows everything that goes on in the village," she said. "He'll be back after lunch."

I bought the *Herald Tribune,* read it in the park, had a pizza and beer for lunch, then went looking for papa. Tall and thin with grey hair, a cigarette dangling from the corner of his mouth, he stood by the entrance to the boutique. After his daughter introduced us, Papa led me inside, picked up the phone, spoke rapidly, and now and then glanced and winked at me, which I took to be a good omen. His conversation over, he motioned for me to follow him. We passed the wooden barriers controlling the village motor traffic, reached the busy Valbonne highway, skirted a small art gallery, a pottery shop, a diminutive park with a Byzantine chapel, a large apartment complex, and arrived at a stone house with green shutters. A short, middle-aged man with receding hair waved at us from the entrance. We shook hands and he introduced himself as Giuseppe.

"*E Italiano?*" I asked.

He nodded. "*Allora possiamo parlare Italiano,*" ("Then, we can speak in Italian,") I said, being familiar with the language.

Giuseppe explained that he had partitioned his house into two halves. The part available for rent was the one facing the street. After papa excused himself, Giuseppe led me into a large, dark room that served both as the kitchen and the living room. It was mid-morning. The day was bright and sunny. Yet the apartment, even with the single window open, failed to offer sufficient light to read a newspaper. The street noise was deafening. Eyeing the discolored, Salvation Army-like furniture, I reflected that it was tolerable. My furniture in Santa Fe had also seen better days. But the darkness, the humidity, and the musty smell sickened me. As if reading my mind, Giuseppe said, "The electric heaters are more than adequate."

The refrigerator and the stove were up to American standards. The bedroom at the opposite end from the apartment entrance, to my immense surprise, had plenty of daylight, and it opened up to the view of a valley studded with tall trees and homes perched on a sunny hillside. With the door closed, there was a quiet that a Yoga master would find agreeable. Adjacent to the bedroom were the shower and the toilet.

Visualizing myself playing computer chess while eased in the armchair, I reflected that should I rent the apartment, I would make the bedroom my headquarters. Giuseppe informed me that the rent came to three thousand five hundred francs or seven hundred fifty dollars, which was two hundred dollars less than the amount I received for renting my house in Santa Fe. The price was fine, I said, but the traffic noise and the darkness in the kitchen-living room were unbearable. Would he consider letting me have the other half of the house, with a south-facing balcony? His wife, Nina, wouldn't allow it, he replied. That was going to be their retirement home.

I went looking for Papa. "Okay?" he asked. I shook my head. "Too dark and too much noise." His daughter translated. He knew of no other available apartments. I thanked him, dialed Giuseppe, and offered to rent his apartment on a month-to-month basis. He agreed. The next morning, dodging the maddening Valbonne motor traffic and reflecting that I would rather live in a dungeon free of Marie than in a sunlit apartment with her as my housemate, I arrived at Giuseppe's home.

A short, middle-aged, stocky woman, stood by his side. I smiled and offered her my hand. Ignoring my gesture, she barked, "I don't rent to his kind."

"Nina, he isn't one of them," Giuseppe protested.

"He is. Just look at him."

Stunned, I asked, "Giuseppe, what's going on?"

"Nothing to worry about," he answered, then reached out for her hand holding the keys to the apartment. She backtracked as a group of bicyclists came riding up the road. One with a number 10 engraved on his purple shirt applied brakes to avoid her and fell. The one behind him skidded and landed on top of him. A large Mercedes came to a hard stop. Cars behind the Mercedes blew their horns. Drivers screamed, raised their fists. Giuseppe rushed to help the bicyclists. Nina seemingly untouched by the pandemonium, kept her biddy, brown eyes glued onto my face. The bicyclists, seemingly unhurt, departed. The motor traffic resumed its chaotic flow.

Giuseppe, his brow covered in sweat and his hair in disarray re-joined us. "Thank God no one got hurt," he mumbled.

"Your wife keeps staring at me." I said. "Why is she doing that?"

"She thinks you are one of the people we rented the house to last year. They also had beards, only theirs were black."

"Pigs," Nina yelled. "They slept on the floor, partied all night, sold drugs, and turned the place into a Casbah."

"We don't know that they sold drugs," Giuseppe protested.

"They were Arabs, weren't they?"

The crazy woman thinks I am an Arab because I have a beard. "*Signora*," I said in a reassuring voice, "*Io sono Americano.*"

"You're as much an American as I. Get out of my sight."

"I have had it, Giuseppe," I cried. "I don't want your fucking apartment."

"Wait!"

"*Abaststanza con chiachere. Andiamo via*," Nina yelled. ("Enough babble. Let's go.")

Red in his face, breathing hard, Giuseppe grabbed her hand, retrieved the keys, and handed them to me. 'Don't worry about her. She'll calm down soon enough."

"One wild party, and out you go!" she yelped.

Nina was crazy. Marie was crazy. But whereas I had to share living space with Marie, I didn't have to share anything with Nina. The rest of the day I packed, read, and slept. At the dinner that evening I informed my housemates that I planned to move out first thing in the morning. "How much do I owe you for the rent and utilities?" I asked.

"Nothing," Roberto said. "You stayed a short time. Buy us a dinner."

"My new apartment has a great kitchen."

"Call us after you get settled."

Glancing at William I said, "*Au revoir, mon ami. C'était formidable de pratiquer le français avec toi.*"

"You speak gooder French now."

"No, no, not 'gooder.' You want to say 'better.' *Est-ce que tu veux continuer à étudier la langue Anglaise?*"

"Yes, I like to practice study of English with you."

"*Tu es un brave homme, William.* I'll be looking forward to seeing you soon. Now I think I'll go to sleep."

"A *tout à l'heure, Adam,*" Roberto said.

"A *tout à l'heure,* Roberto, Marie et William."

"*Bonne chance,*" Marie said, I thought, with much relief. Later, in bed, I mused that all her coldness vanished the moment I announced my departure. Roberto had expressed an interest in dining in my new home. Taking that to be an invitation for a friendship, I vowed to serve him an unforgettable meal to be accompanied by the best Cote d'Azur wine.

7

Headache, watery eyes, mucus kept me awake. Believing I had succumbed to an allergy attack, I picked up my flashlight and went looking for the cause of my plight. Under the bed lay a thick packet of dust. I was allergic to dust but had never experienced such a severe reaction before. Behind the large dresser, there was more dust and two large cobwebs. One held a fly in its delicate lacework. After having inspected the bathroom where I found nothing suspicious, I returned to the bedroom, slipped, and landed on Nina's blanket stretched on the bed. A smell of sweat and manure invaded my nostrils so intensely that I almost fainted.

I threw the blanket on the shower floor, closed the door, opened the window, and to keep warm, put my jeans over my pajama, donned a sweater and a ski cap, and covered myself with the flimsy blanket I had brought with me from the States. Free of allergy but chilled, I slept fairly well.

Sunlight on the ceiling greeted me in the morning. I shut the window, dressed, poured antibacterial liquid soap on Nina's blanket, and washed it thoroughly. Afterward, water dripping, I dragged it across the kitchen and the living room and opened the door.

At the sight of Nina standing a few feet from me, I exclaimed, "What the heck."

Had she been spying, seeking evidence for her paranoiac notion that I was an irresponsible Arab? But she couldn't see what was happening inside. More likely she had been waiting for me to open the door in order to steal a peek into my private world.

"What do you think you are doing with my blanket?" she barked.

"It should be obvious," I answered. "Do you own horses?"

"What difference it makes to you if I do?"

"It makes a big difference if you're allergic to them."

With her stocky build, thick neck, broad shoulders, and strong arms, Nina reminded me of the peasant women I had seen stamping grapes during my early adolescence in northern Italy. Giuseppe had told me that both of them grew up on a farm. She would probably find the blanket smelling as sweet as flowers.

"This thing is dripping all over me, Nina," I said. "Follow me to the clothesline, and we'll chat there."

To my surprise, she came. To my even greater surprise, she helped me hang the blanket.

"I would have washed it had you asked me," she said, wiping her wet hands on her black cotton skirt.

"An American on the Côte d'Azur, the land of the rich and famous, doing laundry in the shower, now that's stuff legends are made of," I grinned.

Her countenance softened. I detected a trace of a smile. "Do you like fresh eggs?" she asked.

"Who doesn't?"

The next morning six eggs and a bottle of wine lay by my door. A note explained: "Eggs come from my chicken, wine from Giuseppe's preserve." After securely installing earplugs to subdue the infernal street noise, I made an omelet garnished with Parmesan cheese, onions, garlic, *herbes de provence,* and tomatoes. It went superbly with Giuseppe's wine.

In an uplifted mood, I vowed to call Julie and not ask any personal questions. She accepted my invitation to visit the Cannes' flea market on Sunday. The mid-November day was sunny and soothingly warm. We met mid-morning at the market. After a friendly handshake, I asked, "Is there anything you would like to buy?"

"Hm . . . let me see. I could use some prophylactics, but I doubt they have them here."

My stomach tightening, I said, "You're joking, right?'

"In this day and age, you never know what kind of shit your partner might pass on to you."

"Are you thinking of herpes?"

"Of herpes and everything else."

"Have you been infected?" I asked.

"Who the hell you think you are to ask such personal questions?"

"Calm down. It isn't every day that someone comes to the flea market looking for prophylactics."

"I am not an ordinary someone. Anyway, I said I doubted I would find them here. What kind of shit are you looking for?"

"Maybe a tool or two to make jewelry with."

We began walking. The market was adjacent to the harbor. Sailboats with flags from different countries fluttered in the wind. Seagulls danced above our heads. A table with tools suddenly appeared.

I picked a pair of industrial caliber scissors. Heavily rusted, they were unusable. I dropped them on the table when the owner, who was sitting on the other side, lifted his head from above the newspaper he was reading and screamed.

Julie pulled me by the arm. "Let's get away. He says if you don't apologize, he'll cut your balls with the scissors you dropped.

"Apologize for what?" I asked.

"Move on, will you?" Safely out of the range of the crazy Frenchman, I asked, "What did I do wrong?"

"You didn't ask his permission to pick up the scissors. This is France, not America."

Unnerved, I moved on and unexpectedly succumbed to fatigue. Julie hadn't answered if she had herpes. Irrationally fearing that she might contaminate me, I moved a couple of inches away from her.

"You are frowning. You look worried. Is something bothering you?" she asked.

"I'll tell you if you promise not to get mad."

"Fuck, what's that supposed to mean?"

"You never answered if you had herpes."

"I don't have them, you asshole. Anything else you want to know?"

I nodded. "Just one more thing."

Coming within a couple of inches from my face, she yelled, "No, the guy who answered my phone is not my lover. I have my standards. I don't fuck losers."

Her comment reassured me, but the vulgar sound coming from her mouth turned me off. "Why do you call him a loser?"

"I met him at a party in London. After I came here, he begged to join me. He said the humidity was killing him. It turned out that he was impotent. Not just impotent. Depressed, hooked on anti-depressants. The guy was pathetic. I didn't have the heart to throw him out. So, I made him cook and clean the apartment while I worked. Now he's got a place of his own. We are still friends. Got it? Friends, just friends. Are you satisfied? Anything else you want to know?"

"Well . . . yes. Were you serious about finding prophylactics in the flea market?"

"Are you a Jew or something?"

"What does that have to do with my question?"

"Everything. Jews have no sense of humor. They're into their heads. Give a Jew a book and he goes into a cave until he finishes it. Well, are you, or aren't you?"

"I'm afraid I am, but not a practicing one."

She burst into a voluptuous laugh. "I knew it. I knew it. Come, I want to kiss you." I closed my eyes, expecting to be kissed on the mouth. Instead, she kissed me on the forehead. Pleasantly surprised, I mused that her tough exterior might be but a cover-up for a sensitive and delicate soul. I felt lonely. I wanted a female companion. *Could Julie be the one?* I wondered.

Enjoying the sun as much as I do, it puzzled me that I found tolerable living in a tomb-like apartment. But after my ordeal with Marie, I would have willingly resided in a hole. Freeing myself from Marie hadn't given me the peace of mind I had hoped for, however. I missed the opportunity to build a friendship with Roberto. The day of my departure he expressed an interest in dining in my new apartment. Deciding to turn the wish into reality, I dialed him a week later. Marie answered. "How have you been?" I asked.

"Teaching and planning lessons. And you? Are you happy in your new home?"

"I'll tell you all about it when you come over for dinner. Are you, Roberto, and William free this Saturday?"

"Roberto is in Nice. I'll talk with him and apprise him of your invitation."

"And don't even think of bringing anything. It's the least I can do to show you my gratitude for your hospitality. Please, tell Roberto to let me know by Thursday evening."

"I will. Be well. Bye, Adam."

Thursday came and went. Friday passed and not a word from Roberto. Saturday, sitting on the wobbly armchair in my bedroom, I wondered if Roberto had come down with the flu, if he had a car accident, if Marie was ill-disposed. Unable to come up with a reliable explanation, I considered calling. But not wanting to appear overly eager, I decided to wait for a chance encounter. The wait was brief.

Monday morning, while I was reading the newspaper at the bench by the obelisk, Roberto stepped out of his apartment building.

"Hello Professor," I called. "Your hair is short. You're all dressed up. What happened to the old hippie?"

"Oh, it is you," Roberto said, glancing at his watch. "How do you like your new accommodations?"

"You would have found out if you had called me."

"I've been very busy with teaching and recording sessions."

Everyone deserves a second chance, I reflected. "Can you come this Friday? We'll have a shrimp stew and homemade wine."

"It sounds wonderful. Let me talk with Marie and William. I'll let you know."

"No later than Wednesday evening, please."

"But of course. I've got to be going now. Have a good day."

Watching him head for the village traffic barriers I berated myself for my lack of faith. If it hadn't been for him, I would have spent my first three weeks in France all alone in some impersonal, dreary motel.

Tuesday afternoon, under a clear, blue sky, I drove to the Intermarchè supermarket in Villeneuve Loubet, half an hour from Biot. I bought the juiciest, plumpest shrimps, the reddest tomatoes, the sweetest-looking baby greens, the plushiest peppers. I bought clover honey and rum for the chocolate-banana desert. Back home I got down on my knees and scrubbed the kitchen-living room floor.

Roberto didn't call Wednesday. He didn't call Thursday. Friday came and went without a beep from him. My anger boiled over. I visualized puncturing his car tires. I visualized feeding him food that would give him diarrhea. I visualized throwing dog shit into his convertible. The fantasies, while gratifying, troubled me. Never before had a rejection unglued me to such a degree. Had he called and said he couldn't come, I would have been hurt but gone on with my life. But being rudely dismissed by the very person I longed to form a friendship with was more than I could tolerate.

For two days I read, played computer chess, and napped. The third day, I took the local coastal train. Gazing at fishermen with poles as long as those holding street lights, at seagulls pirouetting and diving into the ocean, and at sailboats sinking and rising out of the swell cheered me up. But it wasn't until I arrived at Menton, the warmest town on the Riviera, where lemon trees blossom in winter, and gazed at the whimsical creations in the *Musée Jean Cocteau* that my spirit began to recover. It continued to improve in Villefranche Sur Mere as I strolled through the haunted vaulted old town which in medieval times had sheltered the inhabitants from marauding pirates, and as I marveled later at the Russian cruise ship, Maxim Gorky, sailing into the harbor gracefully as a swan. My spirit fully recovered at the sight of exquisitely executed sea life in glasses, ceramics, and canvases in the Picasso museum in Antibes.

That night in bed my mind turned to Voltaire's Candide. He spent tortuous years traveling the world before finding his true *garden*. I liked Biot. *Will Biot become my very own garden?* I wondered. The next morning, in a mood for sunshine, I ventured into the park with the fountain. Moments after I sat down on a bench and opened the *International Herald Tribune,* a bird-like female voice squeaked, "*Ça va?*"

The sight of a small child with obsidian eyes, with a dress imprinted with flowers, covering her from her neck to her ankles, brought fond memories of a journey to Albania. A look-alike, barefoot, gypsy girl, had agreed to pose for me. But to my surprise and amusement, she snatched the money I held in my hand and took off before I had a chance to click the shutter.

"*Ça va,*" I replied.

"*Comme t'appelles-tu?*"

"Adam, *Et toi?*"

"*Je m'appelle Marianne.*" Marianne was the symbol of France. Marianne decorated French currency. Delacroix had painted her bare-breasted, leading French soldiers into bloody combat.

I rose, dropped the paper on the bench, and motioned for her to keep an eye on it. She nodded. At the nearby general store, where I had earlier purchased the *Tribune*, I bought a dozen chocolate candies. Upon returning I said, "*J'apporte des bonbons.*"

"*Oú sont-ils?*"

"*Dans la poche de ma veston.*" She put her tiny hand inside my jacket pocket, retrieved a candy, removed the paper covering, and placed it inside her mouth. That my French pronunciation was atrocious didn't seem to faze her a bit.

"*C'est bon?*" I asked.

"*Oui. C'est très bon.*"

Wiping off her chocolate-stained mouth with her hand, she asked, "*D'où êtes-tu?*"

To tell her that I came from the United States would have, in all likelihood, confused her. So, I said, "*Je viens apres Biot.*"

She tilted her head in the direction of a brick house housing a pottery shop on the street level. "*J'ai habité là-bas.*"

Could she be an Arab? I wondered, *or perhaps a Pied Noir, a French ex-colonialist from Algeria.* Marianne waved at a heavyset, dark-skinned woman sitting on the wall surrounding the fountain in the company of two other dark women. "*Ma Maman,*" she said. The woman waved back. A constable appeared and Marianne joined him. They chatted for a few seconds, then he got down on his knees and kissed her on both cheeks. She returned, ate half a dozen more candies, jumped, cried "*Au revoir,*" and took off.

"*A tout à l'heure, Marianne,*" I yelled, as she headed toward a group of children at the fountain. I closed my eyes, surrendered my face to the sun, and imagined joining Marianne at play.

9

Julie lived in Vallbone, a well-preserved medieval village, some ten kilometers north of Biot. With a large old plaza with restaurants, crafts shops, bakeries, real-estate agencies, a small English bookstore, and renovated homes in the adjacent cobblestone streets, it was an expensive and showy expatriate enclave, which I frequented mostly when in a mood for the mouth-watering *Mille Feuilles*, the thousand-leaves chocolate-topped vanilla dessert. Julie's apartment was on the second floor of a renovated brick house with rain-stained walls. I climbed the steps and knocked on the door. Receiving no answer, I knocked again.

"Hold your horses, will you?" she screamed. "I'm on the phone."

Opening the door, she said, "Mark is having one of his depressive episodes. Talked of suicide. I wish he would do it and get it over with."

"You're joking, right?"

"What do you think? I feel sorry for the poor bastard, but he needs more tender loving care than I can offer him. Make yourself at home. There is a bottle of whiskey on the end table. I'll be back in minutes."

The apartment was Scandinavian teak modern, comfortable in a somewhat austere way. Flower urns on mantels and tables added a touch of warmth. Family photographs stood pinned on one wall, on another hung a large painting of two attractive naked women at an outdoor café. They smoked and held hands. Soft porn, I thought.

"Where did you get that painting on the wall?" I yelled.

"A present from old pals. Why?" She yelled back.

"It is sexy."

"You can masturbate while I'm getting ready. But be fast. I shouldn't be very long."

Taken back by her coarseness, I yelled back, "I think it would be more fun doing it with you."

Coming in moments later, she snickered, "Men—all they think about is sex. Except for poor Mark. He can't get it up."

"If you keep talking like this, I won't be able to get mine up either."

"But that's how men talk to each other. Women do it too when alone. All I'm doing is breaking down the barriers. Let's go."

"You look lovely wearing a skirt. You should do it more often, especially with your high heels on."

She ran her hands down her side, glanced at her skirt and her shoes, and said, "I know how to be a woman when I want to."

We headed for San Remo, Italy. Along the way, we listened to Pavarotti singing Neapolitan songs. The Italian customs agent waved us through. Friday evening, the center of the city was bustling with people. Pedestrians ran into each other. Cars blew their horns to keep striders out of their way. We parked in a side street near Victoria Casino and reached Pizzeria d'Amore in no time. A waitress in a black suit escorted us to a table by the window. I helped Julie to her chair, sat down, and picked up the menu, more out of habit than necessity, as I knew what I wanted to order. A vegetarian, except for seafood, I winced when Julie ordered a pizza with sausages. Sharing pizza was as satisfying as sharing a kiss. But Julie's choice of food obliged me to settle entirely on a pizza Napolitana with extra spinach. The waiter took my order, I thought, with a touch of puzzlement. I explained that I was short of iron, which was a lie. I just liked pizza with added spinach. He nodded with understanding. To make the evening special, I ordered a bottle of Chianti.

Julie removed her shoes and ran her toes up to my thighs. I looked around, but I shouldn't have worried. The tablecloth almost reached the floor. Aroused, I imagined us in bed embracing passionately.

We returned to her apartment in an ebullient mood largely, I suspected, because of the copious wine we consumed. I sat on the sofa while she went to change. Minutes later she returned wearing felt slippers and a cotton robe with a low neckline. She poured whiskey into two small glasses, passed one to me, then placed a CD in the player. Melodies from Beethoven's Ninth Symphony, my favorite composition, reverberated between the four walls. "Thanks for the excellent dinner," she said, sitting next to me.

"It was great dining with you. Let's do it again."

"Yes, let's do it," she said and rested her head on my shoulder. Ever so gently I lifted her head, kissed her neck, her ear lobes, and her eyes, then fondled her breasts. To my great surprise, tears ran down her cheeks. "Am I hurting you?" I asked.

She shook her head. "You know nothing about me. My life has been one disaster after another. My mother was a mouse, my father an alcoholic. Once, when I was eleven, he walked into my room as I stood naked. I covered my private parts with my hands. He smiled and said, "You don't want your father to see your sweety, is that it?"

"Was he drunk?"

"I was too scared to notice if he was or wasn't. I just wanted him to leave me alone. From then on, I locked my door at night. As an adolescent, I mistrusted boys, and grew fond of girls." She cleared her nose with a tissue, and went on, "Girls weren't angels by any standard, but they were trustworthy. Some gave me affection and love."

"Are you a lesbian?" I asked, with a knot in my stomach.

"That's a misused word. I had sex with girls if that's what you mean. Later, I had sex with boys too. Depending on how I felt, I did it with either sex. Fraternity boys raped me. I kicked several in their groins. With girls, I smoked pot and got high on acid. It's a miracle I survived."

"You sure had a hard time reaching full adulthood," I said, removing my hand from her breast.

"I feel so much better now that I got all that shit off my chest," she said and wiped the tears off her face with the palm of her hand. "You took really good care of me."

"You made me feel welcome. It was easy."

Suddenly, to my chagrin, she ran her hand up my thigh. "And you touch as nicely as some of the girls I had known."

"Please, don't," I said, removing her hand. "All that talk about your sexual abuse has changed my mood. I just feel like being close to you. Let's hold each other and listen to the music."

"But you got me all aroused. Tell you what. You eat me, and I'll give you a blow job."

"I am really not up to it. I'll take a rain check."

"I can't wait for a rain check. I want to fuck now."

"Julie, cuddle next to me. That will be as good as having sex."

"Like shit, it will. You're as bad as Mark. All you do is think of yourself."

"Only minutes ago, you told me that I took good care of you."

"I was wrong. You used me. You took what you wanted, and then dropped me like a used washcloth."

I rose. "I don't deserve that. I think I'll go home now."

"Go, you shithead, and don't even think of calling me again."

10

Some men get drunk to get over disappointments. Others dive into promiscuity. I hike. Actually, I had been thinking of going on a major trek even before things went sour with Julie. In my two months in Biot, I had only hiked to the train station a few times, four miles round trip. While there was no visible snow on the Maritime Alps, the cold nights indicated that winter was fast approaching and that if I intended to trek in the mountains, I would have to leave soon. I opened the *Michelin Guide to the Riviera* for ideas on where to go. One entry excited me. It said, "To the west of Tende, around Mount Bego (alt. 2872 m - 9423 ft) lies a region of glacial lakes and valleys, rock cirques and moraines, cut off by the lack of roads and the severe mountain climate . . . The peaks and valleys and lakes make a grandiose spectacle, but the region which is part of the Le Mercantour National Park is . . . famous for the thousands of rock engravings . . . some of which could be traced to the Bronze Age."

Further reading revealed that the *Refuge des Merveilles* offered meals and accommodations. I closed the book filled with anticipation, but my excitement diminished fast as I reflected that I was cursed with plantar fasciitis. The three-hundred-fifty-dollar shoe insert provided by my Santa Fe pediatrist hadn't ameliorated my heel pain. Because the pain varied in intensity, I decided not to allow it to affect my plans and to depart the following day.

Torrential rain woke me up the next morning. Trees in the valley below twisted as if rammed by a wild bull. Windows rattled uncontrollably. Clearly not a day for driving and hiking in the mountains, I threw my gym clothes into a bag and drove to Top Fit, on the outskirts of Antibes.

A young woman, with long black hair tied with a red handkerchief, worked on a stair stepper with an uncanny singularity of purpose, her breasts rising and falling as if propelled by a supernatural force. After forty-five minutes of a workout on the muscle-toning machines and weights, I stopped. The woman kept going. I got on a stationary bicycle and, as I started pedaling, she stopped, wiped her brow with a towel, and took a long swallow of Evian water. When she approached me, I smiled in the hope that my smile would convey my admiration for her indomitable will and finely tuned physique. After she returned my smile, I almost yelled to let her know that tomorrow, rain or sunshine, I would head for the *Refuge des Merveilles*.

I departed at noon in a drizzle, my foot mildly hurting, for the coastal highway that I had taken with Julie a week earlier. At the Italian border town of Ventimiglia, I turned north, re-entered France, and reached the Lac des Mesches, a subalpine lake at the foothills of tall mountains, the site of the trailhead. With my backpack, containing antihistamines, earplugs, a sweatshirt, rain gear, drinking water, figs, and dried chunks of soya, I took the broad, gradually rising forest trail. Knowing nothing about overnight stays in a refuge, I thought the clothing, the medicine, and the food would come in handy.

To protect my heel from added injury, I picked up a branch, cut off the protruding projections with my Swiss army knife, and turned it into a walking stick. Half an hour into the hike, heavy rain started. I donned my Gore-Tex pants under a large tree. A short while later the rain stopped. I took the pants off. The rain returned in no time, continuing like this until I arrived at Neige et Merveilles, a 60-room inn, a couple of miles from the trailhead. At my request, the innkeeper called the refuge. "Plenty of room," he said. "No need for reservations."

Back on the trail, my heel got worse. Wet gravel, dripping branches, and a deeply overcast sky continued monotonously. I longed for the inn. But then I thought of the woman at the gym. She wouldn't have quit. She would have gone on no matter what the difficulty. I pressed on, reached a cave, crawled inside, removed my backpack, ate dried figs, and drank water. It was a cozy spot and I closed my eyes intending to take a nap, but the awareness that dusk was approaching fast compelled me to rise and resume hiking.

To one side of a treeless valley studded with boulders appeared a small, crystal-clear lake. On its edge rose a wooden cabin with a stone chimney. The weathered walls looked as if they had been erected centuries ago. Plastic curtains blocked the view of the interior. Thinking I had arrived at the refuge, yet finding it hard to believe that refuge would be so small, I reached out for the door handle. It didn't budge.

On the ground by the door lay a wallet. Curious, I picked it up and noticed the picture of a smiling middle-aged woman and, deeper inside, a bundle of French currency. Placing the wallet inside my backpack, I reflected that a fellow hiker must have dropped it and that returning it to her would partially redeem me from my fiasco with Julie.

A larger hut appeared a short distance away. A sign above the entrance read: "Refuge des Merveilles, Club Alpin Français, 2200 meters (7200 feet)." The elevation gain from the Lac des Mesches was 2500 feet; from Biot, it was more than 7000. No wonder I was out of breath.

Inside, in an alcove to one side of a small dining room, a burly young man stood by a stove. I asked him if I could have accommodation and a vegetarian meal.

"Of course," he answered, and pointed at a staircase. "You won't find sheets, but will have all the blankets you'll ever need. The toilets and the showers are outside. There is no hot water."

After drying myself by a wood stove I ventured up to the dormitory, consisting of two long wooden platforms with dozens of foam-rubber mattresses piled on top. A bin in the center contained woolen blankets and pillows. A small window at each end offered a bit of lighting. Leaving my backpack on a mattress, I returned to the dining room.

Two couples and a single woman, all in their early fifties, sat at a long table. The burly attendant placed a container of meat stew on the table. The single woman filled her bowl with the stew, then passed it to me. Shaking my head, I was explaining that I was waiting for my vegetarian dish when the attendant appeared with a bowl of pea soup.

"Excuse me," I said, "But you told me I would have a vegetarian meal."

"It's in front of you."

"The pea soup?"

"That's vegetarian, isn't it?"

"Yes, but not enough to fill me up. Do you have any eggs or cheese?"

"Everything is gone. The refuge closes tomorrow. You may want to eat extra bread."

I filled my plate with the watery potage, dipped bread into it, took a drink of red wine, and wished that I, too, were a meat-eater.

"You aren't having much of a dinner," the woman, whom I recognized as the owner of the lost wallet, said. "It's cold and rainy. You need energy. Why not compromise and have some meat?"

I shook my head, "One compromise leads to another. Before you know it, you are in compromises up to your ears."

She wiped her mouth with a napkin and went on, "What would you do if you were starving and meat was all you had to eat?"

"Dalai Lama explained that in matters of life and death, it's justified to temporarily surrender one's values."

"A wise man, for sure."

"By the way, my name is Adam."

"I am Julie."

"Oh, no, you couldn't be."

"Did someone named Julie cause you harm?"

"It's a long story. But tell me, if a compromise is acceptable, would it be alright to keep a bundle of money you found and knew whose money it was?"

Laughing, she responded, "It might, depending on how much money there is in the bundle."

I rose. "Please excuse me, but I have to get something from my backpack. I'll be right back."

On the way to the dormitory, I contrasted the Julie from Valbonne with the Julie at the table. The Julie at the table radiated warmth. She soothed my nerves with her smile. She gifted openness and spontaneity. I removed the wallet I had found from my backpack, returned to the table, and said, "Guess what I have in my hand?"

"A chunk of dried meat?"

I laughed. "Something much more tempting. Your wallet."

"Oh my God. You found it. Where?"

"On the floor of the cabin by the lake."

She leaned over, kissed me on the cheek, and exclaimed, "I am so happy that you're a man of integrity. Stick to your watery pea soup. Don't eat meat. Suffer for your beliefs."

"Amen," I exclaimed. "Words befitting a messiah."

"Julie, we have to be going if we want to see the surrounding landscape before the night sets in," the woman next to Julie nudged her.

Julie grabbed a pen and a piece of paper, "Here is my email. I am returning to the States the day after tomorrow. Keep in touch when authentically wishing to have my company."

I laughed, "May God be my witness, I'll do that."

We hugged and she left with her friends.

I finished my pea soup, returned to the dormitory, sat on my mattress, munched on figs and chunks of dehydrated soya, then crawled under three woolen blankets. To my sorrow, my fast-beating heart stopped me from falling asleep. I took an antihistamine, closed my eyes, and shortly after lost consciousness. At sunrise, Julie's and her friends' noise woke me up. After they left, I slept another half an hour then, bleary-eyed, dragged myself to the dining room, ate bread with jam, drank Chamomile tea, and went out in search of the rock art.

During the tourist season, rangers lead hikes to the stone age drawings. I had no idea which way to go. Glancing at the 9,422-feet-high *La Cîme du Diable* (The Peak of the Devil), with its massive, jugged, peaks, I thought, for no clear reason, that heading toward the mountain's base I would stumble on the ancient inscriptions. My intuition proved to be correct. For, a half a mile into the hike, there appeared small human figures, flanked by animals with long imposing horns on an orange-hued boulder. Executed less elaborately than those made by the Native Americans centuries ago, the figures stood out in their stark, austere simplicity. Moments after I photographed the exhibit, it began to rain. I rushed to the refuge, put on my Gore-Tex pants, picked up my walking stick, and headed for the return trail. Halfway into the trek, the sound of a car engine stopped me. The refuge guardian in an old jeep waved. I waved back.

I tripped against stones. I slipped. My heel hurt badly. I could have asked for a ride, but an inner voice commanded that I complete the hike on my own. I arrived at the trailhead barely able to stand. In the car, I turned on the heat and mused that I had redeemed myself from my fiasco with Julie from Valbonne and that Julie from the refuge would have been proud of me. I had hiked the length of the trail, in each direction, hurting badly, hungry, and deeply fatigued. I had behaved like a giant of a man. I had been the most daring and the most authentic since my arrival in France.

A week after my hike to Le Mercantour National Park, a sunny but cool morning, Giuseppe knocked on my door.

"Nina and I are headed for Carrefour, the biggest grocery market on the Côte d'Azur. Would you like to join us?"

"I'll be ready in fifteen minutes. Let's go in my car. Nina might enjoy riding in a large vehicle."

She sat in the back, Giuseppe by my side. We drove toward the Biot station, followed a winding road for a mile, then turned right up a hill. An old Peugeot began tailgating me. I pressed on the breaks repeatedly to let the driver know I wanted him off my back. He blew the horn and gave me the finger.

"The son of a bitch," I exclaimed.

"Give him room to pass," Nina said.

"A car might be coming from the opposite direction, and it will be the end of all of us. He'll just have to wait."

The idiot nudged his bumper against mine. Nina made the sign of the cross.

"On the Côte d'Azur the auto insurance rates are as high as those in Paris," Giuseppe said, grabbing the support handle above his head.

Some twenty yards from the top, the man swung to my left and accelerated. I pressed hard on the brake pedal, causing our heads to thrust forward.

"You'll get us killed," Nina wailed.

"It isn't I who will kill you. It is that crazy French driver. I have this urge to go after him the way I went after a guy on the expressway to Italy."

"You chased someone?" Giuseppe asked.

"A week after my arrival, I was in the passing lane in one of the tunnels going to Italy, driving 100 kilometers per hour, when this man in a Mercedes got inches from my back. Because of the heavy traffic, I couldn't turn into the slow lane. I waved for him to be patient. Outside the tunnel, the moment I turned into the slow lane, he cut in front of me, slowed down, gave me the finger, and took off."

"Was he an Arab?" Nina asked.

"How was I supposed to know? I caught up with him at 150 kilometers per hour, pulled in front of him, slowed down, and flexed my arm the way Italians do to convey contempt for a fellow human. In the rearview mirror, I saw the guy gesticulate as if he had gone mad."

"Mio Dio," Nina exclaimed. "Don't do anything so foolish while I am in your car."

"Don't worry. The experience made my heart beat so fast that I thought it was going to escape from my ribcage. I vowed never again to let other people's insanity drive me insane."

In the enormous Carrefour parking lot, Nina dropped a 10-franc coin into a stationary slot, released a cart, and said, "This is for your use. Meet me at the fish counter in half an hour."

Stepping inside the market, I froze as a young woman on roller skates with a name tag on her blouse and a walkie-talkie in her hand zoomed by. She stopped to say something to a young man also on roller skates, who was talking to a woman in a wheelchair, then disappeared in the thick crowd. A Humpy Dumpty stood on a wooden crate. Children screamed and ran around him. I half expected to see Mickey Mouse appear.

At the vegetable stand, a petite, gray-haired woman stood on her toes, picked tomatoes, eyed them carefully, kept two, and replaced the others. A short man in a suit and tie examined several green peppers before choosing one. Men and women stretched their arms and necks in search of the ultimate heads of lettuce, cucumbers, carrots, lemons, oranges, and apples. Never before had I witnessed such passion for quality food.

Inspired by my fellow shoppers, I bought Greek yogurt, Parmigiano Reggiano cheese, a round, multi-grain organic bread with the crust the color of chocolate. Then at an aisle with a sign *Biologic, (Organic)*. I grabbed tofu, muesli, soya drinks, raisins, and figs. That the items were twice as expensive as those sold in Santa Fe didn't stop me. Filled with enthusiasm, I rushed to the fish counter.

Nina pointed at a package in her cart and said, "For our dinner Friday."

"Our?"

"You, Giuseppe, my son, Umberto, and me."

Her words sounded warm and inclusive. I liked that.

In the car, Giuseppe asked what I thought of *Carrefour*.

"A carnival. A place to dream impossible dreams. The French love of food is contagious. Let's try my bread. It's made with whole wheat organic flour."

Nina shook her head. "I prefer my baguette."

"But whole wheat is healthier."

She patted her well-rounded belly. "My digestion is so good I could eat iron."

We were chatting like old friends. She had invited me for dinner. And to think that only two weeks earlier she had refused to rent me her apartment.

Saturday, the day of my dinner with Giuseppe and Nina, the sun cast a blanket of warmth over Biot. After a hearty breakfast, I placed a dozen bracelets and pendants I had brought from Santa Fe into a leather pouch, and headed for St. Paul-de-Vence, the premiere art center on the Cote d'Azur.

Fishermen stood still as statues at the edge of the sea. Children played ball. Adults sat on blankets. Seagulls shrieked and dived. Regretfully, I exited the coastal highway at Cagnes Sur Mer and headed for the hill country. A castle graced with turrets beckoned me to stop for a visit. I ignored the invitation, pressed on, passed several sloping emerald fields with luxurious homes with swimming pools, and arrived at a rest stop which opened up to a view of parapets and watchtowers on the top of a hill: St. Paul de Vence.

No vehicles being allowed in the village, I left the car outside the ancient wall, then ventured into a maze of narrow alleyways lined up on each side with restored medieval homes. Gallery after gallery displayed in windows museum-quality art. I stepped inside one, introduced myself to the owner, and asked if he would be interested in seeing my jewelry. A New Zealander named John—he nodded. I passed him a large silver bracelet, partly smooth and partly textured, with a carnelian on its top. After eyeing it from different angles for several seconds, he asked how much I was asking for it.

"Two hundred fifty dollars. I would be willing to leave it on consignment," I replied.

Arching his thick eyebrows, he shook his head. "That's a lot of money for that amount of silver."

"The bronze statue of that man on a horse, do you sell it by its weight?" I asked.

"Of course not; that's art."

"And my jewelry is what?"

"You obviously aren't aware that jewelry, even that made with gold, isn't considered art in France. Try Oliver, in Old Antibes. He sells craft."

I wrote down Oliver's address and left. Owners of other galleries displayed even less interest in my jewelry than John did. Reflecting that I was wasting my time in St. Paul-de-Vence, I got into my car and headed for Old Antibes. I wasn't particularly discouraged. I had come to France mostly to make jewelry. As I approached Cagnes Sur Mer, the Mediterranean suddenly exploded with the splendor of crushed diamonds. Filled with excitement, I veered right into the littoral highway and watched with sailboats rolling in the swell and adults and children frolicking in the sand. The Old Antibes port was filled to capacity with yachts displaying international flags. Opposite them, on the *terra ferma,* elderly men played "bocce," the Italian game of throwing balls at stationary ones. Past the park, an enormous parking lot skirted a Roman wall. I left my car in the lot, walked through an arch, and arrived at a frenzied world of horn-blasting cars, roaring motorcycles, and rushing pedestrians that brought to mind a Middle-Eastern city.

The two-foot-wide sidewalk offered minimal protection from the traffic. Rubbing my shoulder against walls and windows of shops selling everything from electronic gadgets to flowers, I arrived at Silver Cloud, Oliver's emporium.

Colorful saris, shawls, and gowns hung over the sidewalk. Inside, carved brass boxes, leather billfolds, carpets, tall candlesticks, and Asian jewelry added to the exotic atmosphere. As I bent over to examine pendants, earrings, and bracelets in a large box, a young woman dressed in a black suit and white silk blouse lifted her pretty head from behind a small desk and asked in accented English, "May I help you?"

"My name is Adam. John, from St. Paul de Vence, suggested I show my jewelry to Oliver."

"I'm Claire, the manager. I'll be glad to take a look at them."

Something strange happened inside me. I felt as if I were in the presence of a human being endowed with divine grace.

"You are French, aren't you?" I said.

"But, of course. What else would I be?"

"You're so fit and nimble."

"Most French women are. We watch our diet."

I felt like complimenting her to the end of time, but my business acumen prevailed, and I pulled out of my leather bag a narrow, sinuous silver bracelet adorned with a small turquoise. She glanced at it intensely, then and asked its price.

"Five hundred francs or a hundred dollars."

"There isn't one piece of jewelry in-store that sells for that much."

Eyeing her display, I mused, *No wonder. Everything is mass-produced Asian junk.*

A sudden shriek in the street made me gasp. Claire ran outside. I ran after her. An elderly woman was screaming, grabbing pedestrians, and pointing at a disappearing motorcycle that was vanishing in a cloud of black smoke.

"Arabs," Claire said, a twitch forming below her left eye. "A week ago, as I walked to the back of my car to retrieve a package, a guy on the back of a motorcycle got off, opened the passenger's door, grabbed my purse, and remounted the bike, and took off. I didn't lose much money, but what upset me was that he took my passport and driver's license. French bureaucracy can drive you crazy." She paused, then exclaimed, "Here comes Oliver."

The middle-aged, heavyset man with no neck to speak of, wore a pair of trousers in need of pressing and a military-style shirt buttoned up to his neck.

"How did we do today?" he asked in the way of a greeting.

"Same as yesterday. Lousy." Claire answered, then pointing in my direction said, "This is Adam. John sent him over to show his jewelry. He wants five hundred francs for this bracelet."

"It's handmade, one of a kind," I said.

He glanced at it cursorily and shook his head. "Our bracelets are handmade too and cost one-third of what you're asking. The most you would get is two hundred francs. In France, domestics wear silver jewelry."

"But that's only forty dollars."

"Welcome to the Côte d'Azur. Go to the English bookstore near the Roman arch, and ask the owner how much she would be willing to pay for it."

Convinced that the owner of a bookstore would appreciate my beautiful bracelet, I left Claire and Oliver filled with optimism.

The bookstore owner—I assumed she was the owner because of diamond rings on her fingers—was busy collecting money from a customer. After she finished, I introduced myself and told her the purpose of my visit. She weighed the bracelet in her hand, then passed it to an attractive, younger companion. "What do you think, Ruth?"

Ruth weighed the bracelet and said, "I would guess about four ounces."

My instincts told me to grab my bracelet and run, but my reason said to give the women the benefit of the doubt. The shelves were stocked with volumes on art, French language, history, philosophy, and novels by well-known authors. They had to have an appreciation for the finer things of life.

"Let's see, the price of silver is six dollars an ounce," Susan said. I would guess the bracelet is worth about forty dollars."

"What about the stone and the workmanship?" I asked.

They shrugged. Filled with bitterness, I returned to the Silver Cloud. Oliver lifted his eyes from a mystery novel.

"I could try to make simpler pieces, but they wouldn't be as interesting," I said.

"Would they be stamped? In France, all jewelry made with silver and gold weighing more than 10 grams must be approved by a state inspector."

Oh well, I sighed, there is more to life than selling jewelry. John, the gallery owner from St. Paul-de-Vence, told me that Oliver and Claire were lovers. Imagining that Oliver talked French at home, I said, "You must be fluent in French,"

Oliver raised his thin eyebrows. "Not really. Claire prefers to speak English. I take French lessons at the Cagnes Sur Mer Cultural Center. If you would like to give the French language a try, meet me here on Monday at two o'clock."

In my adolescence in Rome, I had read Camus, Sartre, Zola, Voltaire, and a host of other French literary luminaries. I considered myself a Frenchman at heart. One reason for coming to France was to share with natives my love of the country's literature and philosophy. Claire must have studied my favorite authors in school. I imagined us strolling on the Boulevard des Anglais in Nice, listening to the spilling waves and discussing the human condition as only the French knew how. With her large blue eyes, cascading blond hair, high cheekbones, and slender build, she stood out in body and hopefully in mind. But she was enamored of Oliver who wore a military shirt and looked as interesting as stale bread. *C'est la vie*, I reflected, shook hands with Oliver, kissed Claire on both cheeks, and returned to the parking lot at the port.

A young woman in a mock sailor outfit was polishing brass fittings on the lower deck of a Greek vessel. A film by Roman Polanski about a married couple and a hired hand on a sailboat crossed my mind. The hired hand took a fancy to the wife. The wife welcomed the attention. Passion and mayhem broke out on the high sea. Did the woman in the mock sailor suit have more intimate duties than polishing brass? My fantasy annoyed me, first Claire and now this woman. I shook my head to banish the thoughts that, like dead leaves scattered by the wind, went nowhere.

12

At home, I took a long and restorative hot shower. Afterward, dressed in jeans and a woolen sweater, I went looking for Giuseppe and Nina's home in the countryside. At a crumbling Romanesque chapel, I turned my flashlight on to warn oncoming drivers of my presence, as there was no sidewalk. I progressed slowly, keeping my shoulder close to the stone walls and wire fences. But I wasn't really worried. Frenchmen drove like maniacs, but they were skilled maniacs. Rarely did pedestrians get hurt.

Giuseppe's wrought-iron double gate appeared softly lit by a small bulb. A gravel path led downhill toward, I presumed, Giuseppe's and Nina's cabin.

"Hello," I yelled at a cluster of light some twenty yards ahead.

"We're in the chicken coop. Come down," Nina called.

Half a dozen chicks stood by her rubber boots. Giuseppe pointed at them. "Nina always wanted to have a large family."

"Don't listen to him," Nina said. "He is all talk and no action."

A rooster, twice as large as the largest hen, held its beak high and displayed its green, yellow and gold plumage with the pride of a CEO wearing a Savile Row custom-made suit.

"Crazy bird!" Giuseppe offered. "A few days ago, I was fixing the fence, and the brute attacked me."

"And you ran for your life?" I teased.

"I came back with a paddle and took over its harem."

Nina shook her head, sighed, placed the chicks inside their cages, and motioned for me to follow her. Moments later rabbits in their pens twitched their ears, and glanced at us with their beady eyes. Nina picked up a large white one with black patches on its ears, pressed it against her ample bosom, and said, "My favorite."

Giuseppe winked. "Tomorrow she will slaughter it."

"She will what?" I cried.

"Slaughter it."

"I don't believe you."

"If he were man enough, he would do it," Nina said, putting the rabbit back in its cage. Now we eat dinner."

I followed her and Giuseppe to their small cabin nestled in between trees and bushes. From the outside, it seemed better suited for dwarves than for people of Nina's and Giuseppe's sizes. Moss covered the walls. Inside, thankfully, a wood stove let out a blanket of warm air. I placed my back near the stove and gazed at the four chairs pressed against a table in a manner to facilitate pedestrian traffic. At opposite corners two antique credenzas that had seen better days held dishes. A television rested on top of another credenza. To the right, beneath a small, curtained window, stood a worn-out velvet sofa with matching pillows, and an ancient gun above it. Cozy, with the charm of Salvation Army furniture, the place was ideally suited for a single, unpretentious individual, but there were three of them: Giuseppe, Nina, and their son, Umberto. And the bedrooms, where were they? Perhaps, in the back of the door adjacent to the credenza?

"Giuseppe, get the wine," Nina said from the tiny alcove that passed for the kitchen. The door in the back opened and Umberto stepped in, holding a bottle of Coca-Cola. More than an inch taller than Giuseppe, fair-skinned and broad-shouldered, he could have easily passed for a Scandinavian. But his pronounced aquiline nose and unstoppable hands clearly betrayed his Italian origins.

"Have you toasted yet?" he asked.

"We've been waiting for you to grace us with your presence," Giuseppe said, opening a bottle of his homemade red wine and filling my glass with it. "To our friend, Adam."

"To my illustrious landlords, Giuseppe, Nina, and Umberto," I intoned.

"Now, the trout," Nina said. She went to her cubicle and, moments later, returned with a large plate holding a whole trout.

"Olive oil and *Herbes de Provence,* a splendid combination," I said.

"With lots of garlic," Nina corrected.

Giuseppe took a swallow from his glass. "The wine turned out good this year, largely thanks to Umberto's labor. He worked the press machine."

"The hard labor killed my appreciation for wine," Umberto said and took a long sip of his Coca Cola.

"The trouble with today's youth is that they shun honest labor," Giuseppe continued. "Take Umberto. He would rather read books than sweat."

"Leave the boy alone," Nina barked. "He's trying to get an education."

"There's more to life than an education," Giuseppe corrected.

Umberto lifted his bottle. "To my hard-working father, whose sweat is enabling me to gain a degree in accounting."

A drawing of farmhouses, fences, trees, stone walls, and a grassy field, executed so precisely that for a moment I thought it was a photograph, hung on the wall behind Umberto. Pointing at it, I exclaimed, "Masterful art. Who is the artist?"

"Papa," Umberto said, his fork holding a chunk of trout in midair. "It's his village in Italy."

"Were you commissioned by the elders to do it?" I asked.

Giuseppe laughed. "By the mayor and the town council."

"Don't listen to him," Nina said. "He likes to clown. He did it for his own amusement."

"Amusement? But that's high art. You could easily make a living with your drawing."

"Art is okay, but I prefer honest work."

A peasant will always be a peasant, I thought. "I am an artist, and I do honest work."

"Giuseppe wasn't talking about you," Nina said. "How do you like the trout?"

"The best I've ever had." But I wanted some satisfaction from Giuseppe. "So, you think farming is nobler than painting?"

"Art doesn't fill our stomachs."

"Art fills our souls with delight," I cried. "It would be a dreary world without it."

Giuseppe shook his head. "The bounty of the earth, yes. As far as art is concerned—"

"Eat your trout and stop jabbering nonsense," Nina snapped.

Giuseppe and Nina had come to France from Italy in their early twenties to work as caretakers for a Frenchman and his American wife. Nina had cooked for the pair and maintained their large stone house near the wrought-iron gate. Giuseppe took care of the flowerbeds and trimmed the growth in the six-acre spread. In exchange, the landlords gave them a rent-free cabin, a small stipend, and a parcel of land to raise vegetables.

After the landlords died, the property was passed to a Parisian nephew. Unable to find a buyer for the estate, he agreed to let Nina and Giuseppe live rent-free in the cabin in exchange for property maintenance. Nina and Giuseppe had one major expense: Umberto's graduate education. They received state pensions, which they supplemented with the rent they charged me. In addition, Giuseppe made some money doing carpentry and yard work for friends and acquaintances, and Nina made money selling chicken eggs, and rabbits.

Nina's brusque manner had silenced Giuseppe at other times, and not once did he complain. With me, he held his ground. An old-time socialist, he stood for justice and human dignity, yet he allowed himself to be trampled all over by his wife.

"Giuseppe, do you ever visit your village in Italy?"

He shook his head. "Nina can't stay away from her rabbits and chicken."

"Somebody has to take care of them," she spat out.

"Then you'll never come to visit me in America?"

"I will," Umberto said.

I clicked my wine glass against his soda bottle. "To our meeting in Santa Fe, the city of art."

Nina brought in chocolate mousse. Giuseppe opened a bottle of homemade liqueur. I took a long swallow and felt my head spinning.

"Everything okay in the apartment?" Nina asked.

"It's great except for the darkness, humidity, and street noise."

Nina eyed Giuseppe. He said nothing. "How about letting me have the adjacent apartment?" I said. "The kitchen there is alive with the sun."

"That's our retirement home. It's not for rent," Nina shot back.

She rose and began collecting the dishes. Giuseppe pushed the cork into the liqueur bottle. Umberto drained his Coke.

"I'll have to start looking soon for a more cheerful place," I said. "I would sure hate to see our friendship come to an end."

"That's nonsense," Nina protested. "You can still drop by for a visit."

We smiled. We laughed. We joked. But my heart grew heavy. As much as I looked forward to moving to a more cheerful residence, the thought of leaving my landlords saddened me. Trading an inhospitable apartment for a comfortable one struck me suddenly as not being such a desirable option after all.

13

The French language—with its cadences, nasal sounds, and inflections—pleased me no end. Listening to the natives exchanging greetings and pleasantries awoke in my mind images of cascading waterfalls, lilies floating in ponds, monarch butterflies at flight. But to my chagrin, the love was far from mutual. In the arts and crafts shops, in the grocery stores, even in the tourist information offices, whenever I spoke in French, the staff would immediately respond in English. I forgave them the discourtesy, as I was aware that my pronunciation hurt their ears.

English was the second language on the Riviera. The Brits had been colonizing the Cote d'Azur for decades. They bought the choice property, thus, sending real estate prices sky-high. As an American, I was not particularly resented, merely tolerated. Oliver had invited me to join him for his Monday French language lesson in the Cagnes Sur Mer Cultural Center. On the way to the bus station, at the three-story low-income housing development, some forty yards from my apartment, a rat-like dog charged me and sank its teeth into the cuff of my trousers. I kicked it and inspected the pants. There was no damage. The dog barked wildly and ran in circles around me. An elderly, obese man rose from a bench in the lawn, dropped the newspaper on the ground and, huffing and puffing, came over, grabbed me by the shoulders, and screamed in my face, *"merde"* and *"cretin,"* (shit and idiot), and some other words I didn't understand. In a mixture of English, Italian and French, I explained that it was his dog that had started the pandemonium. Either not understanding or not interested in an amicable resolution, he kept shaking me. Pushing him away, our feet tangled, and we fell on the sidewalk.

Staring blankly ahead, the man looked as if intending to remain on the ground forever. I offered him my hand. He shook his head. I got up and was about to leave, when he nodded. I helped him get up. Without as much as a "thank you," unsteadily, he headed back to his bench, the dog following him closely. I resumed my journey thinking that I had handled my first street fight quite honorably.

The bus driver collected my eight francs, turned the radio to a rock-and-roll station, and lit a cigarette, in disregard of the sign above his head that said, *Il est interdit de fumer.* Forty-five minutes later, after riding in and out of residential areas populated with small neat houses with fenced gardens, we arrived at Place General-de-Gaulle in modern Antibes.

I descended down a wide street, bought half a pound of dried figs in an open-air market, and walked to a small park crowded with children. A little boy in long pants and sneakers suddenly threw a handful of sand at a smaller one dressed in shorts. The smaller boy threw himself at his tormentor. Both fell. Then, as suddenly as they began to fight, they topped, and walked hand in hand to a box filled with sand. They sprinkled water and began building a castle.

Impressed by the civilized way they resolved their differences, I reflected on the French children's maturity. Not once did I see a child in the streets, playgrounds, or shopping mall pull at his mother's skirt or at his father's pants, and requesting loudly to have his or her way. The state provides free medical care and education. The schools offer gourmet meals. On the rare occasions when school administrators complain about the expense of feeding their charges with choice food, the parents rise in protest, their argument that quality food is a basic staple of the French way of life prevailing.

Continuing my way to the old Antibes, I stopped at a store window displaying art works. The reproductions being startlingly well done, I stepped inside, and immediately took notice of Matisse's

"Red Room," an exuberant painting of a woman dressed in black, sitting by a table with a fruit bowl, and a window to her left, opening up to a mysterious green garden. The walls in my bedroom being blank, on impulse I bought it. Years later, to my immense joy, I saw the original hanging in the Hermitage Museum, in St. Petersburg.

Oliver, dressed in his military-style shirt buttoned to his neck, stood by the entrance of his store. We bade farewell to Claire and took off in his Mercedes. Seagulls cast moving shadows on the sand. White-cupped Alpine peeks eerily rose above clouds far in the distance. Sailboats glided lazily over smooth swell. It was a propitious day, I thought, for the start of my venture into the French language.

At Cagnes Sur Mer, we turned north in the direction of St. Paul de Vence, drove through a dreary industrial zone for a few minutes, and came to a stop before a weathered two-story-brick building. Oliver went to get a cup of coffee from a vending machine. I stopped to register, then joined him and two middle-aged women in the classroom. A tall, and thin woman in her early thirties, wearing a tight-fitting gray skirt and a yellow blouse walked in, said her name was Françoise and, without further ado, pulled out a series of pictures from her briefcase. She pointed at a turtle.

"*La tortue de mer*," Oliver said with ease.

Françoise nodded, then placed her finger on a butterfly.

Oliver's face opened up in a smile. "*Le papillon.*"

I was impressed. Not only did he know the words, but he pronounced them faultlessly.

"*Le cheval*," Oliver said, acknowledging the picture of a horse.

Pointing at the picture of an egg, she eyed me. "Uff," I said, uncertainly.

"*Oeuf.*"

"Uff."

"*Oeuf, oeuf,*" she said, smiling from the corners of her eyes.

"Uff, uff," I repeated imagining myself a seal.

"*Oeuf, oeuf, oef,*" she corrected, and winked at Oliver.

"Uff, uff," I persisted, with a growing sense of embarrassment.

Outraged, I felt like spitting at her pretty dark face. Out of respect for Oliver, I remained in the classroom to the end. After a coffee break, Françoise made us practice simple phrases. Now and then she directed a question at me and at the two middle-aged women, but her comments were primarily reserved for Oliver.

On our way back to Antibes, I asked Oliver how long he had been attending the class.

"A couple of months. There were eight people at the start."

"What happened to the other students?"

"They dropped out."

"I am dropping out too," I said. "Should you wish to have private lessons in Françoise's home, I promise not to say a word to Claire."

"Claire and I have a mature relationship."

An open-ended one? I was going to ask but decided that it was none of my business.

The next day, after receiving a partial refund from the Cagnes Sur Mer Cultural Center, I stopped at the Biot Tourist Information Office and asked the Italian-speaking woman if she knew where I could take French lessons.

"At the Sophia Antipolis Cultural Center, about half an hour from here," she replied. "Sophia Antipolis is an industrial park in what used to be a forest. It houses computing headquarters, airline offices, business consulting firms, and high-tech enterprises. A branch of the University of Nice is there."

That's where Roberto teaches, I reflected the next day on my way. Past the small commercial plaza home to my favorite pizzeria and a traffic circle, I turned right and entered an architectural wonderland. One building, with the roof slanting to the street level, and with a tall, perpendicular facade made of glass and textured concrete, looked like something out of a science-fiction movie. Daring abstract structures rose in between chunks of trees and dense bushes. The Cultural Center, a rectangular, pre-fabricated building in a small plaza housing a travel agency, a restaurant, and an arts and crafts shop, stood out as an anachronistic relic from another era.

A young, thin woman sitting by a computer greeted me with a smile and offered me tea, which I gladly accepted. She explained that she was a British volunteer and that the center, in addition to offering French classes, sponsored weekly hikes of different levels of difficulty, excursions to museums, potluck socials, and other activities of interest to foreigners. Her words cheered me up, as my life in France had been so far on the dull side.

The next morning, I headed for Biot's old town, hoping that Tonio would have a change of heart and offer me workspace in his atelier. He was sweeping the floor. An electric heater glowed by the side of his workbench. I waved a greeting. He acknowledged me with a nod and went on with his cleaning. After he finished, he pointed at a stool, and sat down by his bench.

"How is life?" I asked.

"It couldn't be better," he responded.

"Mine leaves much to be desired," I said.

"Did you come here to seek emotional support?"

"Something like that. Just joking. Did I tell you that I met Oliver from the Silver Cloud? in Antibes. He said the business was slow."

"That asshole!" Tonio barked.

Thinking that he was referring to Oliver's views on Arabs, I said, "He does appear to hold some prejudicial views."

"I don't know anything about his prejudices, but I do know—"

A boy stepped in, pointed at a bracelet on display in the case by the entrance, and said he wanted to buy it for his mother. After he left, Tonio said, "I gave him a 20% discount."

"You have a big heart, Tonio," I said, wishing his heart would envelop me as well.

"You seem surprised. Do I impress you as being heartless?"

"Not heartless, just protective of your space."

"Why did you visit that asshole?" he spat out.

"What . . . what was that?"

"You shouldn't mess with the bastard."

"Why do you call him names? Has he hurt you in some way?"

"He took a couple of pendants to the inspector's office in Nice to be stamped. They damaged the finish of one, and authorized him to bring it to me for repair. Afterward, he accused me of having made the pendant worse, and I never received payment for my labor."

"His jewelry is flimsy, that's for sure."

"Asian *merde*."

"He told me that every piece that weighs more than ten grams has to be officially approved and stamped."

"First you have to get a license to manufacture jewelry. Then, after you receive an official emblem which you put on your pieces, you submit them for approval. A few days later you pay a fee and get them back."

"And if I sold them un-stamped?"

"See that book on my desk? I list all the silver I buy. And then I list all the jewelry I sell. That way the inspectors give me a clean bill of health."

"I could call my pieces wearable sculptures, and sell them as art."

"You can do anything you want, *mon ami*."

I wasn't getting anywhere. Carla's words echoed in my mind: "Make Marie feel important; compliment her."

"Did anyone ever tell you that you look like a lion?" I asked.

"A lion, you say?"

"With your full beard and long hair, a very majestic one."

"Hm . . ."

"You must have been born in late July or early August."

"As a matter of fact, I was, August 7th."

"That's why you're fulfilling your destiny as an overbearing beast."

"What was that?!"

I grinned. "We've got to laugh now and then at the sorry state of our lives."

"There is nothing sorry about my life."

"I know. I know. You are destiny's favorite child, Tonio. You have an atelier in the heart of Medieval Biot; you make fine jewelry which you sell nonstop; you have a lovely twenty-year-younger wife; you were born under the sign of a lion; I could go on, but you get the idea."

"Thank you, my boy. This is the nicest thing you have said to me since we met."

"Tonio, have a heart. Give me workspace. I'll pay you rent."

"All you ever think of is money. Treat yourself to a fancy dinner and a bottle of good wine, and you'll feel better."

14

Winter had arrived. Daytime rain and nighttime snow held Cote d'Azur in a merciless vise. For two days no flights took off or landed at the Nice airport. I read, played computer chess, and waited for the sun to return. The third evening after a chess game, which I lost to my invisible opponent, the phone rang.

"I've been reading in the newspapers that *Côte d'Azur* has been flooded and that flights to and from Nice have been canceled," my sister, Carla, said.

"My house is intact."

"What do you do for food?"

"I eat bread with jam and butter for breakfast. Bread, cheese, and apples for lunch. Sardines for dinner."

"You need salad, vegetables, and meat."

"Didn't I tell you that I haven't touched meat in more than two decades?"

"Come to Rome. I'll make you tofu-burgers with homemade tomato sauce."

I visualized my sister in her living room, wearing her old green cotton gown, her back hunched like a Kokopelli, her face lined with age. "And you, how are you?"

"I don't expect much out of life. I take things as they come."

"And the weather, is it any better in the Eternal City?"

"Sunny, but cold. Your grand-niece will be gone for Christmas. You can have her room." Falling in and out of love, she had presumably found a new match. Her bed was narrow but satisfyingly firm. "I'll come after a stopover of a couple of days in Venice."

"Venice is inhospitable in winter. The cold, the wind, and the stench will depress you."

"In Piazza San Marco, they build wooden planks over the water this time of the year. I want to walk on water like Moses. I will arrive in Rome Christmas Eve."

"As you wish." Carla sighed. "Be careful on the train."

"I haven't read of any recent wrecks."

"Gangs invade at night. Make sure to engage the bolt before going to sleep."

I thanked my sister for her advice, then called Giuseppe. He agreed to drive me to the Antibes train station. "Make sure to hide your billfold and your watch," he warned. "Criminals release sleep-inducing gas to rob more effectively

Two days later, as I was settling down in the upper berth of a four-person couchette, a short and stocky young man in gym clothes and a baseball cap walked in. He dropped a carry-on bag on the opposite lower berth, pulled a cell phone out of his shoulder bag, and started talking loudly in a strange dialect. With his low forehead, bushy brown eyebrows, muscular arms, and hair doused in Vaseline, he fulfilled my fantasy of a "mafioso." Half my age, the man frightened me.

The rotund, balding cabin attendant stepped in. Wiping the sweat off his forehead with a dirty handkerchief, he told us to have passports ready for the Italian customs in Ventimiglia and to make sure to bolt the door at night.

"That's what my sister told me," I said.

"Better listen to her. A month ago, one guy put a knife to my throat and said that if I as much as squeaked, he would slash it."

"Aren't the police aware of what goes on?"

"What police?" the Mafioso snickered. "The gangs have them on their payroll."

An uneventful hour later, after completing customs formalities at Ventimiglia, I bolted the door, climbed on my berth, placed my passport, jewelry, and Swiss Army knife under my pillow, and waited for sleep. The Mafioso's gentle snoring filled the cabin. I considered putting earplugs on but decided that full hearing was safer.

The call of nature woke me up at two in the morning. The train stopped at a station. Through an opening in the curtains, I noticed half a dozen young men in black overcoats holding what looked like violin cases. Rifles! No doubt. Thankfully, the train resumed its journey without them. I got up and was about to unlatch the bolt, when the Mafioso yelled, "Don't!"

"I've got to go to the bathroom."

"To do what?"

"The usual."

"The usual, what?"

This guy was not a criminal. He was a clown. "Piss, okay?"

He got down on his knees, rummaged in his travel bag, pulled out a Classic Coca-Cola bottle, opened the window, emptied it, and passed it to me. "Use this."

"You crazy?"

"Be sensible, man. You go outside and we'll arrive in Venice in our underpants."

I stared at the bottle and waited.

"What now?" he asked.

I wanted to tell him that I had no intention of being watched while urinating. As if reading my mind, he turned his back and mumbled, "When you get done throw the damn thing out the window."

Somehow, I managed to fill the bottle, got rid of it, and returned to my berth. The clickety-clack sound made me drowsy and I soon fell asleep. When I woke up, an hour after daylight, my travel companion stood by the door window applying Vaseline to his hair.

"Good morning," I said. "Did you sleep well?"

"I did after you gave up the idea of going to the toilet." He put his comb into his pants pocket and said, "I hope Venice is still there. It's been sinking ever since they built the industrial complex in Marghera."

"Is Venice your home?"

"Born and raised there. I am a gondoliere."

"And I thought you were a Mafioso."

He laughed. "And I thought you were a moron."

Two whistles announced our arrival at the Santa Lucia station. I grabbed my backpack and headed for the exit. Cold, foul smell and hissing wind accompanied me to the *Vaporetto,* the water taxi, some thirty yards away. Shaking with cold, I watched Baroque and Renaissance palaces unfold their magic in the morning sun. Regretfully, the 15th century *Ca d'Oro,* the most splendid of them all, lay hidden behind scaffolding. Bundled up in scarves, overcoats, and hats, people watched the water traffic from the Rialto Bridge. I waved. A woman waved back.

The lion statue keeping vigil on the top of a marble column announced our arrival at the Piazza San Marco. I exited the *Vaporetto,* gazed at waves splashing under wooden scaffolding, then went looking for a room. After obtaining one in a hotel overlooking the lagoon, I put on long johns, woolen slacks, and a thick woolen sweater and headed for my dream walk. A small boy in a heavy yellow sweater and a blue ski cap, stood in front of me next to a matronly woman.

A spur of sunlight lit the basilica door as a priest, with a belly the size of a wine barrel, stepped out. He raised his arm, I thought to bless the flood but, instead, he shielded his eyes from the sun.

A pigeon landed on the boy's shoulder. *"Pane, dami pane,"* ("Bread, give me bread.") he cried, scaring the bird away. The woman passed him a chunk of bread which he broke up into morsels and dropped by his feet. A flock of pigeons dived to the ground. He jumped and clamped his hands, then ran after them. The woman, wobbling like a goose, cried, *"Alfredo, stai attento. Ritorna qui,"* (Alfredo, be careful. Come back). Moments later, hand in hand, they resumed their walk under an umbrella of screeching birds. I barely restrained myself from begging the woman for a chunk of bread.

My expectation that walking on wooden platforms over splashing water would give me a high proved true. After half-an-hour of thinking myself Moses crossing the Red Sea, I left for the Basilica of San Marco. At the *Pala d'Oro* altarpiece, a masterwork constructed with gold, silver, and precious stones, pilfered by the crusaders in 12th century Constantinople, my stomach turned at the thought of the conquerors beheading innocent men, raping women, and slaughtering children.

With my mind still full of the crusaders' cruelty, I took the *Vaporetto* for the *Academia di Belle Arti*, a seventeenth-century school turned into a museum. There I revisited Hans Memling's *The Portrait of a Young Man.* His confident pose and dramatic presence filled me with gladness I ordinarily experience upon being reunited with a long-absent friend. Giorgione's *The Tempest,* with its magical juxtaposition of two naked, breast-feeding women, and two fully-dressed soldiers at ease, before an approaching storm, affected me no less.

My soul well-nourished but my stomach empty, I headed for a pizzeria. Along the way my eyes fell upon the *Chiesa di St. Giorgio Maggiore* on the other side of the lagoon. With nostalgia I recalled entering the church decades earlier, as an organ began playing a Bach fugue. The cavernous interior being empty, I had made myself believe that the sound unfolded in my honor.

The chilly but sunny day was made for hiking, so after lunch I headed for the vaporetto to the Lido, the beach of Venice. Along the the way, I stopped at the *Ponte dei Sospiri* (The Bridge of Sighs), the graceful covered little bridge connecting *Palazzo Ducale* with the New Prison. According to the legend Casanova, on the way to the dungeon, had paused at the bridge's tiny opening for a last look at daylight. A small marble relief of a man with a pronounced belly, long hair, and a bunch of grapes in his hands hung on the *Palaza Ducale* wall. As I lifted my camera to take a picture of the statue and the bridge, a blow at my back sent me sprawling on the ground.

A short middle-aged Asiatic man wearing gray flannel pants, a thick white sweater, and a black fedora bowed and said, "So sorry."

"Sorry, my ass. Why don't you watch where you're going?" I yelled.

He offered me his hand. I rose on my own. To my chagrin, he began brushing my butt.

"Cut it out," I barked.

"Just try to be helpful," he mumbled, rabbit-like spaces showing between his teeth.

The woman and the child I saw earlier on the boardwalk appeared and whispered something to each other, as an elderly man appeared.

"What's going on?" the man asked.

"They are fighting," she responded.

"But the Japanese guy is too small to put up a good fight."

"They are a tricky race. They know jiujitsu," she explained.

A *Carabiniere,* his sword ceremoniously dangling by his side, came over. "What's the commotion all about?" he asked.

"The Japanese guy is using martial arts on the other guy," the woman said.

The policeman glanced at me. "Has he attacked you?"

"It was an accident," I said.

"An accident, yes, yes, an accident," the Japanese man echoed and bowed.

"Have you seen them fighting?" the officer turned toward the woman.

"I want my ice cream," the boy pleaded, pulling at her coat. She took his hand and walked away.

"What did it look like to you?" the officer asked the elderly man.

"The woman told me they were fighting."

"Accident, officer, accident," The Japanese guy persisted.

"That's the truth," I said reluctantly, part of me wishing to get the Japanese guy into hot water. "He ran into me and I fell down, that's all."

"Do not disturb the public peace again," the policeman said pompously. "We expect our foreign guests to abide by our laws."

The Japanese fellow pointed his camera at me, and said, "You have good Italian face. Grand beard." Pulling folded Liras out of pocket, he asked, "How much?"

I directed my Minolta at him and pressed the shutter. "You don't owe me anything. We're even."

The picture-taking session over, I strolled to the pier and bought a ticket for the Lido Beach. Milky waves lapped at portholes. Seagulls pirouetted above. *Piazza San Marco* grew smaller, then vanished. In Thomas Mann's novella, *Death in Venice,* the elderly man loses his health and will to live over a boy endowed with classical Greek beauty. That was Lido Beach smothering with summer passion. *Will cold winter give rise to equal drama?* I wondered.

Lido Beach was deserted. Empty taxis parked at the curbs; iron curtains shut tight over store windows; no moving cars in the streets; notes of a tango tumbled down from a second-story house. The ambience had all the character of a Fellini movie set. At a turn in the sidewalk, I collided with an elderly man

"Scusatemi," ("Excuse me.")I mumbled.

"*Va fare un culo,*" (Up your ass) he spat out.

I wanted to give him the finger. but deciding that I had intruded into his domain, did nothing. At a small park, I sat on a wooden horse, ate a chocolate croissant and drank water. Leathery leaves swirled nearby. With my eyes shut, I surrendered my face for several minutes to the sun, then rose, and headed toward the Victoria Casino. The casino and the shore on the opposite side showed no traces of human presence.

Boarded-up cabanas, empty refreshment stands, metal poles with torn flags, plastic bottles, bits of paper, and other rubbish suggested life gone into oblivion. A tattered green sweater lay at the bottom of a pole. On the top of the poll sat a seagull. De Chirico couldn't have created a more surreal scene.

The moment I brought my camera to my eyes, a human shadow appeared a couple of yards ahead. My heart skipped a beat. The seagull took off. From afar the ocean beckoned me. I wanted to respond to its call but feared that alone on the edge of the sea I would be more vulnerable to a possible stalker's attack. As I tried to decide on my next move, a tall, thin young man with long tangled hair, a several-days old beard, jeans with holes at the knees, and a stained sweatshirt suddenly appeared from behind a cabana.

"A lighter. Have you got a lighter?" he said.

"I don't smoke. Stop! Don't get any closer," I cried, and took a quick glance at the street leading to the Casino. There was no one in sight.

Give him your money, and he won't hurt you, my father whispered into my ear.

Run, my mother echoed.

I would have followed her advice but the man, half my age, would have caught up with me in no time. He came a step closer.

"I have told you I don't have a light," I yelled.

"Don't worry. I am as harmless as a pigeon. I don't even shit on people. What's your name?"

Sharing names is the first step toward forming a friendship, and I certainly didn't want his friendship. But prudence prevailed. "Adam, and yours?"

"Gianni." He glanced at the unlit cigarette stub in his hand, coughed, and threw it on the sand. "I really ought to quit. You're wise not to smoke."

He spoke in a friendly tone. Perhaps he meant no harm. "Gianni, you sure startled me."

"Sorry to hear that. Say, that's a fine jacket you have on."

I took a step back. "Thanks. I am quite attached to it."

"It must keep you nice and warm." He slapped his chest and stamped his feet. "Brr. . . it's a cold day."

My legs felt as if made of lead. I removed my jacket and threw it at his feet. To my surprise, instead of picking up the jacket, he glanced at my hiking boots. "Norwegian welt. I like that."

The man wasn't dumb. He knew more about outdoor clothing than most people.

"Yeah," I responded without thinking. "That's why I got them." We were discussing my boots like fellow hikers on a trail. But I knew better than to think that his interest was academic. I could return to Venice without my jacket. But returning without boots?

"I'll die of hyperthermia," I pleaded.

"You can wear my sneakers."

"But they are falling apart," I said. "I am sorry. I didn't mean to disparage them."

"Don't worry. They won't be mine much longer."

"My boots are a gift from my son," I lied. "He'll be mortified to learn that I no longer have them."

"He'll buy you another pair. He loves you, doesn't he?" the man said, getting closer.

As I threw a desolate glance at my boots, my right hand fell on a hard object in my jean pocket. It was my Swiss-Army knife! "Shit," I exclaimed.

"Now, now, Adam, don't get all riled up. Think of yourself as a good Samaritan, giving your jacket and your boots to a destitute, poor man."

"I see your point," I said. "Step back a few feet. I don't want you to pounce on me while I am taking my shoes off."

"Suit yourself, but you really shouldn't worry so much."

I pulled out my knife, opened its two-inch blade, and yelled, "Come on, you son of a bitch. Get my boots."

He bolted as if the devil was after him. I gave chase. I wasn't going to take a chance on having him sneak up on me again. From the street, I saw him running toward the pier.

After I stopped shaking, I put my jacket on and headed for the shore. Seaweeds, clamshells, and flotsam crunched under my feet.

Waves swallowed and spit chunks of sand. I shut my eyes and started walking like a blind man parallel to the waterline, relying on the sound of the swell for direction. Peaking at the sun on and off, then continuing with my head seemingly swimming amidst a canopy of brilliant stars, I persisted at the game until my left foot sank into an incoming wave. Easing down on a log, I removed my wet sock, and reflected on the incident with the derelict. I felt sorry for him, but in the struggle for survival, the stronger prevails. A seagull flew overhead, dived into the water, and rose with a fish in its beak. The seagull was a winner too.

I returned to the *Vaporetto* as the day gave way in to the night. A large group of Spanish tourists mingled inside. Amidst the tourists, suddenly, to my bewilderment, I saw my tormentor. I considered confronting him. And then what? Calling him a thug, a scum, a thief, and getting reprimanded by the conductor—and possibly a *carabiniere*—for disturbing public peace.

The Grand Canal welcomed me with lavish red hues. After a hot shower and a change of clothes, I asked the man at the reception desk for the name of a good trattoria. He suggested *Tavola Calda*, near the Opera.

The *Tavola Calda* was everything I had hoped for: checkered table clothes, Chianti bottles on counters, waiters with black bands around their waists, and an accordionist playing old favorites. I sat by a table near a window overlooking the street, ordered a plate of spaghetti, mixed salad, a rum dessert, and half-liter of red house wine. When the man with the accordion began singing *O Sole Mio*, I closed my eyes and imagined cruising in a gondola down the Grand Canal with my soulmate.

"A peace offering," interrupted my revelry. Above me, the little Japanese man held a glass of brandy.

I shook my head. "It's not necessary. Please, keep it for yourself."

"If no brandy, then money."

"Oh, all right," I said. "Forget the money. I'll take the brandy."

"You good Italian man," he bowed and walked away.

I dipped a piece of bread in a dish of olive oil and brought the bread to my mouth when a strange unease descended upon me. I glanced outside the window but saw nothing out of ordinary. That didn't mean that I wasn't being spied upon. I dropped the bread on the table and thrust my hands into my pockets. My Swiss-Army knife wasn't there. I had left it in the hotel. But did I really see my tormentor? The window reflected images of people and tables. The waiter placed my dinner on the table, said, "Buon appetito, signore," and walked away.

The music and the singing went on. Glasses clinked. Laughter resonated from one corner of the room to the other. I ate with my eyes glued to the window. *Did I imagine him,* I wondered. After finishing my dinner, I gulped the brandy and stepped outside. There was no one on the street, not even a shadow of a human being.

With the hood of my jacket covering my head, I headed toward an adjacent plaza, renowned for holding the status of a man and a woman on an iron bench. A street lamp lit the couple with a touch of melancholy. I sat down and put my arm on the woman's icy shoulders, half expecting to be cursed by her companion. The joke was short lived. Thinking that befriending a statue on a freezing night was utterly stupid, I rose and headed for an old church at the other end of the square. Near the church's entrance stood an isolated kiosk. I had to pass it to get to my pension. I couldn't see the bum but I felt in my guts that he was there.

"Adam, do you have a lighter?" he asked from the penumbra.

"You want a lighter?" I mumbled. "Why do you want a lighter?"

"Don't act stupid," he said getting closer.

I thrust my hands into my pockets, knowing that my knife wasn't there.

"You forget to bring your weapon, didn't you?" he snickered.

A sense of the absurd took hold of me, and I broke into a hysterical laugh. He joined me, our laughter echoing from wall to wall in the ancient plaza. When he got within six feet of me, I wiggled out of my Gore-Tex jacket, threw it at him, and ran.

The aria, *Ridi Pagliacio,* and wisps of tobacco and sweat followed me into the night. Past alleyways, across bridges, through plazas, I ran and ran. Soaked in sweat, breathless, my legs about to give up, I stormed into my hotel. The man at the desk opened his mouth, but I was gone before he had a chance to utter a word. I collapsed on my bed. After my heart regained its normal rhythm, I filled a tumbler with Chartreuse, walked to the window, eyed the gondolas swaying in semi-darkness, and mused, *Age is not an obstacle in situations of danger.*

I had outrun a man young enough to be my son. What surprised me, though, was that I continued to feel sorry for him. He needed my jacket more than I did, and he looked as lonely as I had been in my childhood. Still, I wished I've had my Swiss Army knife when he asked for a light in the square with the statues.

16

Early the next morning, I boarded the train for Rome. I didn't fear being robbed as the journey took place in the daytime. There were four of us in the third-class compartment: myself, a middle-aged man, and two women, one young and one old. The young one, sitting across from me, read a Polish newspaper. She dropped the paper on her lap and smiled. I returned the smile, and said, "You Polish?"

"I Polish, yes," she said, pulling a pack of cigarettes out of her cotton shoulder bag. A sign above the entrance said, *E proibito a Fumare*—smoking forbidden. Perhaps, she didn't understand Italian. When clouds of smokes reached me, I stepped out of the compartment, sat on a folding chair in the corridor, and watched farmhouses, barns, and horses pass by.

Upon returning, I took another look at the woman. Dressed in a modest cotton dress and plastic sandals, with hair in a bun and no makeup, she made me think of a refugee from WWII. The notion appealed to me, not because of her seemingly poor circumstances, but because of her unassuming demeanor. But she smoked. The savior in me wanted to confront her about the perils of self-indulgence, but I held my tongue in conformity with Carla's perennial advice: "Let people be who and what they are. Don't expect everyone to be like you."

She opened a paper bag and pulled out bread and sausages. The question I had been struggling with seemingly forever came back to haunt me. Would my soulmate smoke and eat met? I thought and thought and, as usual, came up with no answer.

At the Termini Station, I bought the *International Herald Tribune* and boarded a bus for Via Nomentana, Carla's street. She lived on the fourth floor of a massive apartment building minutes away from a park with gigantic trees, landscaped grounds, and shaded wooden benches which, at one time, Mussolini had used for his pleasure.

Turning the pages of the paper, I came upon a matrimonial advertisement:

> "A genuine Trophy Woman! With INTELLECT, natural BLOND BEAUTY & REFINED TASTE! And as enticing as a warm desert breeze . . . Graceful, 32, 5'9" tall. Charmingly feminine, soft-spoken, presenting an effortless elegance and refined approach which will leave you disarmed!
>
> As a fashion historian (MA) and former top mannequin, she has distinctly established herself. Fluent in 5 languages, with an interest in classical literature, music, and the arts, she values a sophisticated, fine traditions-oriented lifestyle. Impressing are her authenticity, her powerful gentility, and subtle wit!"

Hm . . . I thought. I was also well-read, well-educated, knowledgeable about the arts, and committed to authentic behavior. But, whereas I liked camping and frugal travel, the woman clearly preferred five-star hotels and adventuring on the Queen Mary. We were really not a good match, after all.

That evening, in a mood for some amusement, I translated the ad at dinner.

"She is much too good for you," Carla said. "She has money, poise, and sophistication."

"I don't have the money, but I do have poise and sophistication."

"But, of course," she responded sarcastically. "There is no end to your sophistication. By the way, you look different from your last visit. Have you lost weight?"

"Last few days, the weather in Biot was terrible. I survived mostly on apples, crackers, and cheese. I am sure glad to have your veggie-burger on my plate."

"Here, have another," she said, placing a patty on my dish. "Did you befriend anyone else in Biot, besides Marie and Roberto?"

"They betrayed my trust," I said, my fork holding a chunk of veggie burger in midair. "They said they were looking forward to visiting me in my new apartment. When I invited them for dinner, they didn't even bother to confirm the invitation."

"You must have antagonized them with your big mouth."

"Can't you just for once take my side? And please stop telling me I need friends when you have hardly any."

"I'm a woman. Women handle social isolation better than men do. How is Eric?"

"My son is studying engineering at the University of Virginia. Ever since he decided at fifteen that I didn't care much about making money and liked camping, he lost interest in me."

"You made too many demands on him. I never interfered with my daughters' lives. Treat him kindly, and he'll be your friend again."

"I doubt it," I said, my frustration growing. "He's too attached to his mother. He wants me to think of her as an angel, when in fact she's a two-faced bitch."

"There you go with your harsh judgments. Tell him she is an admirable creature, and he will welcome you with open arms."

"Thanks for your advice. What's new with you? How have you been?"

"The usual. I watch television, read the papers, and now and then attend a play. Day after tomorrow, I'll see *Six Characters in Search of an Author*. I ought to be doing more, but I don't have your energy."

"I'm sure glad your granddaughter is in love again."

"Why should you care?"

"This way I can have the use of her room. Sleeping on the living room sofa is not nearly as comfortable as on her bed."

"Your selfishness knows no bounds. I would appreciate it if you kept such thoughts to yourself."

The next day, as was my habit when in the Eternal City, I headed for the center to pay my respects to the historical and architectural sights that had given me much pleasure during my adolescence in Rome. After taking pictures of the Fountain of Trevi, I stretched out on a flat slab of marble and fell asleep. An uncertain amount of time later, an urgent, officious voice woke me up.

"Non e permesso a riposarsi qui," the *carabignere* said, his long sword dangling by his side. ("It's not allowed to rest here.")

"Che male fa? C'e poca gente. E'inverno," I said, annoyed. (What's the problem? There is hardly anyone. It's winter.")

"Signore, le prego di alzarsi." ("Sir, please get up.")

Sighing, I did as I was asked. He tipped his hat with his fingers and walked away. My next stop was my all-time favorite—Piazza Navona, a long rectangular square housing a fountain at each end. Artists sketched caricatures of tourists; vendors sold souvenirs and objects of art spread on the ground and on carts; lovers sat on benches with their hands entwined; solo musicians played music and sang.

In the days of the Roman Empire, the square was a flooded arena for boat racing. A pedestrian zone now, it provided a colorful respite from the hustle and bustle of urban Rome. The "Tre Scalini," once reputed to have the best ice cream in Rome, was located at the northern end. After purchasing a chocolate cone, I ambled to the Bernini's fountain, opposite the Church of St. Agnes, and sat down on the marble enclosure. Agnes, according to the legend, refused at age of thirteen to marry a man chosen by her parents. As punishment, she was made to stand naked on the spot occupied by the church. God took pity on her and covered her nakedness with hair. The miracle impressed the Pope, and he proclaimed her a saint.

Next, I went to nearby Piazza Venezia, and fought my way into a bus heading to the Termini station. Arms, legs, buttocks, and breasts pressed at me from all sides. Sardines had to be more comfortable in their can than I was on the bus. A tall, thin man with red hair, standing by the ticket validating machine, mumbled something.

Grabbing the metal pole to steady myself, I asked him to please repeat himself.

Leaning forward, he said, "Hotel Marcus."

"Ah, you want to know directions to the hotel?"

"Yes, please."

Glad to help a fellow tourist, I said with not a little pride, "Descend at the second stop, make a sharp right turn, then go straight for one block."

"Sharp right, straight, okay?"

"Yes, yes, you got it," I answered, as I felt mysterious fingers caressing my butt. Someone seeking intimacy? Unlikely. Women, not men, are fondled on Italian buses.

I was about to ask the red-haired man where he came from when the fingers intensified their dance. An accident, I reassured myself, just an accident. The bus slowed down. The questioning gentleman elbowed his way toward the exit.

"No, no," I exclaimed. "Next stop."

"Oh, yes, next stop. Thank you," he said and pressed on.

"Remember to turn right," I cried, suddenly becoming aware of a strange lightness in my back pocket. I reached out for my wallet. It was gone!

"Non aprite la porta! Un ladro ha rubato il mio portafoglio!" ("Don't open the door. A thief has stolen my billfold") I wanted to scream, but fear of making a spectacle of myself made me keep my mouth shut. The red-haired man, followed by another in a jacket too big for his small frame, descended in a hurry and disappeared.

That evening at the dinner table, I told Carla about my ill-fated incident on the bus. Carla poured spaghetti on my plate and asked,

"Do you want me to put the Parmesan cheese on, or do you want to do it?"

"Haven't you heard me? I've been robbed!"

"A week ago it happened to Allegra." Allegra was my sister's closest friend. "She stepped in front of her building, got out of the car, and walked to the trunk to pick up a package when a motorcycle suddenly stopped. The back rider jumped out, opened the passenger's door, grabbed her purse, remounted the motorcycle, and disappeared in a cloud of smoke."

"That's what happened to my friend Claire, in Antibes. She said an Arab did it."

"Arabs, Gypsies, Africans, it's all the same. The government opens doors to immigrants, then does nothing to help them make a living."

She was right. At every major street-light, dark-skinned men swarmed over cars washing windshields for donations. Outside the Termini train station, the police patrolled the premises in force, as if fearing a terrorist attack.

"Allegra doesn't dare go out alone anymore," Carla continued. "I stay at home at night. I've installed a new alarm system."

"You would think the police would try to make the streets safe."

"The police like to saunter around in their polished uniforms. The politicians don't care. The hungry immigrants do as they please. Everyone is out for himself. No one wants to pay taxes. The Mafia has the bureaucrats on the payroll. Industrialists make underhanded deals with each other."

"Why don't you move to Switzerland?" I asked.

"Because I like it here."

I scratched my head, then decided she made sense after all. Italy was fascinating with its art, architecture, musical language, and unrivaled cuisine. It had many virtues, but resisting temptation was not one of them.

"You were right about the trains," I said. "On my way to Venice, the attendant told me that a gang member had threatened to slit his throat."

Carla buttered a chunk of bread and lifted it to her mouth. "At least they didn't gas the passengers, right?"

"That's what Giuseppe, my landlord in Biot told me might happen."

"Three months ago as a train was approaching the Swiss border, a gang gassed the passengers and stole everybody's valuables," Carla went on. Now policemen ride German trains at night."

"Why don't the Italians follow suit?"

"That would be the day. How do you like the sauce? I made it with fresh tomatoes."

"Italy is sure a hopeless mess," I said.

"Yeah, and what about the United States? Racial and drug problems are rampant. People carry guns to protect themselves and shoot each other. Don't tell me that life there is any safer."

"Would mass suicide be the answer?"

"There you go with your extravagant thinking. Life has its good and bad moments. You have to learn to accept both." She rose, started collecting the dishes, and eyed me. "You're too much alone. That's what's wrong with you."

"Thanks, for figuring it out."

That night I hardly slept. I played and replayed in my mind the incident on the bus. I had the equivalent of twenty dollars in Lire in the billfold and no credit cards. My driver's license was in it, but I had the international one in another pocket. It wasn't the loss of money that grated on my nerves. It was my passivity. I should have screamed when realizing that my wallet was gone. The thief would have dropped it. I let him get away because I didn't want to draw attention to myself. Never, never again, will I let silly inhibition hold me back, I vowed, but an inner voice said, "Don't count on it."

The next day I visited the Etruscan Museum. The Romans assimilated the Etruscan civilization in the fourth century BC.

The little that is known of them comes from objects found in their catacombs. Roman historians claimed that the Etruscans were bloodthirsty warriors and that they got what they deserved.

Watching dozens of miniature statues room after room, all with smiles on their faces, I couldn't help but question the objectivity of the Romans' version of history. My doubt reached the zenith as I came to a large terra-cotta statue of a man and a woman on the top of a sarcophagus. The woman, radiantly smiling, leaned on the man's strong chest with one hand pointing forward as if intending to make a statement. He, smiling as radiantly, held one hand around her shoulders, and the other on her elbow, enveloping her in an arc of eternal intimacy. If ever there was a couple totally happy together, this had to be it. I sat on a bench with my eyes glued on the lovers when a young, thin woman, dressed in a long green rumpled skirt, a heavy brown sweater that had seen better days, and a plastic handbag stepped into the room. She made me think of the Polish woman on the train.

"Una grande celebrazione d'amore," I said.

She stared at me with her mouth open.

"A grand celebration of love," I said in English, carefully pronouncing each word.

"Yes, indeed," she said, blushing.

"You foreign?"

"From Budapest. I am here on a brief holiday. My name is Marinka."

"I'm Adam. I visited your city a decade ago. On a cruise on the Danube, I felt so safe that I fell asleep."

"Why so safe?"

"The communist government, in spite of its faults, did one thing right. It kept the streets and the waterways free of criminal activity. I remember a huge red star on the top of an impressive building. The city exuded grandeur, but the people appeared depressed. In a nightclub, the musicians played with the exuberance of people at a funeral."

"The star is still there," she said, sitting by my side.

Pointing at the sculpture, I said, "Aren't they amazing? They must have been soulmates."

"Soul . . . what?"

"Soulmates are people uniquely destined for each other."

"A very romantic notion, indeed. Do many people in America believe in soulmates?"

"Not really. The country is too pragmatic for that."

"In Hungary, people worry about making a living. Finding a soulmate is the furthermost thing on their minds."

A teenage girl suddenly walked in and cried, "You wouldn't want to be dragged to a disco, would you?" The gray-haired, matronly woman accompanying her intoned soothingly, "It's good for you to be exposed to a bit of culture now and then."

Marinka and I glanced at each other and rose. In the next room, gazing at a display of ancient coins, I asked, "Are you alone in Rome?"

"No, I came with a friend and her boyfriend. We're returning home tomorrow."

"How would you like to have dinner at my sister's home? I could ask her to set up another plate."

"I'm sorry, but I can't. My friends are taking me to a concert this evening."

"How about us having a bite now?"

Marinka's face darkened. "I didn't mean to be pushy," I apologized.

"No, no. That's not it. I . . . I ran out of money."

"Come," I said, taking her by the arm. "You'll be my guest."

At a nearby trattoria, over a pizza and wine, Marinka explained that she worked as a translator for a state shipping company. Glancing at me shyly, she continued, "My apartment is small, but I have a cot on which visitors sleep. Should you ever come to Budapest, I'll give you an insider's tour of the city."

We had known each other only a couple of hours, and she was inviting me to stay in her home. How old was she? Early forties? Did she truly like me, or was she seeking an American to marry, and thus move to the States?"

Shamed by my doubts, I took her hand, and said, "You make me think of Mimi, from La Boheme."

"Please, don't pity me," she said removing her hand.

"No, no, I don't mean it like that. Just the opposite. In her own way, Mimi had guts. You have a hard life. I know people who bring unneeded suffering to themselves. Your suffering is brought to you by fate."

Laughing bitterly, she replied, "Small consolation."

The waiter with a black waistband collected the dishes. She glanced at her watch. I pushed a napkin toward her and said, "Write your telephone number and address in Budapest. I'll call and get in touch should I ever get back to your city."

She passed me the napkin with the information, and gently touched my cheeks. Waves of tenderness spilled over me. Outside, we hugged. Our lips brushed against each other. "Can't you forget your friends?" I whispered.

"Remember me!" she exclaimed and ran toward an approaching bus.

"You look tired," Carla said at the dinner. "Did you have a long day?"

"No, not really. I had a very enjoyable time. I wish it had lasted longer."

We watched television news as we ate. During a commercial, I said, "I met a Hungarian woman in the Etruscan Museum. I invited her for dinner, but she couldn't come. I didn't think you would have minded."

"Here? You invited her to dinner in my home?" Carla cried. "Did you think I manage a restaurant?"

"You keep telling me I am too much alone. When I finally find someone whose company I enjoy, you don't want her in your apartment."

"I don't know her. If your intent was to impress her, you should have offered to take her to a fancy restaurant."

"You aren't getting it. I thought the warmth of a family dinner would have done us all some good."

Carla shrugged, rose, and walked to the kitchen. I went to my room and thrust my hand into my front pocket. The napkin with Marinka's address and telephone number wasn't there. It was not in the other pockets, either. Vainly, I tried to recall the concert she planned to attend. A deep pang settled in my chest. It couldn't have been caused by love, as I had known her only a few hours. And yet, now that she was irrevocably gone, I would have given anything for a chance to see her again. The next morning at breakfast, I told Carla that I intended to spend New Year's Eve in Capri. "You'll feel isolated and cold. I might be wrong about the isolation, though. Italy is so crowded that revelers might be willing to put up with the freezing weather and go there for the holidays. The cold will be worse than in Venice."

I buttered a toast and spread jam on it. "It's further south. It should be warmer."

"You're forgetting that Capri is an island. If I were you, I would take an extra pair of long underwear."

"You don't mind if I go, do you?'

"Heavens no. I do well alone. It will be less work making meals just for myself."

Suppressing my disappointment at not being missed, I asked if she had visited the famous Museo Archeologico, in Naples.

"Tourists get robbed; police officers get murdered; people are held for ransom. Naples is as dangerous as a Casbah. The further south of Rome you go, the worse it gets."

17

The next morning, stepping into a third-class carriage, I wondered if Carla was right about Naples. Her comments about the night travel to Venice had been on target. Three uneventful hours later, I arrived, got on the bus for the port, and paid close attention to my fellow passengers. They spoke with a melodious twang. Their skins and hair were darker and their bodies shorter and stockier than those found in Rome. A middle-aged woman wore knee-high white socks, black shoes, and a green mini skirt. The heavyset, muscular man by her side wore his shirt sticking out of his pants. Naples is about 200 kilometers south of Rome, yet the folks in the bus looked as if citizens of a different country. Mindful of Carla's warning, I periodically touched my wallet ensconced inside a pocket of my rain jacket.

A little girl, with lovely black eyes, smiled at me. I smiled back. The fat, mustachioed man in overalls by her side said, "Pechato che no ce sole." (Too bad the sun isn't out).

"Si, e pechato," I replied, thinking of the song, "O sole mio," Neapolitan ode to the celestial sphere.

"Da dove viene?" he asked. (Where do you come from?)

"Da Roma."

"Bella cita," he said, taking the little girl's hand. Before descending, he turned and waved. I waved back. At the port, there was no sign of a hydrofoil for Capri. A taxi driver offered to take me to the embarkation station for the equivalent of fifteen dollars. We settled for ten.

Two hours later, the vessel tossed here and there by the high waves, my stomach turning, we arrived at Marina Grande. Its white and pastel homes, perched on a cliff, seemed to sway in mist and rain. With the hood of my jacket over my head, I rushed for the funicular. The postcard-perfect Piazza Umberto was deserted. Following directions provided by the Roman travel agent, I found the nondescript hotel in a side street, identified myself to the clerk and requested a room with a view. The thin mustachioed man released a cloud of smoke through his nostrils, pushed a book for me to sign, and said, "It's raining."

"Will it rain the next two days?"

"Who knows?"

"The Roman travel agent assured me I would get a room overseeing the ocean."

"There is something of a view."

"Something?"

"If it stops raining. If there is no fog. If you look past the rooftops and the trees, you should get a glimpse of the water."

"I really want an—"

"I'm giving you the best room we have. It's free of draft. I'm sure you'll appreciate that."

The accommodation had all the charm of a Motel 6: a double bed, a dresser with a television set, and a table with two chairs. The mattress was reassuringly firm and, as the clerk has said, there was no draft. Pulling the window curtains apart, I noticed a faint light flicker in the distance. A ship? A street lamp? I ate an apple, cheese, and crackers, washed them down with a cup of tea made with my electric heating coil, and went to bed.

The sound of a radio woke me up the next morning. Dressed in multiple layers, I walked to a nearby diner, ordered two soft-boiled eggs, a toast, butter, jam, and tea. My stomach full, I crossed the quaint Piazza Umberto, and headed for the Michelin-Guide-recommended Grotta di Matermania. Rain-saturated gardens led to boarded homes and pathways with protruding weeds. Thick mud grew thicker with every step.

Grotta, a small, flat stretch of land, surrounded on three sides by thick dark growth, and on the fourth by a cave with a sweating wall looked like an illustration from a fable. The lichen-covered rocks, the thick foliage, and the trees dressed in vine suggested a home for goblins and other forest creatures. Startled by an unfamiliar sound, I hurried for the clamoring ocean.

Mist hung over the swell spilling onto the trail for Piazza Umberto. Skirting the sea, picturesque, I had planned to take the trail on my way back. A wall of water suddenly charged me. I closed my eyes, covered my face with my hands, and waited to be hit. Thrown against a boulder, unhurt, I retreated and eased down on a rock a dozen feet from the sea. After taking several pictures of the nature gone mad, I rose and left for home the way I came.

After a quick lunch in a trattoria, I headed for the Giardini Augustus, built by the Roman emperor Augustus in the third century AD, on the other end of the island. A sign on a wrought-iron gate warned that the Augustus Park was closed due to the inclement weather. I squeezed through the bars, passed a boulevard of stately wet trees, and came to another gate with bars too close to allow passage. After gazing for several minutes at dozens of small waterfalls heading for the sea, I retraced my steps, and turned left at the descending road for Marina Piccola.

The small port was deserted. The boarded-up restaurant moaned in the wind and rain. Dry in my Gore-Tex jacket and waterproof pants, I hopped from stone to stone toward a flat rock close to the ocean. At my arrival, I smelled lavender. Turning, I noticed to my left a middle-aged woman in front of a massive boulder.

"What the hell are you doing in this gloomy, godforsaken place?" I cried.

The woman lowered her scarf and replied, "The place may be godforsaken, but it's not gloomy. It overflows with nature's exuberance."

The roaring ocean, the hissing wind, the cutting rain did, indeed, exude life at its wildest. But the woman was not athletic-looking. She belonged in the storm as a gazelle belonged in the arctic.

"If I were a man, you wouldn't be shocked by my presence." She mumbled.

I nodded. My reaction was sexist indeed. "Okay," I said, "But even if you were a man, I would still want to know what you're doing here."

"And you, what made you come out on a day like this?"

Best leave, I mused. *I came to enjoy the storm's infuriating energy, not to chat with a strange woman.* I lifted my hand to wave goodbye when a ponderous wave broke out of the ocean.

"Get down!" I cried, then pressed her shoulder with my hand. The wave hit the boulder I was planning to sit on, spewed clouds of foam, gushed forward, spent itself amidst the rocks, and retreated toward the ocean.

"That was a close call," I cried.

"It's what I had been waiting for."

"You can't possibly mean it."

"But I do."

"Are you telling me that you wished to be swept away?"

She nodded. "That's why I came to Marina Piccola."

"You have a weird sense of humor. You should save your jokes for a calmer day," I exclaimed, my impatience growing.

"We all have to die eventually. I just intended to speed up the process a bit, that's all."

The woman is insane. Best leave her to her demons. "Well," I said, "I've got to be leaving now."

But then reflecting that if she was indeed suicidal, I had the responsibility as one human being to another to dissuade her from taking her life. I wiped rain off my face and shouted. "Did you really wish to die?"

She nodded. "I did."

"But why? What made you so desperate?"

A gust of wind pushed her against the large rock behind her. Steadying herself, she said, "It's hard talking in the rain. Let's go to Capri Town and find a restaurant. I will tell you my story over a glass of wine, and you can tell me yours. By the way, my name is Theodora."

"I am Adam." We shook hands. Her handshake was pleasantly firm, an encouraging sign. Hopping carefully over slippery stones, we reached the boarded-up restaurant, then continued up the steep asphalted road. No pedestrians or cars intruded into our consciousness. The sound of the clamoring ocean grew fainter, then vanished by the time we reached Piazza Umberto. We stepped into a side street restaurant, walked to a table near a fireplace, and ordered a bottle of house red wine and a pizza with anchovies. Checkered tablecloths, pictures of Rome, Venice, and Florence on the walls, wine bottles arranged in a credenza, and lit candles on tables made the place homey.

"I am ready," I said. "Tell me your story."

"It's not a very pretty one."

"I suspected as much."

She glanced around as if worried that onlookers might hear what she had to say, then began, "Ben, my male friend, and I are English. We planned to celebrate New Year's Eve in Capri, but he had a change of heart, so I came by myself. Men! They complain about women being unpredictable."

Oh, my God, I thought, *here comes the tear-jerker.* "So, you got depressed over your lover's rejection and came to Capri to kill yourself?"

"What on earth makes you say that? I would never kill myself over the jerk. He complained about me being pushy. You tell me, is there anything wrong in asking your lover that he read the editorial pages now and then, brush his teeth daily, and regularly change his underwear?"

"Of course not," I said impatiently. "Please, go on."

She took a deep breath and sighed, "I hope you don't mind me saying it, but he turned me on sexually more than any man I had known."

"He drove you to ecstasy?"

"Yeah, he sure did."

"And then he rejected you, and you lost your purpose in life, and decided to do away with yourself."

"No, no, that's not it. He did not precipitate my depression. I did."

I opened my mouth to tell her that I had trouble following her when the waiter arrived with our orders. "I am confused," I said after the waiter left. "You told me that you got addicted to the man's sexual ministrations. You told me that he refused to come to Capri. You—"

"I did indeed but I never said that he precipitated my hopelessness. I brought my misery upon myself. I despised him. He was dirty, smelled bad, and cursed a lot. He had the manners of a drunk sailor. Yet, I let him touch me. I behaved like a bitch in heat, a cunt, a slut. Seeing my reflection in the mirror I felt like puking. Once I hit myself with my fist so hard that I bloodied myself. At night I cried in bed for hours."

"I get it. You sinned against yourself. You betrayed your innermost values. You shit on your very being."

"That's why I couldn't go on living."

"But why Capri? Why not end your life in England?"

"I used to come to Capri on vacations with my family. I love the island. It just seemed the most natural place to end my miserable existence. Now, it's your turn. What caused you to come to Marina Piccola in such awful weather?"

"I came to France to make jewelry. I had been cozying up shamelessly to an Arab-French jeweler in order to get workspace in his workshop. I kissed his ass. I humiliated myself time and time again. I hoped the storm would cleanse me, fill me with energy, and help me recapture my dignity and self-respect."

We were the only patrons in the restaurant. The waiter kept looking at his watch. I suspected he wanted us to leave, so he could go home to his family. "In three hours, it will be midnight," I said, "Let's get a bottle of champagne to usher in the New Year."

"Will I be safe with you?"

"Reformed sinners are the most trustworthy people on earth. We'll be like two children, playing the game of life innocently, trusting our instincts to point the way."

"Let's hope that our paths are on a parallel course for the night," Theodora murmured. Now, that I have decided to go on living, I must catch up with my teaching responsibilities. I should leave for England first thing tomorrow morning."

"But—"

"Let's not dwell on the future. Let's concentrate on the moment."

I wanted to query her about her planned departure the next day but found it unbelievable that she really meant to leave. We had become quite close to each other in a very short time. So, I said nothing. The waiter informed us that he would gladly sell us a bottle of champagne. Unwilling to seek an open liquor store in the rain and wind, I accepted the offer and paid him twice what a liquor store would charge. Theodora split the cost of the pizza and wine with me. With our heads lowered to shield ourselves from the cutting rain and gusty wind, we arrived at my hotel. I placed the champagne on the window sill and asked, "Why don't you take your coat off?"

"Because I want to go back," she said.

"Back where?"

"To the Marina Piccola. We'll listen to the ocean. We'll celebrate life, you and I, along with our hopes and dreams."

"That's crazy. If we don't get run over by a car on our way there, we'll slip on the rocks and drown."

"There will be no traffic. It will be fun."

"We might make it if we had a flashlight, but we can't purchase one because the stores are closed. You'll have to come up with a better idea."

She opened her purse, pulled out a flashlight, and said, "Voilà! We'll be able to see our way."

I hesitated but then reflected that returning to Marina Piccola might be enjoyable. I did cut short my stay there upon meeting Theodora, after all. "Okay," I said, "But first I'll put long underwear on."

"Do you have an extra pair?"

"I do, but they will be too big for you. Then, again, in this kind of weather, the size doesn't matter, does it?"

She took the long johns and went to the bathroom to change. "How do they fit?' I yelled.

"A bit long but otherwise fine." Minutes later, she returned. We hugged and I had an erection. Glancing at the bed, I said, "It's still early. We could—"

"We could, but we won't. Maybe later, if we develop the right feelings for each other. No more recreational sex for me."

"But I love you," I said, smiling mischievously.

"Sure you do. Let's go."

After crossing Piazza Umberto, I turned the flashlight on and pointed the beam a few feet ahead. I felt strong. With Theodora by my side, I felt like a giant of a man. And to think that when I first met her, I had found her unattractive. The soul beautifies the body, and Theodora was a woman with a soul. The sound of waves reached us. Theodora stopped, let go of my hand, and began to dance. She twirled on her toes; she kicked her legs into the air; she threw her arms in front of her; she bowed her head, then threw it back, all along with emitting incomprehensible sounds. Gazing at the surrounding darkness, I half-expected a ghostly audience to break into applause. Part of me wanted to stop her. Another part wanted her to go on forever. Her energy passed through me, rose into the night, and embraced me again and again. I felt as if a cloud of butterflies had landed on me, their quivers sending pulses throughout my body. I felt out of control, yet happy to surrender to Theodora's wild ways.

"The ocean is calling us," she suddenly exclaimed, stopped dancing, grabbed my hand, and pressed on.

I wanted to ask her the meaning of her dance. Did she witness it in Africa? Did she participate in the natives' dancing ceremonies? Eager as I was to learn, I decided to keep my questions to myself, and thus allow her to carry on undisturbed her dialogue with the crashing waves.

At the Marina Piccola, she took the flashlight and led the way to the rocks where we had first met. Picking her way through the wet stones, she seemed fully attuned to the energy that permeated the celestial bodies, the earth, and all living creatures. Thrilled by the roaring wind and the sharp rain, I stepped closer, and whispered in her ear, "Thanks for bringing me here." She said nothing. I wondered about the time, but not wanting to spoil the mood, refrained from looking at my watch. At the rocks, after gazing seemingly spellbound at the rumbling ocean for long seconds, she turned and exclaimed, "You must leave now."

Thinking that she felt the call of nature, I said, "I'll get out of sight for five minutes, okay?"

"No, no, you must go back to the hotel. Here, take the flashlight."

"Have you gone mad? You will slip and drown."

Wiping rain off her face with her hand, she went on, "I came to Capri covered with mud. You helped me cleanse myself. But there is more cleansing to do, and I want to complete the job on my own." I empathized with her desire to restore her honor and dignity through her own effort. But doing it alone on the shore of a wild sea seemed an insane way of achieving the goal. "You may drown."

"It's a chance I must take."

She appeared resolute, unshaken in her determination. "Okay, I said. But you keep the flashlight. Will I see you again? Will we celebrate the New Year together?"

"I'll be in your room before midnight. Keep the champagne at the ready."

She lit the way to the boarded-up restaurant, hugged me, turned, and headed toward the shore. I watched the beam of her flashlight grow smaller. When it disappeared, I started my trek for Capri Town. It was the loneliest walk of my life. I wished Theodora well. I wished that someday I would have the courage to be as true to myself as she was to herself.

18

I arrived at my room disoriented as if I had traveled through several time zones. I took my shoes off and plopped onto the bed with my clothes on. Sometime later, a knock on the door woke me up. It was five minutes before midnight.

"It's really you?" I said, rubbing my eyes. "Your face is as white as snow." I walked to her, took her hands in mine, and started massaging them when she glanced at the clock on the wall and exclaimed, "The bottle! We've got only minutes before midnight."

Laughter and the sound of clinking glasses resonated from somewhere in the hotel. I grabbed the bottle and pried the cork loose. It landed on the ceiling, then fell on the carpet. Theodora held two paper cups at the ready.

"To us," I said. She echoed my words. We drank, put the cups on the table, embraced tightly, and kissed. I came to Capri to find inspiration in its magic landscape. Instead, I found it in Theodora's arms.

"Aren't you going to take your clothes off?" she asked, then embracing me whispered, "I'm ready for you."

"I am surprised to hear you say that."

"But why? Don't you want me?"

"When I first met you, I didn't. Then, the more I came to know you, the more desirable I found you. But we aren't in love yet. Sex without love culminates in emptiness. I don't want to experience emptiness with you."

"So, what are we going to do?" she asked, sitting on the bed.

"We care about each other, don't we?"

"All night? You want us to spend all night holding each other . . . and do nothing else?"

"By the time we wake up in the morning, we might be in love."

"Adam, I am already in love."

"Just what I was hoping to hear. Now let's go to bed."

Minutes later, no gaps, not even a breath separated us. I was holding in my arms a woman I desired, yet wasn't making love to her, because . . . I didn't love her. I felt proud of myself. I thought of myself a giant of a man.

I dreamt of being on a tropical island with Theodora. We hiked on silky paths. We broiled fish on the makeshift fire. We drank coconut juice. We covered ourselves with palm leaves. Then, on a sunny and breezy afternoon, a sailboat cast anchor close to the shore.

"Theodora," I exclaimed, "We have visitors. They have come to take us back to civilization."

"Not us, just me."

"Don't say that," I screamed.

"Try to understand. You are on the path of your destiny. You have found your home. I still have to discover my true path. I still have to find the place I belong to."

"But we have each other. That should be enough."

"I wish it were that simple." She sighed. "Look, a rowboat is coming. I am sorry, Adam, I really am, but I must leave. Think of me now and then. Bye, my love."

"Wait!" I reached out for her but my knees had turned into rubber, and I collapsed on the sand. She got into the dinghy assisted by two sailors. The dinghy headed toward the sailboat. Upon arriving, Theodora climbed up a ladder, waved, and disappeared. The sailboat, graceful as a swan, left for the wide-open ocean. Tears spilled down my face. I felt as if the core of my being had departed as well.

Upon awakening in the morning, I reached out for Theodora but she wasn't by my side. She wasn't in the bathroom. Her things were gone. There was no note. Dropping onto a chair, I reflected that her mysterious disappearance conformed with her odd behavior. She had danced in the darkness of the night. She had revisited Marina Piccola alone. I felt no anger, no bitterness, only deep gratitude for the memory of the transcendental moments we shared.

I dressed, walked to a trattoria, drank tea, ate chocolate croissants, and reflected that I had sufficient time to visit Anacapri, the village on the top of the island. The bus going to Anacapri was empty. I sat down by a window and wondered if I would be able to have positive moments without Theodora by my side. A cargo vessel appeared in the distance. I had been dreaming seemingly forever of someday cruising the world in one, lounging on the deck with Tolstoy's *War and Peace* in my hands, watching cranes load and unload merchandise in exotic ports, and reflecting on the finished and unfinished tasks of my life.

Fearing incompatible travel companions and a lack of a vegetarian regime, I never undertook the journey. With Theodora by my side, I would have taken my chance and traveled to the end of the earth.

"Let's go!" she suddenly exclaimed. "Dreams are meant to be realized."

"You weren't in the bus when I boarded it. How did you get into the moving vehicle?"

"Questions, always questions. Let's concentrate on the present and get ready for a big journey."

"On a cargo boat?"

"That will have to wait until another time."

"Where to?"

"To the sun."

I had taken off for the luminous globe a decade earlier on my own but had failed to complete the journey. To this day I hadn't forgiven myself my lack of will to face the challenge of becoming one with the sun.

I was sitting in my kitchen armchair, mid-morning, my face aglow with sunshine when, to my amazement, I saw myself leaving my body and departing for the sky. Light as a feather, at an incredible speed, I zoomed into a tunnel of light with walls painted in orange, green, yellow, purple, and blue. Free of worries, free of doubts, free of regrets, awash in beatitude and joy, I twirled happily toward the welcoming celestial globe, when suddenly fear stopped me.

I thoughts of what I left behind, of never again seeing my house, my car, my books, my stereo, and my friends. The kaleidoscopic display and the caressing sun rays enticed me to go on. The objects and the people I cared for urged me to return home. Moments later I found myself back in my armchair—the unwashed dishes, the overflowing garbage bin, a puddle of water on the vinyl floor, half a loaf of stale bread on the table. For years I had been cursing my neediness. For years I had been longing to resume my journey, and now, thanks to Theodora, I was realizing my longing.

Theodora," I exclaimed. "You're taking us on a voyage beyond the beginning and the end of time, outside the earth's boundaries, toward a realm saturated with gladness, joy and merriment."

With her eyes afire, she shouted, "Yes, yes, forever and ever."

I embraced her, let her go, and embraced her again and again, exulting at the sight of her shapely body, fiery eyes, and smiling face. Then, driven by tenderness, I caressed her breasts. She removed her clothes and tossed them away. I removed mine and did the same. Weightless, inebriated by colors and speed, I glanced momentarily at the yellow circle at the center of an exploding sea of light we were headed to, then leaned over to consummate our love, when she shouted, "Adam, the bus is entering *Piazza Vittoria*. Our journey is over. I must leave. I'll miss you, my darling."

Like a celestial wizard who had finished painting the sky with colors of the rainbow, and who had to attend to new tasks, Theodora suddenly disappeared. Shocked, on shaky legs, fully clothed I exited the bus and headed for a wooden bench. Easing down I asked myself whether I would be able to attain fulfillment without Theodor by my side.

Anacapri had the Church of St. Michel, an eighteenth-century sanctuary, packed with luxuriant blue and yellow tiles of cats, dogs, and all sorts of other real and imaginary animals, the Neapolitan Solimena's vision of an earthy paradise. Yearning to revisit the magical realm, yet questioning my ability to fully enjoy the display, I stepped inside the church. To my delight, I felt immediately uplifted as in the past. Theodora's absence didn't get in the way of my joy. I felt whole. I felt fully alive.

"But she was with you," an inner voice protested. "She was in your heart and in your spirit.

I stopped to think. The more I thought, the more obvious the conclusion became. Theodora had indeed been with me as I embraced Solimena's paradise. She had been inside my soul. She will be there to my last day on this earth.

"Theodora," I murmured. "I wish you fulfillment wherever you are. May your days be laced with magic and mirth."

19

I left Capri rejuvenated and fully alive. At dinner that evening I described to Carla my adventures without mentioning Theodora. Placing a veggie-burger on my plate, Carla said, "You should have gone with a woman."

"What for?"

"A man your age needs someone to watch over him."

"I have you, don't I? Anyway, my lifestyle places me in a marginal category. I like camping. Most women of a suitable age prefer to travel in comfort. Also, Santa Fe is New Age mecca. People go to shamans, astrologers, and tarot readers when in a mood for adventure."

"Not all Santa Fe women could be New Age followers. There are bound to be a few with minds of their own."

"I am sure there are. I just haven't met any." I took a bite of the veggie-burger. "This is excellent. If I could find a woman with your talent for cooking I would . . . no, I wouldn't. Anyway, as long as I have the strength and the desire to travel, I can endure my solitude."

"Age will catch up with you, as with the rest of us."

"I aim for eternal youth. Do you think my goal is attainable?"

Carla ignored my question, began collecting the dishes, and said, "My life is much simpler than yours. I'm content to spend evenings watching television."

"How about doing something different for a change? Let's go and see *Il Postino*."

133

"I've seen it."

"You enjoyed it, didn't you? You might find it even more enjoyable the second time."

Il Postino was a movie about a simple, inarticulate mailman, a delightful mixture of neo-realism and romanticism. I had read several reviews and had a good idea of what to expect. The actor portraying the main character had died before the film's completion. Cleverly, the director managed to have him die in the film too.

Half an hour later we sat in the darkened theater. Carla pulled out a handkerchief and pressed it against her eyes. I cried silently.

On the way to her apartment, I said, "You took good care of me. I couldn't have asked for a more caring sister. I'll miss you."

I left for Biot the next morning. Giuseppe welcomed me in the Antibes train station. I passed him a box of chocolate candies. "My sister, Carla's, gift for Nina."

"Nina is twenty pounds overweight. I'll keep it to myself. You'll be pleased to know that the apartment is warm. The electric heaters have been on since yesterday."

The following morning, I headed for Tonio's atelier. A green Citroen with Parisian plates blasted its horn and passed inches from me. I flinched and gave the driver my middle finger.

Tonio was polishing a bracelet at the wheel. "A son of a bitch," I said, "Almost ran me over."

He turned the motor off. "What was that?"

"The driver with Parisian plates came so close that I thought I was going to land in the emergency room."

"Bitch, bitch, bitch, that's all you ever do."

"Did you ever see anyone in America drive as they do here?"

"They shoot each other on the Los Angeles freeway, don't they?" Staring at me with his beady eyes, he barked, "I haven't seen you in a week. Where the hell have you been?" I sat down on the bench by the large iron anvil. "What difference does it make? You don't give a shit."

"Stop feeling sorry for yourself, and answer my question."

"O sole mio," I sang.

"What's with 'O sole mio'?"

"I walked on wooden platforms in flooded Piazza San Marco, visited family in Rome, and celebrated New Year's Eve in Capri."

"La bella Italia. Some day the poor slobs will learn how to govern themselves."

"Would you suggest a leader of De Gaulle's stature?"

"De Gaulle was a fascist."

"How about Torez?"

"It takes more than a communist to save Italy from itself. Look," he lifted the bracelet he had been polishing. "Not bad, eh? It's for an exhibition at the Biot Cultural Center."

"Congratulations," I said, the green monkey of envy crawling on my back.

A matronly woman walked in and asked to see his earrings. Tonio complimented her on her sweater, her perfume, and her excellent French. She bought two pairs and left. More people came in. Tonio regaled everyone, even children, with the honor one bestows on the royal family. Every sale he made added to my misery.

"And how is the Pope?" he asked during a lull in business.

"You know about him as much as I do."

"Why the bitterness, my boy? Could it be that you're jealous about my exhibit?"

"Fuck you, Tonio."

"How many times do I've to remind you that in France men like women, and women give it to them just for the asking."

"Okay. Okay. You've a blessed life. What else is new?"

"As a matter of fact . . . but I am not sure I should tell you." He paused, took a deep breath, and went on, "You miss jewelry making, don't you?"

"You know darn well that I do. And you know darn well that I've been idle since my arrival in Biot."

"Well, no more, my boy. Starting tomorrow half of the workbench will be yours."

"What . . . what was that?"

"Don't play at being stupid. You heard me."

"You've decided to let me use your atelier? You really have? Tonio, you're brilliant, an asset to mankind, deserving of the Legion of Honor. And to think I imagined you with a heart of stone." I grabbed his arm. "Dance with me."

"You crazy? Let go! Had I known you would lose your marbles, I wouldn't have made the offer."

I rushed out with my feet light enough to take me in the air like a balloon. At the village liquor store, I purchased a bottle of Champagne and hurried back. "Do you have a bottle opener?" I asked.

"Do you think this is a bar?"

"Well, then take the bottle home and drink it to the good health of your young wife. I'll begin my jewelry career tomorrow afternoon. In the morning I've got to go to the Préfecture to renew my residency permit. Oh, one more thing. My apartment is depressingly dark and noisy. Do you know of a sunny and quiet place for rent?"

"Did you talk to the village realtor?"

"He has nothing I want."

"C'est la vie."

A Frenchman who doesn't have an answer, or is unwilling to help is more likely than not to say, "C'est la vie." Tonio offered me space to make jewelry in his workshop. That he didn't want to take an interest in my other problems was something I had to live with. Perhaps I should do as the French do—shrug my shoulders, say, "C'est la vie," and whistle a happy tune.

20

Renewing my long-residency visa was the ultimate drag. The bureaucratic stranglehold that applied to jewelry and registering cars, applied to the renewal of residency as well. Upon my arrival to Biot, I had paid a car dealer the equivalent of two hundred dollars to register my Legend, and I still hadn't received the plates.

At the Prefecture's entrance, men in fezzes, women in white robes that covered them from their toes to their foreheads, giggly girls in miniskirts, men in business suits and ties, teenagers in leather jackets pressed from every side. The instant a burly gendarme opened the door everyone raced into the cavernous hallway to a large room holding two counters, several rows of chairs, and a machine dispensing numbered tickets.

I grabbed a ticket and settled down at the end of the last row next to a sweaty man in a rumpled suit. He pulled salami and a loaf of black bread out of an Arabic newspaper, opened a can of Coca-Cola, and lit a cigarette. I rose and went to the other end of the aisle and sat by a pregnant woman. She lit a cigarette too.

People spat in their handkerchiefs. They spoke in incomprehensible tongues. A young hourglass blonde, wearing a tight-fitting dress with a low neckline, lifted her hand. The racket stopped. She called a number. Those like myself who sought an extension of the residency permit were directed to the left counter; those who applied for the first time to the right one.

A mustached middle-aged man with stooping shoulders walked to her. She asked him something, then pointed at the counter to the right served by a squinting man in a suit and tie. A young dark-skinned fellow in reflecting black sun-glasses jumped and pointed at his stub. The Hourglass spoke sternly. The fellow protested. The Hourglass raised her voice. For reasons beyond my grasp, I wanted the young man to prevail. But he sat down, lowered his head, and stared at his muddy boots.

After two hours of waiting, the Hourglass called my number. I passed her my completed forms and said, "In America, if you have a long-term residency permit, you don't have to renew it every three months."

"We treat American citizens the same way French citizens are treated by the Americans."

I looked at her in disbelief, but as I knew nothing about how the American government treated foreign visitors, kept my mouth shut. Half an hour later, with my renewed residency permit in my hand, I passed a room reserved for the European Union citizens. The few well-dressed people lounged on comfortable chairs. The smoke seemed bearable. There was no shouting or crying.

Patches of blue had broken through the gray sky as I drove home. A jetliner passed with a white smoke tail in its wake. By the time I arrived at Biot, sunshine had spilled its warmth over the rooftops. After a quick lunch, I retired to my quiet bedroom for a nap. In Biot, like everywhere else in France, businesses opened after a midafternoon siesta. I dreamed that a jazz quartet welcomed me into the old town. Musing on my dream, I dressed, filled my backpack with silver sheet metal, pliers, files, and sandpaper, and headed for Tonito's atelier.

"Where is the jazz band?" I asked.

Sitting at the workbench, he barked, "Jazz band? Here? Did you have marijuana for lunch?"

"It was a dream, Tonio, a wonderful dream. I thought for sure a French-Arab would appreciate it."

He shook his head and pointed at the chair by his side. I sat down, emptied the contents of my backpack on the bench, and closed my eyes. Images of bracelets swirled in my mind like a pack of silver birds.

"Dolores, this is Adam," Tonio said, interrupting my fantastic journey. "He's from Santa Fe, the city of art."

"Are you an artist?" the tall woman with a few gray strands of hair asked.

Tonio pointed at a huge ceramic green pepper on a pedestal. "She made that."

"Magnificent," I said. "You sculpt vegetables?"

"Yes. My art is in Paris galleries." She shook her head to dislodge a curl from her eyes. "What art you make?"

"Sculptured jewelry."

"Qu'est-que c'est?"

"Bijou sculpture."

"Oh, bien. Je voudrais les voir." ("Oh, great. I would like to see them.")

I asked Tonio to translate that I would be glad to show her my work at her convenience. I kept to myself the thought that I would be just as glad to buy her dinner. She turned her attention to Tonio, and the two of them talked in a subdued tone, like two people who had been through a lot together. After she left, I said, "Charming, talented, and sexy, a true French woman."

"She's the mother of my son."

"Ah, your wife?"

"I told you my wife is twenty years younger than I," he mumbled and sighed. "Those were the days. I'll show you." He walked to the small storage area in the back of the workshop, and returned with a picture of a young dark-haired woman, naked from the waist up, her breasts as ripe as melons at high season.

"That's when she was in her twenties. She must be close to fifty now."

"She doesn't look a day older than forty."

"I was sitting at the café across from the park," he continued in a rapturous voice, "when this fabulous creature came with a short, skinny guy. She sat down. He went inside. Our eyes met. I smiled. She smiled back. I went to her and asked her if she would like to join me for a motorcycle ride. She nodded and off we went. We spent the afternoon cruising up and down the Mediterranean coast."

"What about the man she was with?"

"Who gave a shit about him?"

"And that night you conceived your son?"

"That night, and every night after that, for several weeks."

"How old is your son?"

"He is twenty-two, spoiled rotten. Dolores can't say 'no' to him. After he gets out of the army, she'll pay for his modeling school in Paris."

"That was a great story, Tonio. Thanks for sharing it with me."

"What do you mean, 'story'? Americans doubt everything. How come this? How come that? You tell a Frenchman something and he believes you."

"I didn't mean it like that. Tonio, I swear—"

"I know how your mind works. You think I am full of hot air."

He was right. I did think he was bullshitting me. But I wasn't sure. Just because I wasn't the type to dare a strange, sexy woman to elope with me, it didn't mean that he couldn't do it. To my relief, he didn't press the subject further. We focused on our work. I felt odd sitting next to him in silence. Now and then I eyed him from the corners of my eyes. He seemed to give his entire attention to the silver in his hand. At the end of the day, as I was placing my tools into my backpack, he said, "See you tomorrow, my boy."

"Yes, dad." He could have called me 'shithead' or 'asshole' for all I cared. At that moment he was my prince, my savior.

Moments after entering the apartment, the phone rang. "Nina agreed to rent you our retirement home," Giuseppe said. "Now you'll have the sun you've been craving for. The apartment will be ready in a week."

21

The following morning, I drove to Sophia Antipolis for my French class. Four women and two men sat alongside a long rectangular table. I took a chair close to a tripod with a paper pad.

"Hi, I'm Lisa," the bleached blonde of uncertain age, sitting by my side, said. "My husband and I moved to the Riviera from Los Angeles. I just love it here. Don't you?"

Nodding, I asked, "You speak with an accent. Where are you from?"

"Finland. My husband is British. And you come from where?"

"Santa Fe."

"Never been there, but I've heard that it's an exciting town, very colorful and filled with cultural activities."

The whole time I was talking to her I kept my eyes on a young woman in the last stage of pregnancy, sitting across from us. Her soft facial features and gentle ways with her hands made her strangely endearing. Curious about her nationality, I opened my mouth to ask her where she came from, when a wiry, dark-haired, middle-aged woman walked briskly to the head of the table, raised her hand, and said, "I'm Marie-Chloé, your teacher. I am a volunteer."

She spelled her name on the pad above me and said, "Now I want you to take turns telling us in French your name, your profession, and your nationality. Let's start with the gentleman to my right."

"Je m'appelle Ingar. Je suis Suédois. Je travaille à Digital Computing," the tall blond young man said. ("My name is Ingar. I am Swedish. I work at Digital Computing.")

Marie-Chloé nodded, "Formidable."

"How long have you been in France?" the pregnant woman asked in English.

"Nous voulons parler Français," Marie Chloé corrected her. ("We want to speak French.")

Her turn, the pregnant woman said, "Je m'appelle Tara. Je suis Israeli. My husband works for a computer research firm in Sophia Antipolis."

And so it went. Marie Chloé prodded, helped when necessary with the pronunciation, wrote words and sentences on the big pad, and now and then said something in English to facilitate the communication. When my turn came, I said in English that I was from Santa Fe and came to France to make jewelry.

An hour after the start, we took a coffee break. "Marie-Chloé is sharp," Norbert, a German retiree said, running his fingers over his gray beard. "We'll learn fast with her."

Tara nodded. "I took the class to learn the language, but I also came to make friends."

"Friends are so . . . important, my dear," Lisa said. "Let's get together for tea, but not any time soon. I am going crazy looking for a home. The one we had in Los Angeles cost four-hundred-thousand dollars. It was on a hillside overlooking the ocean. Here we can't find anything we like for less than five-hundred-thousand. Meanwhile, we are staying at the Hôtel de Cap-Eden Roc."

"Wow," Tara said. "That hotel was the setting for F. Scott Fitzgerald's *Tender Is the Night*. It's the plushiest resort on the Riviera."

"Unreal, my dear. It's all show and no substance. And you, my dear, where do you live?"

"In Valbonne. The Medieval plaza is a relaxing place to take my two-year-old girl for a stroll."

"A patisserie in Valbonne serves mouth-watering Mille Feuilles," I offered.

"My, my," Lisa said. "You have a little girl, and now you are expecting another child. One of these days I'll get pregnant too."

"You'd better hurry," Tara said. "After a certain age, it is hard."

"What do you mean 'after a certain age?' How old do you think I am?"

Tara blushed, then glanced pleadingly at Norbert and me. "I think what she meant," I said, "is that in Israel the government encourages women to have children when they are very young."

"That's it," Tara said. "That's what I meant." She glanced at a table with a pot of boiling water. "Does anyone know where I can get herbal tea?"

I took a bag of mint out of a plastic bag I had brought with me and offered it to her She shook her head. "Please, take it," I smiled. "All my life I had been waiting for a pregnant Israeli woman to come along so I could share my favorite tea with her."

Laughing Tara took the tea bag and walked to the percolator. Lisa shook her head. "In Israel men and women serve in the military for two years. No privacy. Drab clothes. Day in and day out living amidst sweaty bodies."

"They know from childhood that someday they will be inducted, so it is no big deal to them," Norbert said.

"My dear," Lisa said to Tara after she returned with a steaming cup of tea. "Tell us about your stint in the army. Was it dreadful?"

It was easier than carrying this load." She patted her very pregnant belly. "There is a debate in Israel about women soldiers joining the combat units. I am against it. I hate the sight of blood."

"My father was a Nazi official," Norbert said. "I'm ashamed at what he and others like him did."

"My Polish grandparents died in a concentration camp," Tara said, "I thought all Germans were bloodthirsty." Touching Norbert's arm, she added, "Thanks for confiding in us."

"Now, now," Lisa cried. "We've come to study French, not to get depressed over events that happened half a century ago. Tell us, Norbert, where do you live?"

"In a studio with a view of the Mediterranean in Juan-les-Pins," he said. "It's in a quiet neighborhood, and I pay only five thousand francs a month."

"And you, Adam, where is your home?" Lisa asked.

"Outside Biot, on the grounds of a small vineyard. My landowners make wine.'"

"That Legend with New Mexico plates belongs to you?" I nodded. "We brought a Lexus and a Land Cruiser with us from California. But a Legend isn't bad either."

"There is too much method in the world," I blurted out.

"What was that?" Lisa asked.

"It's from *The Rebel* by Camus. Camus said when the character is weak, appearances take over."

She smiled. "You speak in riddles. I like that."

Marie-Chloé clapped her hands. "Okay, folks, let's take our places at the table."

Sophia Antipolis cultural center was an expatriate's heaven. It offered potluck dinners, ping-pong, excursions to museums and theaters, all-day treks in the mountains, and relatively short Friday-morning hikes.

I joined the Friday hiking group the week of my French lesson. A dozen elderly gents, wearing hiking boots, sweaters, parkas and backpacks formed a circle in the Sophia Antipolis Cultural Center parking lot. My expectation that peoples of different nationalities would attend the event was proved wrong. All the participants, except for me, were French. The day was cool but sunny.

A tall, muscular, middle-aged woman, with a writing pad in her hand, asked my name. "Ah, un Americain," she said and added that I would be riding in her car.

Monique spoke even less English than I spoke French. One careful word at a time, she explained that she had been leading the

Friday morning hikes for several years. She snow-shoed in the winter, hiked year-round, and played tennis in the spring and fall. She was an excellent swimmer. I found her account of herself interesting enough, but one-sided conversation tired me fast. New Age acquaintances in Santa Fe were as absorbed in themselves as she was.

We took a trail which in a matter of minutes led to a densely covered thicket. The sun played peek-a-boo with tree branches creating a magic chiaroscuro effect on the narrow trail. After the sun vanished altogether, the moss attained the upper hand, covering rocks and trees with equal vigor. Humidity clung to our skins. Gentlemen offered their hands to the ladies when the trail became steep and muddy. I grabbed trees for support. Rushing to catch up with the rest, I hit a stone and landed in the muck. Someone called Monique. She ran over and gave me tissues to wipe my legs. From that point on, she would periodically stop to ask, "Ç a va?" ("okay?"), to which I would automatically answer, "Ça va."

Then an unexpected patriotic feeling rose in me. Not wanting her to think that Americans were wimps, I accelerated my pace and joined her. A gurgling sound came from behind some bushes. It was La Rivière they had been talking about in the parking lot. Eating my snack by the water, I told Monique about my hike to the Les Vallée des Merveilles, and my night at the refuge.

Monique made a sound that I took to be the French equivalent of "wow." Had my French been more fluent, I would have told her that I had hardly eaten anything in the refuge, that I had hardly closed my eyes during the night, that I hadn't asked the refugee guardian for a ride back, and that I had arrived at the trail-head more dead than alive.

After lunch, a gray-haired, stooped gentleman, who had been lagging behind joined me. My attempt to start a conversation led nowhere, as he was hard of hearing and didn't know a word of English. Suddenly, he stopped and pointed at a skinny bush. I nodded politely, wondering what was on his mind. He bent over, pulled out a stem, and started chewing it. Had he lost his marbles?

Was he eating weeds? He picked up a stem and passed it to me. Suppressing my revulsion, not wanting to appear ungrateful, I ate it. It was delicious. When we got to the parking lot, Monique thanked me for taking care of the "old man." I told her that the "old man" had been engaging company and that he had fed me good-tasting weeds.

"No, not weeds," she said. "Wild asparagus."

Monique was a tough lady, brusque, almost rude, but as efficient and as protective of her charges as a sergeant would be of his recruits. Shaking hands, she said she was looking forward to seeing me again on her next hike.

A few days later, on an invigorating sunny morning, as I was placing the key into my door lock, a voice behind me said, "Bonjour monsieur." A tall, erect gentleman, dressed in a suit and tie, introduced himself as Monique's husband. He told me in broken English that they lived fifteen minutes north of my apartment. We met several times after that, and each time went through the lovely French greeting ritual:

"Bon-jour, Monsieur. Comment allez-vous?" ("Good morning, Sir. How are you?")

"Très bien, Monsieur. Et vous. Comment allez-vous?" ("Very well, sir. And you? How are you?")

"Merci, bien. Est-ce que vous plaisez ici?" ("Very well, thank you. Are you having a good day?"

"Oui, je me plais beaucoup." ("Yes, very good.")

"Au revoir, Monsieur. A bientôt." ("Goodbye, Sir. Hope to see you soon.")

"A tout à l'heure, Monsieur. Au revoir." ("Same here, Sir. Goodbye.")

22

The last Saturday in January, a freezing and windy morning, I moved into my landlords' retirement apartment. The credenza was peeling; the sofa was wobbling; the plastic-covering the dining room table was torn; the chairs more unsteady. The interior was a far cry from what one would expect to find in the glamorous Riviera, but I had come to live like a struggling artist, and the accommodations suited me just fine. The grease on the wall behind the kitchen stove, the useless oven, the small unheated bathroom, and the continuing maddening traffic, however, depressed me.

Giuseppe eventually fixed the stove and removed the grease, but he couldn't enlarge the bathroom or silence the street noise. The rent was only six hundred dollars a month, less than what I received from the folks living in my home in Santa Fe. The south-facing kitchen was the apartment's saving grace. It was blessed with sunshine. I didn't sign a lease, hoping that a silent and sunny apartment would eventually appear, in no time, on the horizon.

My first evening in the apartment, I stretched out on the floor by the fireplace, rested my head on a pillow, and read the *International Herald Tribune*. The dollar was losing its value against the franc. England resisted closer association with the European Union. Warlords in central Africa battled for land and natural resources. Arabs and Israelis were at each other's throats. Gossip columnists reported that the French prime minister had an illegitimate daughter.

I read every page, the good and the bad news, with passionate interest. All events mattered. The world was my home.

After the fire died, I made a cup of mint tea and retreated to the bedroom for a game of computer chess. Easing down onto the armchair, I almost hit the floor. An inspection revealed broken springs. From the armoire, I picked up a rough, thick woolen blanket, folded it four times, and put it under the cushion. And voila! The armchair felt as comfortable as my favorite one in Santa Fe.

I went back to my chess, but Giuseppe kept intruding into my consciousness. It wouldn't have taken too much of an effort to fix the fucking chair. But then he could have removed the grease in the back of the stove and repaired the oven before letting me into the apartment. Was I being too critical? He grew up on a farm, after all, amid horse and cow manure, chickens squealing, rabbits fucking and pigs eating shit. A filthy wall and a broken chair had to be the least of his worries.

That night I covered myself with a thick woolen blanket. In the middle of the night, I added another one, and a third before sunrise. By the time I woke up, the air streaming down from the chimney had turned the place into an icebox. With long johns, jeans, a heavy sweater, a ski cap, and the electrical heaters turned to their highest settings, it was still too cold for comfort.

Midmorning, I dialed Giuseppe. "It's freezing here," I said. "The electrical heater can't handle the cold air coming down from the chimney."

"You need a cardboard over the opening. I'll bring you some if you don't have any."

"I have a better idea. Sell me firewood. That will take care of the problem once and for all."

Giuseppe sighed. "Sorry. I need all the wood to heat my home."

"Just a few logs. Certainly, you can spare a dozen?"

"And then? What will you do after they are gone?"

I scratched my beard. "You have lived here for forty years. You must know where I can buy wood."

"Hm . . . let me see . . . I cut my own from fallen trees in the field behind my house. Drive around. You might stumble on a sign that says 'Wood for Sale.'"

Giuseppe brought the cardboard, which I cut to fit the fireplace opening. Less air came in, but it was still too cold for comfort. I drove up and down the hilly roads north of Biot, across country lanes, and through business districts, and returned home empty-handed. Turning the heaters on high hurt my pocketbook badly. Electricity in France costs twice as much as in the States.

After Giuseppe repaired the oven, I started baking. One bunch of energy bars, made with whole-wheat flour, dried fruit, nuts, and honey turned out particularly tasty. Such a harvest called for sharing. I offered some to Giuseppe, but he said Nina liked her sweets made with sugar. I knew better than to give any to Tonio. On the few occasions I brought him food, he sneered as if I had intended to demean him. Eyeing my plateful of energy bars on the kitchen table, smelling the baking air, and feeling sunlight on my face, I thought of the protagonist of Camus' *The Stranger*. He felt alienated in Algeria. I felt alienated in the glamorous Riviera. A woman would have made all the difference. But I hadn't even been able to find wood.

My mind drifted to Claire. In a country where the majority of females rated a solid ten, she rated a twelve. She was slim and graceful and exuded charm. Her smooth blonde hair cascaded luxuriously down her neck. Her upturned nose conveyed hope and optimism. Her one defect was smoking which, strangely, didn't yellow her teeth. But she was a mystery. Oliver, her lover, was overweight and clumsy. Did she offer her exquisite body for the privilege of managing his gallery?

I called her. "Claire," I said. "I've got something that will improve your ballet lessons tenfold."

"A pair of silk slippers? How wonderful. We're closing for lunch in minutes. Come after three."

"Don't eat any desserts."

"I love desserts. Why on earth should I give them up?"

"Just do as I say."

I left my car in the lot adjacent to the yacht marina, walked through the ancient arch, elbowed my way through thick pedestrian traffic, arrived at the Silver Moon, and noticed a sixteen-gear bicycle with elaborate shock absorbers by the entrance. Oliver sat by his small desk playing cards. A tall, lean, middle-aged man stood by his side.

"This is Edward," Oliver said. "He used to manage the Lucas franchise in Brazil."

"I'm Adam. You have an impressive bicycle."

"I only use it in town," Edward said in a British accent. "I live and travel in my caravan. And what do you do on the Riviera?"

"I make energy bars for Claire," I answered.

"So, that's the gift that will fuel my way into the ballet world," she said straightening up from the jewelry case.

With her black net stockings, high heels, miniskirt, and a golden silk blouse, she radiated enough body heat to fry eggs. Oliver, clad in his usual cream-colored military shirt buttoned to the collar looked like a Buddha.

Claire took a bite of my bar, munched for several seconds, said, "Tu es très gentil," leaned languidly against an Afghan carpet on the wall, and eyed the ceiling, "Oliver is thinking of not renewing the lease. I've heard a lot of good things about Santa Fe. Do you think I could get a gallery manager job there?"

Claire in Santa Fe, needing me, depending on me for orientation and perhaps a home? Electricity ran down my spine. "Well . . . there are some 146 galleries in town," I said. "You do speak excellent English and have considerable experience. I would be willing to help you, but what would I get out of the deal?"

"Eternal friendship. Eternal gratitude."

You would need a 'green' card and that takes time."

Her eyes sparkling, she smiled, "There is another way. I'll marry you and become a citizen."

"You'll what?"

"Marry you, like being your wife."

She couldn't mean it. She was too beautiful and too young for a man of sixty-two. And she belonged to Oliver. Several silent seconds later, I asked, "Would we sleep in the same bed?"

"I'll clean and cook. I'm a great housekeeper. Ask Oliver."

"She's the best. Her escargots are as good as those found in a four-star restaurant. She irons like a pro. There is not a trace of dust in our apartment," he said without lifting his head from the cards.

"But wouldn't you miss her?"

"She's grown up. She can do what she thinks is best for her."

"Were she mine, I would lock her up inside a gilded cage," I said. What had possessed me to say that? No human being would want to be kept in a cage, golden or otherwise. Claire was frowning. Oliver's face showed no reaction. I laughed nervously. "And there would be no threatening cats around."

"You were born somewhere in the old Balkans, weren't you," she said coldly.

"What I meant, Claire, is that I value you so much that I wouldn't mind spending a fortune to keep you safe from hazards. There are bad people everywhere. A mugger stole your purse, didn't he? There are rapists and thieves on the loose. Your butt must be sore from all the pinching you get in the bus."

"I don't take the bus. I drive my own car."

I couldn't tell her that the real reason for wanting her locked up was to keep her at an arm's distance from younger men. "Claire, think of it as a fantasy, something out of a fable, about a maiden in distress and a—"

"Ugh," she interrupted.

"Okay, okay, I promise from now on I'll think of you as a fancy-free pigeon."

"Pigeon?"

"I meant a falcon."

"I like falcons," Claire said in a conciliatory tone.

"Yeah, they are graceful flyers," I said. "But let's get back to our business. Would we share the same bed?"

"A spare bedroom would be better. I would wear oversize clothes. I wouldn't put perfume on. I would wash my hair only once a weak. No lipstick. No mascara. I would have the look of a Muslim woman in a caftan."

"It wouldn't do. You would look divine in a sack. I would have to get a pacemaker."

She burst into a loud laugh. "You have weird notions, but you are an adorable senior citizen." She stepped toward me. Thinking she was going to kiss me on the mouth, I glanced at Oliver. She pressed her lips on my forehead.

My head was swimming and my heart was beating fast. Could she be truly considering moving to Santa Fe? Claire returned to the jewelry case. Oliver focused his attention on his solitaire. Edward watched him play, his shoulders bent, his arms dangling by his side. He hadn't said a word in ten minutes. I turned toward him. "Do you have a lady in your caravan?"

"A Gypsy woman with a floating skirt and smooth black hair cascading to her waist, but she is gone. I thought Claire might want to replace her."

I threw an anxious glance at Claire. From the jewelry case, she replied, "I prefer the guest bedroom in Adam's home."

"Don't feel bad, Edward," Oliver said. "There must be a legion of women waiting in line to move into your camper."

"I wish it were so but tell me, am I being paranoid to think that the local merchants are trying to cheat me? Yesterday I bought a small loaf of bread and the baker charged me for a large one."

Oliver dropped the card in his hand and cried, "The French! They find out that you're a foreigner, and they try to squeeze your last penny out of you. I bought a pair of shoes. When I got home, I found they were too tight. They refused to take them back. It was only after Claire confronted the store owner that he agreed to refund the money."

"Claire, will you take such good care of me if I marry you?" I asked.

"I'll do better than that. I'll bring you a mug of tea, the paper, and slippers when you get home from work. And I'll entertain you with dancing. Watch me. I learned this movement only yesterday."

She removed her shoes, stood on her toes, and began to pirouette, leaning this way and that way, her arms forming graceful circles over her head. Oliver, Edward, and I applauded enthusiastically.

"That was wonderful," I said. "And you're so slim. Most French women are, yet they eat chocolates, ice cream, and sweets."

Bending over to put her shoes on, she exposed her full round breasts. I admired them with a touch of guilt. It wasn't as if she had intended for me to see them. Standing up again, she said, "We don't eat in between meals, and then always in moderation."

"I have a more original explanation. The reason the French women are so fit and graceful is that for centuries unsightly female infants have been drowned, thus assuring charm and beauty for the future generations."

Oliver hit the table with the palms of his hands, rose, and barked, "Do you have any other mental gems you wish to share with us?"

I took a step back. Was he jealous? "I didn't think you would mind me kidding with Claire."

"Ah . . . so you are kidding." He turned to Claire. "Are you being entertained? I don't see you bending over with mirth."

"Oliver, you have been open-minded about me marrying Claire, and now you are getting angry at me for having fun with her.".

"You have been blabbering for the last hour. Enough is enough. Your sense of humor stinks, okay?"

Claire looked nonplused. "What makes you think that your British humor is any better?" I dared him.

"You're in my store, you know!" he shouted, ripples of sweat forming on his forehead. He clenched his fists. Hastily, I joined Claire at the jewelry case. From the corners of my eyes, I watched him sit down and resume playing his solitaire game.

"Have you found a place to make jewelry yet?" Claire asked.

"I have in a French-Arab's atelier in old Biot. Things are shaping up. But I am freezing in my apartment. I desperately need wood for my fireplace."

"I know where you can find all the wood you'll ever want and for free."

"You do? Are you suggesting I go to a construction site and steal an armful?"

"Steal yes, but legally. On the beach, behind the Biot train station, you'll find enough wood to fill a dozen fireplaces. Trust me. I know what I'm talking about."

I thanked her for the tip, kissed her on both cheeks, then offered my hand to Edward. He shook it firmly. Oliver ignored it.

"Come on Oliver," I said. "It's not easy for me to plan marriage with the woman you're living with. Put yourself in my shoes."

A trace of a smile spread over his meaty face. "Just leave, okay?"

The sun spread a blanket of warmth behind the Biot station. Far in the distance snow-capped Alpine crests toyed with a flotilla of white clouds. Seagulls rose, dived, and rose. The slow-going coastal train chugged by. I left my car on the hard pavement and ventured into the sand. Having no idea where to look for wood, I decided to entertain myself with a game. I closed my eyes, surrendered my face to the sun, and walked slowly like a blind man, my mind free of all uncertainties, longings, and doubts.

My magical journey ended when my feet hit something hard. Before me stood the upper half of a piece of driftwood. Digging to uncover the rest, I thought of Claire, and sent her a warm thank you for advising me to look for wood behind the station.

With every second, the driftwood grew larger until it attained the size of my thigh. I picked it up, placed it in the trunk of my car, and drove to the Géant supermarket, three kilometers away, where I purchased a hand saw. Invigorated by the thought that in a few short hours, I would be stretched by my lit fireplace with a glass of wine and a book, I began looking for more driftwood.

Unused to hard physical labor, I ran out of breath in minutes. After a brief rest, I applied myself harder, found another piece of driftwood, which I promptly cut it into pieces. Sweat forming on my forehead trickled down my face. My throat yearned for water, and I had none. Exhausted, I stared proudly at the fruit of my labor: two dozen chunks of wood piled on top of each other.

The following morning, I returned to the beach with a flask of water and a bagful of energy bars. Cheered up by the sight of Alpine peaks glowing in the distance, I worked with growing passion. A few yards away. a piece of driftwood in between two concession stands, winked at me. I approached it wondering from wat part of the world did it come from.

I exerted myself harder than at the Top Fit, my gym in Antibes. In the gym, compared with the other athletes, I was a midget. Here, alone in the wide-open space and in the clear air, I was a giant, the master of a broad realm.

I split my time between jewelry making and wood gathering. While days were getting warmer, the nights were still quite cold and I wanted to accumulate all the wood I could before the work crew started preparing the beach for the summer crowd. That's what I would have told anyone asking me why I was accumulating so much wood. The truth was that at the beach I felt totally grounded, immersed at the moment, and fully alive.

All that was missing was Claire, my muse. "I'll marry you and become a citizen," she had said.

I dialed her the moment I returned home. "Claire, your advice produced a great harvest. I've got enough wood to last us until summer."

"Us? What am I going to do with it? I heat the apartment with electricity."

"Is Oliver with you?"

"No, why are you asking?"

"I would like to talk to you in private. Okay if I come over?"

"Sure. No problem."

I put energy bars into a paper bag, got into my Legend, parked by the Roman arch, fought my way through a sea of pedestrians, and arrived breathless at the Silver Moon.

Claire was behind her small desk, reading the *Nice Matin* and smoking. She wore a beige Angora sweater that accentuated her appeal. I wiped off the sweat on my brow with my handkerchief and said, "I've enough wood to last me several winters."

She let go of the paper, "So, what's on your mind?"

"Well . . . let me see . . . were you serious about wanting to relocate to Santa Fe?"

"Oliver has decided not to renew the lease. In a few months, or maybe just weeks, I'll be out of work."

"The talk about the marriage was a joke, right?"

"Would you want it to be serious? Do you think we could make it as a couple?"

"I don't know what I think. I am much older and you are so beautiful, so. . . French."

"I suspected as much." She eyed me from my toes to my forehead, sizing me up, studying me. Unnerved, I asked, "What are you doing?"

"Trying to figure out if you are . . . promise you won't be upset if I tell you."

"I have no idea what's on your mind, and I have no idea if I'll get upset. Say it, and we will find out." But my intuition told me that I would be crushed.

"Okay. Here it goes. I was wondering if you were impotent. You talk a lot, and the men who talk a lot, you know, tend to cover their weakness with chatter."

I stared at her wide-eyed, as embarrassed as if my pants had dropped to the ground. "You . . . enjoy sex, don't you?"

"But, of course. I am a French woman."

"Suppose we try and see what happens."

She laughed. "Don't you know?"

"It's different with every woman. Do you reach orgasm with every man?"

"Hm . . . let me think."

"How about with Oliver?"

"He's a Brit. He does the best he can," she said matter of factly.

"Claire, Claire, what am I going to do? You make every cell in my body tingle with excitement. You are deliciously sexy, but I don't feel safe with you."

"Most men don't. That's why I got involved with Oliver. His notion of a 'mature' relationship gives me the breathing space I need."

"So. What's the answer for us?"

"You know as well as I do. A platonic relationship. A friendship. Continue the way we have been going."

My mind turned to Theodora. I had been longing for intimacy with a woman, pure of heart and pure of mind. Claire was pragmatic, very wise about the ways of the world. Then, there was the age difference. I sighed. I ran my fingers through my hair. "I have an older sister. You could be my younger one."

"You'll let me stay in your spare bedroom, then, won't you?"

"Only if you make appetizing dishes and keep the house clean."

"I accept the offer! It's a deal."

I opened my arms. She came over, and we hugged. To my dismay, my member rose. Did she feel it? She let go of me and said, "What's in your bag?"

"Energy bars for my favorite ballerina, what else?"

24

At the end of the month, when Giuseppe came to collect the rent, I pointed at the crackling fire. "Not bad, eh?"

Staring on the piles of wood on each side of the fireplace, he sighed, "That's more wood than I keep in my house. I'll bring you two cardboard boxes to put it in."

The next morning, as I readied myself for more wood gathering, Giuseppe and Nina came over. Giuseppe handed me the promised boxes. I invited them in for a glass of wine. From the sofa, Nina looked at the wood, frowned and shook her head. They left without finishing their wine, something they had never done before

The following day, seeing Giuseppe working on his old Renault in the garage below my apartment, I asked him to come over and take a look at what I had done with his boxes. Glancing at them, he said, "Nina left your apartment in a bad mood yesterday. She's worried you'll set the house on fire."

"I think of your retirement home as if it were my own. I couldn't live with myself if I caused any damage to it."

Giuseppe murmured something indistinguishable. "Is there something wrong?" I asked.

"We'll see. Let's hope for the best."

I wanted to ask him to explain himself but I had something else on my mind. "That monster van with the Swedish license plates has been parked across the street for the last two days. Are the people moving in or getting out?"

"The owners are packing what's left of their belongings and returning to Stockholm. Two weeks ago, upon their return from a vacation in Majorca, they found their stereo and most of the furniture gone. Their alarm didn't do them any good."

"What about the police?"

"They investigate. Arab gangs steal and the police investigate."

"How do you know Arabs did it?"

"There are ten million Arabs in France, and they are on the edge of society. In Vallarus, the police don't dare enter the old town. Not long ago they came to make an arrest, and the youths chased them away with stones. In some villages, life is akin to a lawless Casbah."

The next morning, I found a note from Nina affixed on the veranda door. It said, "The fire inspector has concluded that your wood presents a major hazard, and has requested that you immediately dispose of it." When I confronted her, she admitted that she had written it, but insisted that I get rid of the wood.

"Why did you rent me an apartment with a fireplace, if you're opposed to me using it?" I asked.

"You have turned the veranda into a dump. This is a high-class neighborhood. People will think we're renting to transients or Arabs."

"I thought the Revolution had made France a classless society. Your aristocratic neighbors have fences behind which to store their wood. All I have is my veranda. Let them come to me with their complaints."

"I don't want the wood on the veranda!" she screamed.

"And I want it there!"

It was a draw between an expatriate Italian peasant woman and a naturalized, American Jew. When Nina had first met me, she had thought I was an Arab drug dealer, because I sported a beard. She refused to let me into the apartment. Giuseppe had to use all his power of persuasion to impress on her prejudiced mind that I was a respectable American. The current confrontation didn't entirely displease me. As with Tonio, I had agreed with Nina too many times to preserve the peace. It felt good, for once, to hold my ground.

Giuseppe, who had been a passive witness to my altercation with Nina, raised his hand. "The world isn't perfect. We must compromise. Let Adam keep as much wood as fits inside the boxes in the living room, and the rest store in the spare bedroom."

He eyed me. I nodded.

He went on, "Adam has been a good tenant. He hasn't caused any other problems. He pays his rent on time. He keeps the place clean. He has no noisy visitors."

"It's my apartment," Nina snapped. "I won't let anyone tell me what can take place in it."

Giuseppe's face dropped. He looked like someone suffering from painful indigestion. Glancing at his watch, he said in a tired voice, "It's time for us to leave."

"But he'll keep the wood on the veranda," Nina said.

"No, he won't." Giuseppe responded.

Both Tonio and Giuseppe liked discussing politics. With Tonio, I mostly listened to his views. With Giuseppe, I articulated mine freely. A seasoned socialist, Giuseppe wished every human to have comfort and dignity. I could not have agreed with him more. It was with sorrow that I watched him cave in before Nina time and time again.

A week after my confrontation with Nina, I asked him, "Is the proletariat still marching to a better tomorrow?"

"Of course, it is. It always will."

"Not if Nina's views prevail," I retorted.

Ah, the blessings of living in upscale Côte d'Azur. Nina was right to demand high standards after all. The proof lay in the discards I found inside the two garbage bins near my apartment. After finding a wearable cotton shirt and a pair of gabardine pants, I made it my habit to examine the contents of the bins whenever I took my garbage out. I did that in spite of the fear that Nina might catch me in the act. She would have never forgiven me for behaving like a gypsy or an Arab. What puzzled me, though, was that I shared in her revulsion. I also wanted the intruders out of the way. Was it because I wished the entire loot for myself? I wondered.

One cloudy morning in May, I found a Sharp CD player. Glancing right and left, to assure that no critical eyes were watching me, I removed the player from the trash, took it home, disinfected it thoroughly with alcohol, drove to Carrefour, purchased a 60 watt Kenwood stereo player, two Wharfedale bookcase speakers, and a CD of Beethoven's Ninth Symphony. After connecting the components, I inserted the CD into the player and held my breath. Beethoven's magical notes bounced from wall to wall. But not all was well. The small screen on the Sharp's player that would have ordinarily displayed the playing channel, remained blank. I shrugged. Just a minor inconvenience.

I turned the volume high enough to suppress the street noise, and for the first time since moving into the apartment, ate my lunch to the sound of music, instead of the maddening traffic. In the late afternoon, after four productive hours in Tonio's atelier, I returned home, turned on the stereo, and heard a loud knock on the door.

Frowning, Nina barked, "The neighbors are complaining about your music."

"It is the only way I know of suppressing the traffic noise."

"Play music in your bedroom with the door closed."

"In the bedroom, I don't hear the traffic."

"You knew what you were getting into when you moved in. You don't like the noise. The neighbors don't like your music!"

"Okay, Nina, I'll do something about it."

Turning to leave, she cried, "Do it now!"

There was no end to her bitching. First, she complained about the wood, and now about the music. What next? I turned the volume high enough to suppress the traffic noise, stepped outside, crossed the street, and walked up a driveway leading to a complex of small, modern homes. The music was almost as loud as inside the apartment. I backtracked my steps, lowered the volume halfway, and went out again. The music blended with the street noise. Inside, it blended as well. I let the new setting stand. It was a fucking compromise, and I hated compromises.

The next morning, I dropped the *International Herald Tribune* on Tonio's workbench, and asked, "Are you having a good day?"

"All my days are good," he said, then glancing at the paper, he barked, "You like reading *Merde*, don't you?"

"What do you mean, *merde*? The paper carries no advertisement, and it covers news from around the world."

"And it delivers news objectively, right?"

"At least as objectively as your *Nice Matin*."

"Oh, yeah? When did it last comment on Israelis torturing Arabs in jails?"

"A week ago. Read it, and you'll be impressed by its impartiality."

"I would rather die than read that piece of capitalist propaganda."

"So, you prefer to guess its content?"

"I don't have to guess to know that Israelis shake the prisoners, their heads rolling back and forth until they turn into idiots."

"I agree, it's a terrible thing to do."

"CIA agents taught them. They run schools for Nicaraguans, South Africans, Israelis, and countless other fascist countries. After graduation, they provide field supervision. I bet your paper doesn't mention that."

"The schools offered training in riot and insurgency control, but not in torture. They have been closed for months."

"Is that so?"

"Yes, it is."

"And where did you learn that?"

"In the *New York Times*."

"Another paper on the payroll of the American imperialists."

"And you? Where do you get your information?"

Ignoring my question, he spat out, "If the CIA didn't train the Israelis, they wouldn't know how to torture innocent civilians."

"You mean hardened terrorists? They have plenty of teachers. Arafat tortures his own people. Saddam poisons the Kurds. Algerian Moslem radicals kill women and children by the hundreds. In Saudi Arabia, they hang a princess for eloping with a commoner. Israelis are mad. Arabs are mad. They all belong in an insane asylum."

His eyes afire, he screamed, "It's in the American interest that the Middle East should be in flames. That way they can exploit its natural resources."

We had gone through the routine before. I enjoyed political discussions, but not when expected to bow before fanatical authority.

"What's the point of arguing?" I said in a conciliatory voice. "You have your outlook. I have mine. No harm in that."

"No harm in arming and training Israelis, you mean? No harm in giving them the money to buy ancestral Arab land?"

"Even if America maintained total neutrality, the Israelis and the Arabs would still be at each other's throats. They have been hating each other for generations. Israeli would love to see Palestinians absorbed by the Arab states; Palestinians would love to see Israelis pushed into the sea. America too often sides with Israel, but it's not responsible for the conflict there."

"You talk like a Jew."

"Well, I am a Jew," I yelled. The moment the words left my mouth, I knew all hell would break loose. "My loyalty is to the truth, as I see it," I went on, trying to keep the dialogue flowing. "Sometimes I side with the Israelis and sometimes with the Arabs. Actually, I'm a renegade Jew. I haven't practiced the religion ever since leaving Yugoslavia."

Tonio opened his mouth. Sweat formed on his forehead. "A Jew, a fucking Jew! That's what you are! A Jew making jewelry in my atelier! Laughing at me. The monkey in a cage, watching him go through his pathetic routine. Go ahead and laugh at the pathetic Arab in his little shop, selling his trinkets to tourists, smiling, doing a monkey dance, so he would get a few coins tossed onto his plate."

I watched him openmouthed. I had no clue what he was driving at. Then, it occurred to me that the whole time he was condemning the Israelis for their atrocities, he was secretly envying them. Raising my hand in a gesture of peace, I mumbled, "Tonio, I've never thought of you any the less for being an Arab. I swear."

"Thank you, my sir, for your kind words," he said and bowed. "I shall remember them to the last day of my miserable life."

"Stop it, Tonio! You have got it all wrong. You have given me an opportunity to make jewelry. You've been generous. I—"

"Fucking Jew!" he yelled and stepped forward.

My back hit the wall. I was about to reach for a long file on the bench to defend myself with, when a young woman walked in, glanced at Tonio, and asked. "Are you the artist?" She spoke with a British accent.

Tonio spat on the floor, some of his spit landing on my shoes. "Yes, I am. What can I do for you?"

"My friend Muriel bought a lovely bracelet here. I was wondering if you had any others."

He glanced at me, at her, at me, and shouted, "Get the fuck out of here."

"Muriel has a wonderful taste in jewelry," I said, somewhat reassured by the woman's presence. "She liked my work too."

Tonio snorted. "Out, out! Do you hear me? Out!"

"Should I come back another time?" the woman asked in a perturbed voice.

"No, no, stay. We'll get down to business after this asshole is gone."

That night I tossed and turned. My Jewish background had caught up with me. The wandering Jew. The disconnected Jew. The alienated Jew. I thought of ways to patch things up with Tonio but couldn't come up with any ideas. That I hadn't practiced my religion for decades made no difference. Once a Jew, always a Jew. In our respective ways, we were both outcasts. My parents brought me up with the notion that I was mentally slow, delicate, and unfit for life. Tonio, I suspected, was brought up to think of himself as a pariah. We ought to form a common front against arbitrary authority, instead of fighting each other. I wanted to call him and tell him that, but my instincts warned me that my friendly gesture would only increase his bellicosity.

Ten days after our altercation, a warm, late spring day, I ventured into the old town. I spied at Tonio bent over his workbench. I don't know what I would have done, had he seen me. I turned right at the fifteenth-century church, and zigzagged through eternally dark alleyways, under laundry fluttering above, and past cats on windowsills. I sat on the bench where a few months earlier I had heard a woman playing the piano. The renovated medieval homes, which had filled me with wonder then now felt strangely ominous.

At home, lying in bed, I replayed, again and again, the scene with Tonio, his anger, and my retreat. I had been deceitful. I hid my Jewish origins. But, what choice did I have? On the wall, he had pictures of Arab youths throwing stones at Israeli soldiers. He bitched nonstop about the Israelis. Had I admitted to my origins, he wouldn't have invited me into his atelier. I thought of going back and apologizing. *Too late for that,* an inner voice cautioned, *too late. There is no going back.*

I picked up the computer chess game and dropped it on the bed. I picked up a book with French lessons, and dropped it, too. I couldn't even concentrate on the *Herald Tribune.* The walls began to close in on me. The first thing the following morning, I took the train to Nice. At the Nice airport, two young men, one short and the other over six feet tall, both with red Mohawk hairdos, stepped into my compartment. They sat down opposite me, pulled cigarettes out of a pack, and lit them.

I pointed my hand at the non-smoking sign above the window.

"Have you got a problem with us?" the tall man asked.

"I am allergic to smoke," I said.

"Move to another car."

"But I chose this one because it's—"

"You are an American chap?" he interrupted.

"And you are a Brit, aren't you?"

"To the last drop of my blood. So, what are you doing on the Riviera?" he asked in a falsetto voice, winking at his companion.

"He's got a job with the French railroads," the shorter man giggled. Leaning forward, he pleaded, "Dear Sir, please, don't report us. My mother would have a fit if she found out I was put in jail for illegally lighting a cigarette."

Other passengers appeared unaffected by the commotion. Across the aisle, a man in a blue suit read *Nice Matin.* Nearby two teens spoke in undertones. A large, heavily made-up woman looked out the window. The little girl next to her cradled a stuffed bear. Feeling painfully alienated, I rose and headed for the next wagon. *Did the two Brits figure out I was a Jew?* I wondered. I do have a Semitic nose, after all.

The compartment allowed smoking. *Better to pollute my lungs than to have a nervous breakdown,* I mused, as I sat on a bench near the door and reduced my breathing to the bare minimum. Apartment buildings covered with soot announced the train's arrival in Nice. At the tourist information center, I picked up a map of Nice and headed north in search of the Matisse and Chagall museums. By the time I arrived at the tree-shaded streets in the heart of Cimes, the upscale residential district, only an occasional vehicle disrupted the quiet.

I eagerly entered the modern, sharply-angled Chagall Museum. Chagall's whimsical compositions had filled me with joy for decades. All of the canvases in the museum were immense and hypnotic. Men and women defied gravity; animals twisted in impossible positions, and deep pastel colors spilled over people's costumes and queer-looking buildings. It was a dream world at its best. As I stood before the Creation of Man, the Garden of Eden, the Story of Noah, Abraham, Jacob, and Moses, I thought of my jewelry and vowed to make, from now on, only veritable works of art.

Then, Tonio came to my mind, and my euphoria vanished. I was a wandering Jew. Chagall was also a wandering Jew. But his art redeemed him; it opened the door to a universal home.

Matisse was my other favorite painter. His dancers, with their flowing lines and exuberant colors, have long been my favorites. If I had the money to purchase a painting by a master, it would be a Matisse. In my bedroom in Biot, I had a reproduction of his Red Room, its bouquets of red flowers, apples looking like overgrown gems, yellow chair, a green landscape behind a window, and a stylized woman in black, creating a magical, harmonious whole.

Villa des Arènes, exhibiting Matisse's work was only half an hour away. To my chagrin, his drawings, engravings, and sculptures hardly touched me. None projected the vitality that I had come to expect from the artist. If Chagall had been high on life when he painted his surreal canvases, Matisse must have been depressed when he created the art in Villa des Arènes.

Disappointed, I left the museum and walked to a small, nearby park to eat my lunch. A shaggy black dog, with no collar or identification tag, its ribs showing, appeared from behind a trimmed bush. I tossed it a chunk of bread. It wiggled its tail, came over and we shared my lunch. After it trotted away, I stretched on the bench and fell asleep. Chirping birds woke me up close to sunset.

My next stop was the American Express office on the Promenade des Anglais. The slim, young woman behind the counter greeted me with her usual smile, then handed me my mail. After a stop at the McDonald's to use the meticulously clean restrooms, I crossed the boulevard, sat down on a chair overlooking the Mediterranean, rested my feet on the metal railing, and opened my mail, all containing financial statements.

On the beach below, a Black man and a blond woman held each other in a tight embrace. Behind them, a speeding motorboat pulled a man harnessed to a silver parachute. He rose some 100 feet, stood suspended for a few minutes, then descended gracefully in the shallow water. Some ten yards away, six women dressed in national Bulgarian costumes danced to the sound of folk music. I rose, watched the performance for a few minutes, dropped ten Franks into a dish, then headed for the Hotel Negresco. The boulevard offered the live entertainment of a theater. Musicians and dancers from around the world performed. Teenagers zoomed on roller-skates. Lovers strolled hand in hand. The vitality was so intense that even a dying man would have found the energy to get up and do a jig. Two things detracted me from the bliss, however: a stony beach and dog shit. As I never used the beach, its rough surface left me indifferent. The dog shit, however, annoyed me no end.

The French enjoy impressing foreigners with the notion that their country is a lovers' paradise. Yet, an article in the *Herald-Tribune* reported that in an interview, half of the male dog owners reported that if they had to choose between their female companions and their dogs, they would choose their dogs. The Riviera is a cesspool. Notices in Antibes and Cannes parks advise dog owners to clean up after their pets, which they seldom do.

Hotel Negresco, at the western end of the boulevard, was a Victorian marvel. Overlooking the ocean, it rose like an immense mirage. A green Ferrari and a sky-blue Rolls Royce Cornice were parked illegally by the entrance. In a narrow, adjacent street a shapely young woman in a very short miniskirt and knee-high boots leaned seductively against a brick wall. With my eyes dancing between the cars and the woman, I asked myself which I would rather have. As I couldn't afford neither, I stopped the absurd musing and headed for the train station.

The sign of the French Alpine Club affixed to a wall of a nondescript building stopped me. As hiking was high on my agenda, I stepped inside and asked the elderly woman behind the counter if she spoke English. She shook her head. I pointed at my shoes and moved my legs,

"Alpinist?" she asked.

"*Avec Sierra Club. Je marche beaucoup.*" ("With Sierra Club. I hike a lot.") I said.

She gave me a brochure in English, which stated that to join the club's activities, I had to receive a physician's clearance. The cost of a medical examination, membership fee, and transportation being high, I returned the brochure with the thought I would continue going on free hikes.

Biot was awash in buckets of red and orange hues when I stepped out of the train. I opened the door to my apartment thinking, *There is life after Tonio after all.*

The next morning, while eating breakfast, the phone rang.

"What are you doing, my boy?" Tonio asked.

"You don't care, so why are you asking?" I answered

"Come over. A couple of pussies have dropped by."

Pussies? Cats or women? I suspected he was referring to women. "You're inviting me to your shop? You are no longer mad at me?"

"Of course not. Whatever made you think that I was mad?"

"There are two pussies with you?"

"Hurry. They won't be here much longer."

He sounded friendly, but that could be a ruse to entice me to come so he could drop more shit upon me. Then again, he might have had second thoughts. I was the only one after all who put up with his obsessive barrages against Israeli's occupation of Arab land, the American imperialism, and the sad state of the French economy. A French-Arab and a Yugoslavian-American Jew, needing each other? Stan Laurel and Oliver Hardy. I headed for the old town resolved to fight Tonio to the death if he tried to shit on me. A middle-aged woman welcomed me with a smile from the stool by the steel anvil. A younger one, with the build of an overweight Sophia Loren, was polishing jewelry at the buffing wheel.

"This is Adam. He's from Santa Fe, the city of art," Tonio said.

The older woman offered me her hand. The one at the buffing machine stopped the motor, and asked, "What do you do?"

"I make jewelry," I answered.

"Look at this," she said, handing me a pendant in the shape of a miniature lobster, small and delicate, something I wouldn't have imagined making in my wildest dreams. "My name is Elizabeth."

"I've never seen anything like it," I said. "An incredible piece of work."

"Thanks so much. What kind of jewelry do you make?"

"Large, tri-dimensional bracelets and pendants, in the shape of miniature sculptures. Where do you do your work?"

"In a gallery at the Cagnes Sur Mer castle grounds. Roxanne is the gallery manager. Because I don't own a car, she brought me to Tonio's workshop to do some polishing. Well, I've got to be going."

She walked to Tonio, kissed him on the mouth, and turned to face me. "When I first came to the Còte d'Azur, Tonio let me use his workshop. He's a sweetheart."

She was young enough to be his daughter. I mused. He let her use his polishing wheel and she returned the favor with a sexual gesture. The two made a fine team. I eyed her overdeveloped breasts, her broad hips, her thick legs, her crinkly black hair, and her Semitic nose.

"Elizabeth, what's your last name?" I asked.

"Goldberg."

Shit! He had befriended a Jewess before I had appeared on the scene. Why had he gone berserk when he learned about my ethnicity? Was it because I had lied? After the two women left, I screamed, "Elizabeth is Jewish."

"So what? I hold no grudges against Canadian Jews. An Israeli I would kick out."

"And a Yugoslavian-American Jew? Do you hold grudges against him?"

"Questioning, questioning, that's all you ever do. What about this? What about that? Yap, yap, yap." He glanced at his watch. "It's time for lunch. Come. We'll eat at my home."

"What about the Israelis and the Arabs?"

"They can go and fuck themselves."

Tonio padlocked the glass door, leaving the shutters open so that the jewelry display could be seen from the outside. We took a cobblestone alley in the back of his shop and came to an old stone house. A 500 cc Yamaha was parked near the entrance. "Is that the motorcycle you used to elope with Dolores?" I asked.

"You must be joking. That one died a long time ago."

Tonio's wife, Madeleine, slender, long black hair resting on her shoulders, in her early forties—stood over the kitchen counter.

"Bonjour," I said. She acknowledged me with a nod without turning her head. The small kitchen was part of the living room. It was cluttered with utensils, bowls, frying pans, and jars filled with white rice, white flour, and beans.

"Smells good, eh?" Tonio said, taking off his leather jacket and dropping it on a stool

The long rectangular room held a wood stove in one corner. Across from it stood a large sofa luxuriously covered with a gold and yellow spread, and rainbow-colored pillows casually thrown over it. The walls were decorated with pictures of Tonio, paintings, artworks, and a couple of small, intricately woven rugs. Between the kitchen and the living room stood a large round table. Tonio eased himself onto a chair at one end, and said, "Now we eat."

Whether his chair was taller than mine was unclear to me, but he seemed to have grown in size. He eyed the cheese, the salami, the bottle of wine, the celery, the tomatoes, the carrots, and the white bread on the table as a potentate might eye a feast spread out in his honor. His wife came over to ask if everything was all right.

Thinking that she had spent three years in Los Angeles with him, I said, "Did you enjoy your stay in America?"

She gave me a blank stare and returned to the kitchen.

Tonio filled his plate with food, poured red wine into our glasses, and said, "She hasn't been to the States. I went there before marrying her."

Pointing his fork holding an olive at a huge ceramic cucumber, he continued, "Dolores made it. She's rich. Her father left her a lot of money."

"Does your wife mind have your ex-lover's art in her home?"

"This is France, my boy. In France, people believe in love. There is no jealousy here."

"Baloney," I said.

He shrugged. "Dolores also made that banana."

The banana was three feet long. "Dolores must have been inspired by a giant's penis," I said.

"She's a good artist, but unstable. She likes to date men half her age."

I wiped my mouth with a paper tissue, "But you're married to a woman twenty years your junior."

"Yes, but just one. A couple of years after my son was born, I met Madeleine. She had been raised in Tunisia by parents who believed that a woman ought to be a woman and a man a man." He smiled. "I am blessed."

Glancing at Madeleine sweating over the sink, at a photograph on the wall of his illegitimate son, and at another photograph of his son and daughter born to him by Madeleine, I said, "Tonio, the sheik of Arabia."

"No, no, my boy, 'The sheik of Babylonia.'"

26

The first Monday of July I woke up with my nose stuffed up, my joints stiff. and my muscles painful. For the next three days, I cleansed my system with gallons of Evian water, ate only fruits and cereal, and spent long hours in bed. In between bouts of sleep, I read and played computer chess. When I came down with a sore throat, I called the Sophia Antipolis Cultural Center and asked if they knew of an English-speaking doctor. The volunteer lady suggested I consult Dr. Ireland, but she warned me that he wasn't affiliated with the National Health Service and that he could charge all he wanted. Dr. Ireland's soft-speaking female receptionist said on the phone that the doctor was attending a serious emergency but that he would be available at six that afternoon. After a long nap, my symptoms abated somewhat. I considered canceling the appointment, but the receptionist had gone out of her way to fit me into the doctor's busy schedule. Moreover, the aches and pains were far from gone.

Driving on the narrow, twisting lanes to Valbonne, I reminisced on my experience with American physicians like Dr. Milroy, an orthopedic surgeon.

I had been reading an old issue of the *Outside* magazine in his waiting room, when a short and thin nurse called, "Adam, Dr. Milroy is ready to see you."

I ignored her.

"The doctor is ready to see Adam. Is he here?"

"Mr. Milan is," I said.

"Mr. Milan?"

"That's my name."

"Will you hurry? Dr. Milroy has a busy schedule."

She led me to a small room at the end of a brightly lit corridor and pointed at a stool. "Adam, please sit down and roll up your sleeve."

"Have we met before?" I asked.

Staring at me as if I had lost my marbles, she asked, "What's that supposed to mean?"

"You're calling me by my first name."

"Does that upset you?"

"Which arm do you want?" I asked.

"Either one." She wrapped the blood test fold, and said, "Adam, please be still."

"Do you call your doctor by his first name?" I asked.

She gave me a look that said, 'don't be a pain in the ass,' then put the stethoscope to her ears, and pressed on the rubber ball.

"What's my blood pressure?" I inquired.

"One-hundred sixty over eighty."

"That's forty points over my typical rate."

"You may consider taking a medication to lower your blood pressure."

"A more effective way would be dealing with a nurse who respects me."

She shrugged, said, "Dr. Millroy will be in shortly," and left.

Dr. Milroy, a portly man with thinning gray hair at the temples walked in, "Adam, I'm Doctor Milroy. How are you doing today?"

"Would you prefer we call each other by our first or last names?" I asked.

He opened his mouth but no words came out. For the rest of the examination, he called me nothing. I wasn't Adam, and I wasn't Mr. Milan. I was a nameless, anonymous patient.

Parking my car alongside a green Jaguar with British plates in front of a one-story white house in Valbonne, I wondered if

Dr. Ireland would also expect to be treated as royalty. Tall, wiry, athletic, in his mid-forties, he introduced himself as Sean, and led me through a dark corridor cluttered with wrapped cardboard boxes. In a large, sunny room he pointed at a chair by a large mahogany desk, eased down on a leather armchair and said, "You're an American? Aren't you?"

"A naturalized one. I was born in Yugoslavia."

"I hear the coast is very scenic. Bernard Shaw referred to Dubrovnik as the 'Pearl of the Adriatic.'"

His voice was soothing. I felt as if in the company of an old friend. But I didn't come to socialize. "A year ago, I consulted an American physician in Rome because of inflamed hemorrhoids," I said. "Twisting in my chair we discussed the pros and the cons of living in the Eternal City. He charged me for the time we spent on small talk."

"I wouldn't do that to a patient I liked," Sean said smiling. He took two apples from his drawer, passed me one, took a bite, and said, "My wife told you I was out on an emergency call, didn't she?"

I nodded.

"She lied. I went skiing for the afternoon." Seeing my startled expression, he went on, "The resort is but an hour away."

"American doctors wouldn't dream of playing hooky on a working day."

"That's why so many of them have ulcers."

"With the money they make, they can afford royal treatment," I said and took a bite of my apple.

"Good, eh? Now tell me what brings you here."

"Weakness, muscle aches, and sore throat for four days, but I'm getting better."

"Why did you come to see me, then?"

"It didn't seem right to cancel the appointment at such short notice."

"Very considerate of you. Let's move to the examining table."

We left our unfinished apples on the desk. He instructed me to sit at the edge of the table and leaned down. "Ouch," he exclaimed.

"Are you hurting?" I asked.

"A bit sore. Now, take a deep breath and hold it."

He tapped me in several places, then said to put on my clothes. Moments later we were back at his desk.

"So, what's the verdict?" I asked.

"You have the flu. Take plenty of fluids and rest."

"But that's what I've been doing. I don't need a doctor to tell me that."

"Obviously, you do. Otherwise, you wouldn't be here."

"The woman at the Sophia Antipolis Cultural Center, who recommended you, told me that you aren't affiliated with the National Health Service."

"That's right."

"So, you can charge all you want?"

"I can."

"Even for the small talk?"

He laughed, filled a form, and passed it to me. "You owe me two hundred francs."

That came to forty dollars. "How much would I have saved if I had consulted a doctor affiliated with the National Health Service?"

"About half. But you wouldn't have gotten an apple."

Three days later, much improved, I went to Sophia Antipolis for my French class. At the break, the discussion turned to the English-speaking physicians on the Riviera. "I like Sean Ireland the best," Tara said. "He's straightforward and has a sense of humor."

"I consulted him last Tuesday," I said.

"But that was the day he injured his shoulder skiing. He shot himself with painkillers. Was he able to treat you well?"

"I guess so, but at one point he grimaced. I wish now that I had been more sensitive to his condition."

After the class, I drove to Carrefour, the grocery store. The circus atmosphere was in full swing. Humpty Dumpty stood on his circular pedestal. Children with wide-opened mouths stared at him. Adults rushed toward their favorite stalls, bumping against each other and apologizing in their gracious French manner. A man hit me in the shins with his cart. I cursed him silently and walked to the Biologique section where I bought tofu, brown rice, spinach noodles, and a carton of chocolate-flavored soya drink. A man bumped into me. *Damn it,* I thought, *the pedestrian traffic here is as bad as the motor traffic outside my home.*

"Sorry," Sean Ireland said. "So, you got over your flu?"

"I have. How is your shoulder?"

"Reasonably well, thank you."

"You wouldn't have said that the day I saw you. You shot yourself with painkillers and went on treating me as if all was well."

"A good doctor can ski, get injured, and practice medicine all in one day."

I gave him a friendly slap on the arm, "I wish American doctors were as easygoing as you are."

"Watch out, not so hard."

"Sorry. But I thought you said you were feeling all right."

"I said I felt reasonably well, not recovered."

We shook hands and I went to the men's clothing section. Several men stood around a huge card box filled to the brim with sweaters. One heavy-set guy with bulging arms in overalls dug deep into the box, pulled out a woolen blue sweater, pressed it against his broad chest, and smiled. I pulled out a gray, woolen turtle-neck one, pressed it against my chest, and smiled as well. *What would Claire think of it?* I wondered.

Back home, I sat on the veranda, inhaled the intoxicating aroma of flowers in full bloom, and thought again of Claire. I longed for a full loaf, and she threw crumbs. *Better crumbs than nothing,* I thought and succumbed to depression. How low can one get? But a man suffering from thirst would drink muddy water if it was the only kind available.

The next morning, I stopped at the Silver Moon. After kissing Claire on both cheeks, I picked up a copy of the *Riviera Reporter*, the weekly paper, from her desk, glanced at the back page, and asked. "Did you place an ad?"

She gave me a puzzled look. "An ad, did you say?"

"Young, attractive, and affectionate Frenchwoman would like to meet an older, wealthy yacht owner for travel and friendship."

"I have a daddy already. He isn't made of sugar, but he'll do. And I have a lover. I don't need a yacht."

"I thought things over, and decided I would be willing to marry you even if you denied me sex. Of course, you would always be welcome to change your mind."

"And you would assist me getting the job of a gallery manager?"

"Of course, and I would help you with the citizenship paperwork. But you must agree to one condition."

"What?" she asked frowning.

"You would allow me to bathe you a couple of times a week."

"Bathe me? You must be crazy."

"Everyone needs a bath."

"Sorry, no deal."

Embarrassed by my foolish proposal, I said nothing. Her rejection of physical intimacy actually reassured me. She was clearly at the height of her sexual prowess, while I was at the low end.

Suddenly, she smiled. "You really like the way I look, don't you?"

"I think you're adorable, especially with your upturned nose."

"My nose?"

"It gives you an impossibly optimistic air."

"Claire optimistic?" Oliver said from the door and walked in. He wore his military-style shirt buttoned to the collar.

"I was agreeing to marry her so that she could become an American citizen. Do you have any objection?"

"Whatever she wants it's fine with me."

"You two have a wonderful relationship. You ought to write about it."

"Maintaining independence is the ultimate romance," Claire said.

"Were you as liberated before you met Oliver?'

"But of course. I vowed in my adolescence never to be controlled by a man."

As I was thinking of something smart to say, a tall woman in a fur coat and a short pudgy man carrying a long sleek violin case walked in. Claire greeted them in English. The French seemed to have a sixth sense about people's nationalities. The woman leaned over the jewelry case and said, "I would like to try those earrings."

Claire handed them to her. The woman put them on, glanced at a hand-held mirror, and said to her companion, "They look nice on me, don't you think?"

"They look lovely, my dear." Her companion rested his case on the ground and lit a cigarette. A cloud of smoke swirled over his bold head.

"Are you Americans?" I asked.

"From Philadelphia," he answered without turning.

"I'm from Santa Fe. In a recent reader survey by the *Condé Nast Traveler,* the City Different was voted as the most desirable vacation destination in the world."

They both ignored my comment. I went on, "That looks like a violin case. Are you musicians?"

The man, in his rumpled suit and stained tie, could have passed for an accountant, a teller in a bank, or a waiter. She had class. While I felt sorry for the animals that had been sacrificed to make her full-length fur coat, I had to admit that it encompassed her slender body with refined gentility. The Louise Vuitton purse hanging from her shoulders conveyed discerning and expensive taste. Could she be a world-renowned violinist?

"My companion is giving a recital tonight at Monte Carlo," the man said.

I considered asking if they would give me a free ticket for the performance but, fearing Claire would be annoyed by my familiarity with her customers, said nothing.

The man was about to throw the cigarette butt on the floor. I grabbed an ashtray from the small desk and passed it to him. He thanked me, squashed the butt, and lit another cigarette.

"How much are the earrings?" the woman asked.

"Two hundred sixty francs," Claire said.

"That's—"

"Fifty-two dollars, my dear," her companion explained.

"But they're made in Asia," the woman protested.

"Everything in the store is handmade. Look at the details of those earrings. Each piece is unique," Claire reassured her.

The woman glanced at the man. "Whatever you think is best, my dear," he said.

"I could let you have them for two hundred fifty francs," Claire said.

"Thanks so much for your time, but I had in mind something less expensive."

Oliver rose, said, "The same old shit," and left the store.

I waved at him, then eyed Claire. "I've been thinking about your jewelry," I said. "They are colorful but lack an aesthetic focus. If I were in your shoes, I would get rid of a lot of the stuff, and turn the store into a high-end gallery."

She dropped the set of keys she was holding on her small desk, glanced at me with fiery eyes, and spat out, "I am the manager. Don't you ever forget it."

"But—"

"No buts about it. If I need your help, I'll ask for it. Do you read me?"

I nodded sheepishly. It was the fighting Claire, the one who cleaned up the mess that Oliver made with the local merchants. But my point was well taken, although I had an ulterior motive when I said it. Were she to turn the store into a high-end outlet, my jewelry could be sold as art, and I wouldn't have to have them officially stamped

"I'm sorry your business is so slow," I mumbled.

"It's been like this for weeks. Americans are the worst. They hate to part with their money."

"I would buy all of you earrings, bracelets, and rings if I could afford to."

"That's what a sugar-daddy would do."

"You would be worth every penny."

She threw me a kiss with her hand. Only moments earlier she had fulminated against me and now embraced me in warmth. "Is your apartment warm? Are you still hunting for wood?" she asked.

"I found so much that my landlady made up a lie that the fire marshal wanted it thrown out."

Our conversations didn't stimulate me. She was very practical. She lived with a dull man. Why was I so drawn to her? She was lovely to look at and feisty, a remarkable combination indeed. I wanted physical intimacy. She offered friendship. We were at a standstill.

27

Mid-morning, rain and wind slammed Tonio's door. I was at the polishing wheel when a young, dark-skinned woman with cascading black hair stepped in. With her brown leather pants and jacket, she looked like a princess from a distant and exotic land. She rested her folded umbrella by the door and glanced at the pictures on the wall of Arab youth throwing stones at Israeli soldiers.

"A heroic confrontation," Tonio said, then noticing her staring at a large sculpture of a tomato on a marble pedestal, he went on, "My ex-lover made it. She exhibits in Lyon and Paris."

"Interesting."

"I used to wear a leather outfit when riding my motorcycle."

"I never rode a motorcycle."

"Women like men on motorcycles."

"You don't say?"

"That's me, over there." Tonio pointed at a photo of a man in a leather jacket and a helmet.

She shrugged, glanced at me, and asked, "What are you making?"

I turned off the buffing machine and handed her my large pendant with little bridges, cones, and small textured areas.

"It looks like a miniature sculpture."

"When it's finished, it will be a wearable piece of jewelry or something to hang on a wall. Would you like to try it on? I can attach a chain to it."

"Don't waste your time," Tonio barked from his bench. "His jewelry is best suited for fat women."

Fat women? The visitor ignored his stupid comment and nodded to me. I pulled a silver chain out of my backpack, attached it to the pendant, and passed it to her. Viewing herself on the reflecting glass of a painting, she nodded appreciatively.

"I make bead necklaces," she said.

"If your necklaces are as exotic-looking as you are, they must be quite a sight," I said, a bit self-consciously.

A faint smile lit her dark face. "They are. People think of them as otherworldly."

Tonio rose, came to a few feet behind her, and asked, "Do you have a boyfriend?"

"Should I have one?" she responded without turning.

"Women need affection." Pointing at me, he went on, "Can't you tell that he's old enough to be your father?"

"Tonio, when you talk to a customer, I don't butt in. Please, restrain yourself," I cried.

"Okay, my boy; go on, spew your nonsense."

"Thanks for your understanding," I said, then glancing at the woman continued, "I come from Santa Fe. Where are you from?"

"The Bronx. I hear Santa Fe is a lovely city. By the way, my name is Fatima."

"I'm Adam. Isn't Fatima an Arabic name?"

"I was born in Gaza. My parents moved to New York when I was a teenager."

Tonio's eyes suddenly bulged with menacing intensity. Foam formed at the edges of his mouth. He threw his arms into the air and began to contort his hips like a belly dancer

"Tonio, stop it!" I yelled.

Fatima turned, just as he quit gyrating. "Forget his jewelry. I've got something that's perfect for you," he said, and left for the small storage room in the back. Moments later he returned holding the gigantic, spider-like necklace, the one he had shown to Muriel, the British woman who had come in the day I had first met him.

"What is it?" Fatima asked, lifting her hands as if to protect herself.

He stepped forward. She took a step back. "Tonio, please leave the lady alone," I begged.

"You would like that, wouldn't you?" He dropped the necklace on the bench, picked up a set of keys, and said, "Take them. When you are done fucking her, make sure to lock up the place."

Fatima gasped. Her face went pale. She took a step toward the door. Tonio followed her. She took another step, grabbed her umbrella, and vanished into the rain.

"Good riddance," he cried.

"You have a wife and two kids," I yelled. "And you go crazy if a woman as much as says a word to me."

He shrugged.

"Would it be all right if I spoke to every tenth woman who walks in?"

He began to whistle La Marseillaise.

"How about every twentieth?"

You son of a bitch, I thought and returned to the polishing wheel.

"Be careful not to get your hair caught," he said and resumed whistling.

"Tonio, wiggling your hips, telling Fatima that my jewelry is best suited for fat women and that I wanted to fuck her, that was . . . that is gross."

"You did want to fuck her, admit it."

"Even if I did, it is none of your business. Your possessiveness and jealousy are disgusting."

"Ok, my dear. From now on I'll behave nicely, so you can be proud of me."

"You are not being funny, you know. You are acting like a stupid, jealous teenager."

"I'm sorry, my dear," he said in a falsetto voice. "I promise I will do better in the future."

"Go screw yourself."

"But I am overwhelmed with guilt. I need forgiveness. Give me another chance, please."

A wish that a bolt of lightning would strike him came over me, but then I reflected that if it hadn't been for him, I wouldn't be polishing a sculptured pendant in Mediaeval Biot, within thirty yards of an ancient church, and with visitors from all parts of the earth dropping in.

"Tonio," I said, in a conciliatory tone, "Let's make a new start, one based on mutual respect and regard. To demonstrate my good will, I will make you a bracelet."

"How much will you charge for it?"

"Free, Tonio, No cost. No money."

"Money, money, money."

"Money, money, money," I sang back.

"Coca Cola and hamburger, American 'merde.'"

"Testing of atomic bombs, French shit."

"Rambo, a film for ten-year-olds."

"Loved by the French."

"Saddam gave America the finger."

"The French army aided the Rwanda butchers."

"Pizza Hut's plastic pizza."

"Forget the bracelet, Tonio. I just wanted to express my gratitude for offering me space in your workshop."

"Don't mention it, my boy. When will you have my bracelet finished?"

So, you want my bracelet, after all? I mused, *wishing I hadn't made the offer.*

The entrance of a big man with a rosy complexion interrupted my revelry. Turning to Tonio, he said, "My mother has rheumatism and she thinks a copper bracelet might do her some good. Can you make one?" He spoke English with a heavy German accent.

Tonio pointed at me. "He will do it. He's a master jeweler. Take a look at the bracelet he's working on."

"Where will I get the metal?" I asked gratefully.

"I've brought it with me," the big man said. He opened a leather bag and dropped a long strand of wire on the bench.

"Hm . . . I was thinking that three wires twisted in the shape of a cord, and soldered at the end with silver would look nice," I said.

"Excellent idea," Tonio said, turning to face the big man. "Adam is a true artist. He doesn't work for the money. He works for spiritual satisfaction. He deserves at least a hundred fifty francs for his labor."

One hundred fifty francs? I couldn't believe my good luck. Tonio had never been so complimentary of my work. I glanced at him with a thankful smile as he discussed the size of the bracelet with the German. Speaking for me, he promised to have it done in two days. I had just resumed polishing my pendant, when Tonio grabbed my hand and exclaimed,

"This is the way you want to do it, my boy. First, you want to press the pendant gently, then harder and harder."

"Tonio, have you gone crazy? Let go of my hand!" I cried.

The German leaning over, his breath reeking of cigarette smoke and sausages, mumbled, "Didn't you say that he was a master jeweler?"

"He is," Tonio replied, forcing my hand with the pendant against the polishing wheel. "But even a master jeweler needs help now and then."

Hard as I tried, I couldn't free myself of his grasp. "Goddammit, Tonio, stop it!" I yelled.

"I would like a word with you," the German said. Tonio let go of my hand and the two men stepped back. "I don't trust him," the German said.

"Adam comes from Santa Fe, the city of art. He knows his stuff," Tonio persisted in a grave voice.

"I know you mean well, but I would really like you to make the bracelet. I don't want to take a chance on disappointing my mother."

"Oh, well, if you insist, but my fee is three hundred francs."

"Of course. You obviously have years of experience, and experience is valuable." They shook hands and the German left.

"Sorry, you didn't get the job," Tonio said, "Better luck next time."

I jumped up and threw my things into my backpack. He raised his arm as if to stop me. "Get the hell out of my way, you son of a bitch." I was so mad that it took an act of willpower for me not to pick up a file and stab him with it.

But along with the rage came a feeling of loss. My artistic career in France was over. What now? Should I remain in Biot or return to Santa Fe? I resolved to wait until my feelings simmered down before deciding on my next move.

The third morning after the fateful event in Tonio's atelier, I was having my breakfast when the phone rang.

"You were right to get mad," Tonio said. "I did act like a jerk. It won't happen again, I promise."

I was stunned. Did he mean it? Was he capable of critical self-examination? Did he truly hold himself accountable? After recovering from the shock, I snapped, "You're bullshitting me. Admit it."

"I wouldn't bullshit my work buddy. Come over before the heat gets unbearable."

"Hm . . . I don't know. The truth is I don't trust you."

"Every man deserves a second chance, my boy."

"Okay," I said, "but I am not going to take any more shit from you."

"No shit, just friendship. Come."

28

In mid-August Claire called. "Oliver is closing the store in a week. I've bought a ticket for Sidney."

Shocked, I asked, "When are you leaving?"

"In two weeks."

"Let me take you out to a dinner."

"When?"

"This Saturday. I'll pick you up at seven. Dress up."

"But, of course. See you then."

I dropped the receiver and eased onto my armchair. Her announcement hadn't taken me entirely by surprise. She had told me that she'd been thinking of moving to Australia. I had wished she had chosen Santa Fe.

Wearing my only suit and tie, I knocked on her door on Saturday with a mixture of sadness and excitement. I passed her my bouquet of roses, kissed her on both cheeks, and said, "Don't go to Sidney. Come with me to Santa Fe."

"We can write to each other, talk on the phone, perhaps even meet once in a while."

"Hardly a consolation. Have you a small statue of yourself?"

"I don't, but why are you asking?"

"So, I could put it in my bedroom and see you first thing in the morning."

"You are joking, right?"

"How about a picture of you in a bikini?"

"Not even Oliver has one."

"I adore you; he thinks of you as temporary human merchandise."

"You're being too harsh on him. He is a Brit, and Brits are reserved by nature."

"I've got my camera in the car. You can pose for me when we come back."

Glancing at her watch, she sighed. "Do you plan for us to spend the evening chatting by the door?"

"I am sorry. When I am with you, I forget how to act in a civilized manner. I become an idiot."

"An aging but an adoring idiot. I'll be right back after I put the flowers in a vase."

What got into me to blubber like that? I asked myself. All I could think of was that I wanted to take her in my arms and kiss her and that, not being allowed to do that, I lost my marbles.

She wore no makeup. Nothing to distract from her natural beauty. I opened the car door for her, and said, "Guess where I made the reservation for dinner?"

Glancing at the bright globe in the sky, she giggled, "On the moon."

"An almost-as-exciting place. At the *Imperial*, a two-star Michelin restaurant in Monte Carlo."

"Did you plan for us to go Dutch?"

"You must be kidding. It's on me."

"It will cost you a fortune."

"You are worth it. Then, after dinner, we'll go to the casino. Ever since coming to France, I've been wanting to do that. How about you?"

"I am not much of a gambler. And after you win a fortune, we'll go dancing."

"Me dancing? I'll be as graceful as an elephant on the floor."

"That's alright. I never let a man lead me anyway."

We stopped talking. I told myself to concentrate on the moment and avoid ruining the evening worrying about the future. More relaxed, I gently squeezed her hand. She squeezed back, sending an electric current over my entire body.

Turning into the downhill road for Monte Carlo, I felt as privileged as the aristocrats inhabiting the principality. My Honda Legend could hold its own with their Mercedes and BMWs, and my passenger surpassed any of their wives or lovers in beauty. I parked the car in front of the restaurant. A tall man in a uniform opened the door, bowed, and said, "Here is your receipt for your car," then rushed to open the door for Claire.

She stepped out queen-like, leisurely eyed the surroundings, smiled at the attendant, and joined me. We stepped inside, went through a wood-paneled bar furnished with thickly upholstered leather chairs and arrived at a large, semi-circular room with chandeliers and floor-to-ceiling windows. A man in a tuxedo bowed, then led us to a table with a lit candle and view of palm trees and the moon-lit Mediterranean.

In the dim light we lifted the menus and examined our choices. Some of the items sounded exotic enough to belong in a fairytale. We ordered green papaya spaghetti with truffled carbonara as the first entrée, frog legs with vegetables as the second, passion fruit, citrus, and meringue for dessert, and a bottle of Champagne.

"Impressive," Claire exclaimed. "I feel like a queen."

"But you are a queen. I only wish I were your king."

She took my hand in hers, "Would you settle for a majordomo?"

"I'll have to think about it," I said, fearful that any movement on my part might cause her to remove her hand.

Another waiter in a tuxedo arrived, filled my glass with an inch of Champagne, and eyed me expectantly. I sniffed at the drink, shook the glass, and sniffed again, then very slowly drank, and nodded approvingly.

The spaghetti arrived in portions best suited for a child. *Quality rather than quantity,* I reflected, as I rolled my fork into the pasta. Claire had already taken a bite and looked blissfully absorbed. I put a forkful into my mouth and felt the same. Never before did spaghetti taste so flavorful. Afterward, we lifted our glasses and toasted silently, I to my yearning for her, and she to whatever was on her mind.

"Do you think the rest of the dinner will be as flavorful?" she asked.

"We're at a Michelin two-star restaurant. There are no compromises here," I replied, then almost blurted out, *you probably taste as good.*

The frogs' legs, sinking in a mysterious and savory sauce, were as delightful. The vegetables added to the inebriating flavor. With every bite of the tiny legs, I took a sip of champagne. My head grew light, and I imagined nibbling at Claire's earlobes. The dessert surpassed in flavor even Zuppa Inglese, my favorite chocolate-rum cake.

Claire burped lightly and asked, "So what comes next? Dancing or gambling?"

"Gambling if you don't mind."

I placed my American Express card inside a folded leather envelope. The waiter returned minutes later with a list of charges. Without as much as a glance at them, I added a twenty-dollar tip, picked up the card and the receipt, and rose.

Claire came over, embraced me, and whispered, "Merci, mon ami."

On unsteady legs, lightly intoxicated, I led us to the Monte Carlo Casino. Roles Royce's, large Mercedes and BMWs drove by as noiselessly as ghosts. The few pedestrians, in their tuxedos and long dresses, spoke as softly as if they were in a house of worship. With my black suit, white shirt, blue striped tie, and a pair of polished black shoes, I projected the appearance of a well-padded bourgeoise, but secretly wished that I looked like a nobleman.

Glancing at the two fountains in front of the Casino, at the two turrets with a clock on the façade, and on the two Greek-like statues below them, Claire whispered, "It looks like a smaller version of Versailles."

"The opera is inside, adjacent to the casino."

"Have you been inside before?"

"I tried shortly after my arrival but the uniformed guard took one look at my jeans and sweater, and waved me away."

The doorman bowed and let us in. Inside the hall with its eight marble columns supporting a ceiling decorated with paintings and crystal chandeliers shaped like a bouquet of roses, Claire whispered, "I never imagined a casino would look so lavish."

"It's the most extravagant in the world."

"And I'll gamble in it?"

"You sure will."

After paying the entrance fee, we stepped into the main gambling hall with its large windows, deeply upholstered leather armchairs, and chandeliers as elaborate as those at the entry. I exchanged five hundred dollars into five-dollar chips, passed them to Claire, and said, "Here you go."

"What about you?"

"I'll be the majordomo at your service."

She sat down at the gambling table and placed a chip on the box numbered 17. The ball landed on the number 21.

"Why 17?" I asked.

"It's the day of your birthday, isn't it? I'll try mine next."

She put the coin on a square numbered 28 and lost again. An hour passed and she was down half of the money I gave her. I said nothing. She seemed to have a good time and that was all that mattered. Then I noticed the man about my age in a tuxedo sitting next to her repeatedly placing his coin on top of hers. After several more losses, he turned toward her, and said, "We should change strategies. Maybe bet on colors for a while."

"Bet as you fucking please, but leave her alone," I said.

Claire squeezed my thigh and gave me a nasty look. Castigated, I left for the toilets. Upon my return, there was no sign of the gent. Claire looked jubilant. Not only did she recapture the money she had lost, but she had doubled the amount.

"This calls for a celebration," I said. "What kind of drink would you like?"

"Champagne. Let's take a break and ease down on those armchairs." I collected the chips in a leather pouch I had brought for this purpose and headed for the bar. Upon returning, distracted by the sight of Claire sitting cross-legged, I lost my balance and spilled one glass on her naked foot. Apologetically, I gave her the remaining full glass, crawled on the floor, pulled out my handkerchief, and began drying her. Then, as if commanded by an irresistible voice, I began licking her wet toe.

"Stop," she grunted. They will throw us out."

Sitting down by her side, I whispered, "I had no idea your toe was so tasty."

She laughed. "You should try the rest of me."

"Here?"

"I don't know what made me say that. Forget it. Let's go back to the table."

The next two hours she doubled several times over what I gave her, lost all, then alternately playing the colored boxes and occasionally the squared ones with numbers, recaptured everything plus some one thousand or so more francs.

Stunned, I said, "Let's quit while we are ahead."

She exchanged the chips for paper money, waved the bankrolls in front of me, and said, "Here, take them. It was a lot of fun."

"Why are you giving them to me, when it was your winning?"

"Because I won with the money you gave me."

"Just give me the equivalent of five hundred dollars and keep the rest."

"But I could have lost all."

"You would have been worth it."

"You are such a dear," she exclaimed and kissed me on the mouth. Encouraged by the sudden intimacy, I considered suggesting we spend the night in the glamorous, nearby Hotel de Paris, but at the last moment decided it would be more romantic driving back through the darkness. After the streetlights disappeared, phantom-like, we drove ever deeper into the boundless Riviera night.

Claire snored as lightly as a child. I placed my hand on her thigh and squeezed softly. She let out a barely audible cry, moved closer, and rested her head on my shoulder. I woke her in the parking lot of her apartment and led her gently to the elevator. Inside she murmured, "I'm going to change and be right back. There is a bottle of Cognac on the table. Serve yourself."

Sipping the beverage, I mused that we had passed the point of no return. The time of friendship had been gradually replaced by a promise of intimacy. She returned in a lowcut silk gown. Curling up next to me, she whispered, "What an evening. I've never had so much fun in my entire life."

Encouraged by her fervor, I kissed her eyes, her nose, then gently bit her ear lobes. She moaned and lifted her head. I kissed her neck, untied her robe, kissed her breasts, then led her to the bedroom where, after undressing, I continued to fondle her. She joined me, and we feasted on each other. When she took me in her mouth, waves after waves of electrical currents ran through my entire being. Parts inside me long asleep woke up. I took off on a blissful ocean journey, waves taking me into timelessness.

"Claire, Claire, Claire," I murmured.

"Yes, my darling," she responded and continued kissing me.

Fearing that any moment I might come, I lifted her head, turned her gently on her back, and entered her. For long seconds we remained still, then we began to move, lightly at first, then faster and faster.

"I love you," we cried in unison, our bodies merging into one.

"I feel like I've been on a journey to paradise," she whispered afterward.

I nodded. "Let's remain there and never come back."

"I'll write to Leslie that I've fallen in love and that I'll not move to Sydney."

"Amen," I exclaimed.

We turned off the lights. My last thought before falling asleep was that I had found my soulmate. Then, awakening in the middle of the night I thought that I was holding Theodora in my arms. I pushed the unsettling thought away but it came back. It came back again later. It came again and again, regardless of how hard I tried to suppress it.

In the morning, watching Claire asleep, I felt like I was next to a stranger. I went over our lovemaking the night before, our kissing, our embraces, our all-absorbing union. Nothing changed. Claire remained a stranger. To my sorrow, I concluded that she was not my soulmate after all.

When at breakfast I shared my unsettling feelings, she broke into tears. Then, after drying her face, she took my hand in hers, and said, "Adam, your notion that Theodora was with you made sense. You and I are very different. You think a lot. I don't. You ceaselessly look for new answers and new explanations. I am comfortable with old ones and have no need to grow wiser. What we had last night was the stuff fairy tales are made of. Pure magic. Something to be cherished to the last days of our lives. But now we have to move on, follow our unique paths. Let's care for each other and be friends."

"Yes," I said. "Let's be friends."

Ten days later I drove Claire to the airport for her flight to Sydney. We held each other tightly for several minutes, vowed to write, and wished each other days filled with joy and fulfillment.

29

I hadn't made jewelry in days. First thing, the day after Claire's departure, I went to the old town.

"Here you are," Tonio exclaimed from his workbench. "I had been wondering if you would ever come back. Get down to work, my boy."

I pulled my large pendant out of my pocket, and sat on the bench by the polishing wheel. "I don't think you realize what an offensive son of a bitch, you are," I said.

"It must be the Arab in me." He wiped the sweat on his brow with the back of his hand. "The heat is killing me. I am leaving tomorrow for a two-week vacation."

"Where are you going?"

"To Corsica. Make sure to take all your stuff with you when you leave today."

We chatted like friends. It was a new Tonio, human and reasonable. Perhaps, he had learned his lesson and decided that I was worthy of his respect. I invited him for a pizza. We ate, drank beer, and chatted casually about nothing in particular.

Late in the afternoon, I finished my pendant, wished him a great vacation, and returned home. Over dinner, I decided that I, too, ought to go somewhere cool and visually exciting.

Ever since gazing from a transatlantic flight at icebergs in Greenland a few years back, I had been dreaming of visiting the island. Unwilling to join organized tours because of their forbidding cost and uncertain human composition, I called a local outfitter about renting a cabin in an ice field. He responded that his wife was in charge of the business, that she had gone hunting, and to call back in a week. Picturing her in the white wilderness on a sled pulled by dogs, and bringing home a harvest of seals, my desire to visit Greenland grew tenfold. But upon deeper reflection, I resolved that those solitary days on ice would be more than I could endure. I thus called the Tourist Information Service in Nuuk, the capital, reserved a three-day stay in a bed and breakfast, and arranged for a week-long coastal journey afterward.

From Nice, I flew to Copenhagen, then to Narsarsuaq, in southern Greenland, an abandoned American military base with jet landing facilities. Learning too late that connecting propeller-driven planes for Nuuk, the capital, failed to accept reservations, and that first-come-first-served practice prevailed, I missed the plane.

"Not to worry," an agent reassured me. "You can take the next flight, in two hours. Just make sure to listen to the announcements on the public-address system."

The day was sunny if a bit on the chilly side. With my Gore-Tex jacket zipped to my neck and the hood covering my head, I took off for the veranda, sat on a step, and began reviewing *The Lonely Planet* guide about travel to Greenland: flights canceled by bad weather, luggage lost, emergency landings, and so on. While reassuring myself that I was up to the challenge, I heard a female voice saying something on the loudspeaker. I rushed to the boarding gate. It was the wrong flight. On the way back to the veranda I stopped at the tiny gift shop, pulled out my bill folder to pay for a pin of a walrus when a male voice made an urgent announcement. I dropped the pin and ran. It was my flight. I arrived in Nuuk late in the afternoon, obtained my backpack and the key to my bed and breakfast from an agent at the gate, and boarded a bus going to the town.

I showed the conductor the address to my bed and breakfast. Half an hour later, he pointed at a quarter-mile-long apartment complex. I was stunned, having anticipated a cozy little house. After going up and down endless stairs, I finally arrived at my small, modernly furnished apartment. I began unpacking when a bundled-up, middle-aged white woman stepped in and began shouting. I showed her the receipt for my stay. She continued screaming, pulled out her cell phone from her purse, spoke into the mouthpiece, and passed it to me. The woman on the other side explained in fair English that her aunt wanted the door to the apartment locked even when I was in because of roaming hoodlums. I presumed she meant the Inuit, the indigenous people, who comprised eighty percent of the thirty-five thousand island's inhabitants.

Nuuk, fifty miles below the Arctic Circle, was a visual disaster. Unremarkable apartment buildings stretched as far as the eye could see. The Danish government's policy of encouraging the natives to abandon their traditional northern villages for the comforts of city life had succeeded all too well. There were no visible fishing boats in the harbor. Except for a few homes dating back to the last century, Nuuk projected the architectural wonder of a contemporary company town.

To cheer myself up, I ordered a vegetarian pizza in a converted van downtown. It came with cheese, tomatoes, onion, garlic, olives, green and red peppers, dried mushrooms, and chunks of pineapple. A main dish and a dessert all in one! So impressed was I by the tasty product that I invited the mustachioed owner to pose with me in front of his mobile establishment.

After three days of aimless meandering, visiting the interesting National Museum, and buying a few souvenirs, I boarded the coastal ferry going above the Arctic Circle. Thankfully, I had the four-person cabin all to myself. That night howling wind and cascading rain made the ferry rise and fall in swells almost as tall as my house in Santa Fe. I had read about Arctic storms but hadn't prepared myself for the ensuing terror. I crawled into my bed and hid my head under the blankets. To my immense relief the ship survived the onslaught intact.

We docked at Sisimut at eleven PM, six hours past our due time. No taxies. No buses. A fellow passenger, after glancing at my reservation, explained that I had booked a room in the Knud Rasmussen High School, a mile away up a rising road. A bed and breakfast in a high school? Booking the room on the phone from Santa Fe, I had hardly understood a word the woman in charge said, and I presumed she hardly understood a word I said. With growing apprehension, I trudged up the dark lane. A poorly lit sign on a wall told me that I had arrived. The door was locked. No one responded when I pressed the bell. A German couple appeared. He pulled out his cell phone and dialed a number. Fifteen minutes later a hefty Inuit woman let us in.

The following morning, after a nourishing breakfast in the school cafeteria, I walked to the Tourist Information Service, obtained a map of the town, and learned that Sisimut, "The fox hole burrowers" in Inuit, is 47 miles north of the Arctic Circle. With 5500 inhabitants and as many dogs, it is the second-largest town in Greenland and the northernmost ice-free port.

The salty air, the billowing white clouds, and the ghostly icebergs floating in the distance filled me with awe. Eager to experience in greater depth the haunting surroundings, I took an isolated gravel road leading to the port. Occasional homes rose in the rocky countryside, their occupants nowhere in sight. But doges, hundreds of them, stood outside their tiny homes. I lifted my camera to record them when they exploded into salvos of anger and fury. They pulled hysterically at their chains. They bared their teeth. Unable to find a stick to defend myself with, I considered retracing my steps but realized I had gone too deep into their territory to find safety in retreat. These weren't ordinary dogs. All alike, looking like small wolves, they were ferocious. In the winter they pulled sleds filled with carcasses of seals and walruses and occasionally fought polar bears.

Something soft suddenly brushed against my ankles. A puppy, a dirt-white puppy trembled between my feet. My one thought now was to assure my visitor's safety. I glanced hopefully at a nearby home. No one stepped out. Worried that in no time one or more dogs would break loose, I took a hesitant step forward, my trembling friend tagging along in between my feet. The beasts jumped and pulled at their chains so hard that the ground shuddered. Gaining in courage from the presence of my little companion, I pressed on and we arrived at the port unharmed.

The racket made by large wooden and metal canisters being loaded and unloaded on the boats was infernal. After several minutes of photographing the action, I glanced at my feet. The puppy was gone. The noise must have scared him. I walked the length of the port looking for him in dark corners and amidst bundles waiting to be loaded, all to no avail.

Saddened, I headed back to town by a safer route. Past several homes perched on steep, rocky terrain, there appeared a field covered with red and yellow flowers. Beyond it screaming children played ball in a school playground. The moment I lifted my camera to record them at their game they stopped playing and rushed over. Laughing, nudging, making the victory signs, they came within a few feet of the camera and posed. With their slanted eyes, oval faces, yellowish skins, and high cheekbones, they formed an assembly exuding joy and happiness.

Greenlanders believe that their children are born with the wisdom and savvy of their ancestors. At the sight of the exuberant, innocent and trusting faces, my sadness at the loss of the puppy vanished. Charged with the kids' energy and enthusiasm, I joined them at their laughter, waved a deeply-felt farewell, and resumed my trek to town. The word must have gone around that there was this stranger who liked photographing kids, for the next morning wherever I went children on foot and bicycles approached me, pointed at my camera, and posed. In the foggy, remote, arctic, I felt more appreciated than in my hometown of Santa Fe.

I bought half a dozen of Tpilaks miniature carvings made from sperm whale teeth. Gruesome, they are legendary weapons directed at evildoers. Thrown into the sea with instructions to reach the loathsome target, they single-mindedly apply deadly punishment. I never learned precisely what punishments they bestowed upon their victims, but judging by their fierce appearance, I imagined them to be lethal.

The last evening in Sissimut, as I was getting dressed for dinner, infernal barking shattered the calm. I ran to the window. On a rise, across the street, dozens of dogs jumped and pulled at their chains. A man in high rubber boots, a bucket filled with chunks of meat in one hand and a whip in the other, descended upon them. The howling stopped. The dogs had prevailed. They had obtained their evening meal.

The following morning, I departed for Ilulissat (population 4,570), one-hundred-fifty miles above the Arctic Circle. To my joy, my bed and breakfast overlooked floating icebergs. The evenings, music, and sounds made by the patrons in numerous downtown establishments made it hard to relax. Ilulissat's popularity was due to the presence of the longest glacier in the world, jutting five miles into the sea.

On my second day, I took a bus to the edge of town, hiked a couple of miles over spongy, moist ground, and arrived at a promontory with a view of an immense tongue of ice spilling into a sea sparkling like a field of diamonds.

Uummannaq (population 1300), 350 miles above the Arctic Circle, my northernmost destination, lay shielded by a tall, heart-shaped rock rising straight up from the sea. During the two hours of the ferry's stopover, I hiked up twisting, steep, unpaved roadways, passed several pastel-colored homes, and watched icebergs colliding in the cozy little harbor.

On my flight from Copenhagen to Nice I reflected that in Illusissat I witnessed the longest glacier on earth. In Uummannaqm, I gasped at the sight of the heart-shaped hill guarding its small, iceberg-infested harbor. Ilulissat and Uummannaqm had dazzled me with glorious scenery. But it was in Sisimut, with the trembling puppy between my feet and the welcoming, exuberant children, that I transcended myself and experienced pure joy.

30

The morning after my return from Greenland, I stepped into Tonio's atelier. Surprised to see him working on a bracelet made with twice the customary amount of silver, I asked, "Are you making a birthday gift for your wife?"

"No, my boy. It's for an exhibit of sculptured jewelry at the Gallium Galerie in Antibes."

"An exhibit of sculptured jewelry in Antibes?" I exclaimed. "And it never occurred to you to let me know?"

"I thought you knew about it."

"Bullshit. You kept silent because you feared competition."

"Will the day ever come when you will stop whining?" He wrote something on a piece of paper. "Here is the gallery's address. Tell Michelle, the manager, I sent you."

I left for Antibes after the afternoon siesta. After viewing my portfolio Michelle asked, "Will you make something special for the exhibit?"

"I was thinking of five large, three-dimensional pendants."

Moments after I spoke, panic descended on me. I was scheduled to fly to the States in two weeks, hardly enough time for such an elaborate project. I considered withdrawing my offer but my artistic fervor prevailed, and I said nothing. An hour later I returned back at Tonio's atelier.

"Why the long face?" he asked. "Did Michelle turn you down?"

"You wish. She loved my work. The problem is I promised to make five large pendants but I don't know if I will have enough time. I am due to leave for Santa Fe in two weeks."

After several silent seconds, he asked, "For good?"

"Do I detect a touch of sadness in your voice?"

"Can't you just for once give a straight answer?"

"Ok, ok, I'll be back after I buy a laptop, and check on the condition of my rented house."

"Why don't you buy a laptop here?"

"Because in America they cost half as much and the manuals are in English."

For the next ten days, working with all my energy and imagination I completed four pendants for the Antibes' exhibit. Large, the silver layered with tiny bridges, balls, and cones, they could have been worn or framed and hung on a wall. The fifth escaped my imagination. At night, waiting for sleep, fantastically-shaped pendants floated on the screen of my mind., but none captured my heart.

Five days before the exhibit's opening, watching Tonio busily working, his mind and callous fingers seemingly in seamless harmony. I rested my head on my palms, and reflected, *Ah, that I could be as certain and purposeful.*

"Did you come to meditate?" he teased.

"I can't come up with the right design for my fifth bracelet. If I could only work as effortlessly as you."

"I don't aspire to be a master jeweler, my boy. I am an ordinary mortal."

"Your style works for you, and mine works for me."

"Except that your style is superior."

"My style is more complex, but not superior. I like your work. Your pieces would sell well in the States. Would you be interested in exhibiting a few in my Santa Fe gallery?"

"Santa Fe, eh? Would it be safe there?"

"Well, I don't really know. Galleries there open and close. It's a gamble. You must decide for yourself."

"Santa Fe, eh?"

"The city of art."

"In your gallery?"

"Our gallery."

"Ok, my boy. Which airline will you fly with?"

"Hm. . . .Would it be too much trouble to ask you to drop half a dozen bracelets in my gallery there?"

"Of course, not. Give them to me."

Later that day, as I watched him complete a bracelet shaped like two twisted serpents, the image I had been longing for finally materialized. Formed like an exotic coat of arms, its right and left sides and the top and bottom bent over to form shafts through which to insert a chain, and at the center a small cube, a little bridge, and a wheel with spokes suggesting rays of the sun, it projected majesty and style.

"I've got it!" I exclaimed. "It will be a small, abstract sculpture."

"Calm down, will you?"

"You are a right. I am a master jeweler."

"And a megalomaniac too."

"But I am running out of time. I only have two days. Will I be able to finish it?"

"Probably not. A master jeweler never has enough time to complete his work."

"That's a shitty thing to say."

"It may be shitty, but it's true. Most of my pieces take only fifteen minutes to complete."

"You sure are a blessed bastard."

"Give up pretension, and you will be one too."

"What pretension?"

"Your notion that your jewelry is better than everyone else's."

"That's bullshit. If I didn't think well of your work, I wouldn't have suggested placing it in my Santa Fe gallery, would I?"

"Argue, argue, that's all you ever do. It must be the Jew in you."

"We both have Semitic ancestry. For all you know, we might have originated from the same tribe. We might be blood brothers."

"God forbid. You're ugly, and I'm good-looking."

"If you are so good-looking, why do you get hysterical when a woman customer takes an interest in me?"

"I don't get hysterical. I get impatient because I can't stand stupid people. Any woman who finds you attractive must have the brains of a child."

"Fuck you, Tonio."

"In France, men fuck women, my boy."

"I'm not your boy."

"My, you sure are grouchy today."

"Anybody would get grouchy hanging around you," I yelled, and began placing my silver and tools in my backpack.

"Where are you doing? You haven't even started working on your fifth piece."

"I thought you found my company bothersome."

"What gave you the idea? We've been working bodies for more than a year, haven't we?"

"We sure have, Tonio. We sure have."

The day before my departure for Santa Fe, I handed Tonio my five pendants to enter the Gallium exhibit. He passed me six of his bracelets to place in Santa Fe and another six in London. I had one project to complete before my departure. Nina's birthday was due the day of my return. When I had asked what kind of present she would like, she answered, "A silver cross made by you."

I had in mind a massive one, with an Australian opal in the center. Hurriedly, I put a match to the acetylene torch, when the flame swept like a miniature tornado. I jumped, fell, and injured my arm. The village doctor put it in a sling and resorted to pantomime to advise me to have the arm checked in Santa Fe. I was crushed. Nina and I, in spite of our periodic confrontations, had formed something of a bond. I hated to disappoint her, but fate had delt me a losing hand.

My plane for the States was scheduled to leave late in the afternoon and, except for mild pain emanating from my injured arm, I felt quite ready for the journey. Outside the bakery, the familiar aroma of freshly baked bagatelles caressed my nostrils. *I'll miss the bread,* I mused, as I stopped at the kiosk to buy the *Herald Tribune.* In the park with the fountain, I sat down on a stone bench to read. Children screamed as they ran playfully around the fountain. Two elderly men played chess nearby. Moments after I opened the paper, a female voice said from behind, "Hi. Nice to see you again."

It was Fatima. She wore the leather outfit she had on the day I met her at Tonio's atelier. Wind-blown black hair partially covered her face. "What a pleasant surprise," I exclaimed, and pointed at the bench. As she eased down by my side, I said, "Later today, I am leaving for Santa Fe, my hometown. But what I really want to talk about is your treatment at the hands of Tonio. Ever since he called you names and threw you out, I've been feeling like a heel for not standing up for you. You see, he offers me workspace and I don't dare antagonize him. I don't mean that as an excuse, just to—"

"Please, don't let it bother you," she interrupted. "I grew up in Gaza and know all about the intimidating power of authority. What I can't get over, though, is that he knew I was an Arab like him. He is weird, for sure. Let's talk of something more pleasant. Is Santa Fe as exciting as I hear?"

"A few years ago, Condé Nast Travelers proclaimed the city the premier tourist destination in the United States. It has about 140 art galleries, good restaurants, arts and craft fairs, a world-class opera, and an abundance of old Spanish and Pueblo architecture."

"That's quite impressive."

"A lot of people think so. Two years ago, a short, broad-chested, heavily-tattooed man with a long gray beard had been leaning against the wall of the Palace of the Governors, in the downtown plaza for days, with his Harley by his side. A journalist from the weekly *The Reporter* asked him what he was up to. 'I lost track of my woman in California,' the biker answered. 'I am waiting for her. 'What makes you think she will show up here?' the journalist wanted to know. 'At one time or another everyone comes to Santa Fe,'" the man replied.

"Did she ever show up?" Fatima asked.

"I don't know. A week after the interview he disappeared. Most likely he resigned himself to a lonely life."

"And you, do you feel lonely in Biot?" After a few silent seconds, I responded. "More solitary than lonely. I came to France to make jewelry and to find—I hope you don't find me silly for saying —my soulmate. So far, fate has led me to Tonio."

"Your soulmate? How romantic you are."

"Bach, the author of *Jonathan Livingstone Seagull,* wrote a book in which he described his passionate love for the woman of his dreams. I wrote him a letter congratulating him on his good luck."

Fatima burst out laughing. "And did he reply?"

"His soulmate did. She sent me a postcard in which she said that I have made two life-long friends. And you, are you looking for your ideal mate?"

She shook her head. "I am too down to earth for that, plus American men I know have difficulty grasping the suffering in Gaza, and my Arab acquaintances try to be like Americans."

"Do you miss Gaza?"

A smile graced her face as she answered, "I certainly do. We were malnourished, but we rejoiced in the wide-open spaces reaching out for a dusty horizon. The silence was palpable. The moon was my playmate. My friends and I greeted its appearance from atop a sand-hill."

"You consider yourself a child of nature?"

She nodded. "I do."

"In my own way, I consider myself a child of nature too. More than once while hiking I transcended my human boundaries and felt one with my surroundings."

"Did this happen in the desert?"

"In the desert, in the mountains, by the sea."

"Can share an instance of it?"

"Sure. Three decades ago, after a long hike on the shore of Moonstone Beach, in Rhode Island, I headed for a nearby swamp. Beach grass stabbed my bare feet. A tunnel of bamboo branches lay ahead. I stepped inside and felt as if in a fairytale."

"And it was there that you had your transcendental moment?"

"No, no. That occurred later. Upon leaving the tunnel I noticed dozen wild rosebushes skirting the shore of a lake. Monarch butterflies, their wings painted in black, red, and orange, looking like tiny stained-glass windows, hovered in the air. One, painted in strikingly deep colors, rested on a large bush, her wings gently undulating in the breeze. Cautiously, I touched her wings with my fingers. She stirred gently but held her place. I touched her again. She gave no sign of distress."

"You mean she didn't fly away?"

"That's right. My presence didn't seem to frighten her. Touching her, a tickling sensation descended down my spine, then spread over my entire body. I felt as if in a new, ecstatic realm. Past and future lost their meaning. I felt totally grounded at the moment. The magic ended when I started worrying if I had injured her. Would she fly again? I released my hold and, to my delight, saw her take off as gracefully as a tiny ballerina. She circled over me a few times, then landed on another bush."

"A lovely story, I must say. I hadn't encountered any butterflies in the Gaza desert. But I rejoice when I see them elsewhere."

Encouraged by her positive response, I continued, "And then I met another one. With her, I experienced greater intimacy than with any human being."

Fatima inched closer. "It happened several years ago in the Tetons National Park. One spring afternoon, I was hiking up a steep trail overlooking a lake surrounded by tall pines. An hour into my trek a rumble from inside a dense grove stopped me, and I went to investigate. A fast-running stream crashed against broken tree branches and rocks of various sizes. Clouds of rainbow rose out of small waterfalls. I remember thinking that it was a complete scene, all the parts in the right place, a splendid natural work of art. I stretched out on the smooth surface of a large, flat boulder, and closed my eyes, and just then something light landed on the back of my hand. Imagining it to be a wasp, I tensed up. It was a small blue-gray butterfly, but my fear incredibly persisted. I twitched my fingers and the butterfly flew away. I felt as if a part of me had died. Back on the trail, I started looking for a butterfly to befriend. None appeared. It was as if the retreating sun had taken them with it. Then, a close replica of the one that had frightened me appeared on a twig some ten feet ahead. Holding my breath, I picked her up by the wings and released her on my left hand."

I stopped to take a deep breath. The children at the fountain screamed. A dog barked somewhere. Fatima glanced at me with wide-open eyes. "Is that the end of your story?" she asked.

"No, there is more. The butterfly had no weight to speak of, yet her pulsations charged my whole body with electricity. Small as she was, she affected me hundred times more deeply than the Monarch butterfly in the Moonstone Beach. With my eyes fixed on her, I resumed my trek down the trail. In the lake below, a boy cast a fishing line from a wooden pier. Tree shadows formed a checkerboard on the tranquil water. In the nearby campground, fires flickered like so many immense fireflies. Voices rose from around a bend.

"A couple and two teenage boys glanced at me walking with the butterfly on the back of my hand. Hoping that they would perceive me as a man blessed by nature and awash in the timelessness and the beauty of the moment, I marched on. The butterfly pressed against my flesh, flapped her wings, and after sending one last wave of electricity throughout my body, she took off toward the darkening forest. I watched her getting smaller and smaller with sadness and joy. But my joy was dampened by a concern that she might not find her way home."

"What do you make of the experience? Did it have any particular significance?"

"All I can think of is that I was born with an uncommon sensitivity to the natural world."

"Yeah, that's how I feel, yet I live in New York."

"Do you revisit the Gaza Strip often?"

"I came to New York as a teenager. After I learned the language, obtained an education, and got a teaching certificate, I returned to my village, and found that all my friends were gone."

I enjoyed listening to her. Her every word seemed to originate in her heart. Her black hair, dark skin, and a pronounced aquiline nose brought to mind a princess from the Arabian Nights. *Enjoy her while you can*, I told myself. *Soon enough she'll depart, never to be seen again.*

Marianne, the little girl I had befriended a month after my arrival to Briot, suddenly appeared, "Ça va?" she said. "Qui est ton amie?"

"Ça va. Mon amie c'appelle Fatima."

After a brief and friendly exchange, Marianne waved and darted back to her friends by the fountain.

"A sweet girl," Fatima said. "Do you know her parents?"

"Just her mother by sight. I believe they live in the brownstone house, next to the post office. She is an Arab."

"I thought so."

"When you were her age did you look like her?" I asked, a bit self-consciously.

"You think all Arab children look alike?"

"I didn't mean it like that. She is pretty and you are—"

"I know you meant well, but I dislike generalizations. So, you came to France to make jewelry?"

"Yes. I came hoping to be inspired by Picasso, Chagall, and Matisse who lived in this area. In a few weeks, I'll participate in a group exhibit in a gallery in Antibes."

"Oh, my God. It's getting late," She suddenly exclaimed. "I am supposed to meet friends for lunch."

Offering her my hand, I said, "Should you ever come to Santa Fe, I would love to buy you lunch."

"Give me your telephone number, and I'll call you."

I wrote it down and passed it to her, but my instincts told me I would never see her again. As I watched her tall, slender figure vanish in the crowd, my mind turned to the tattooed biker, and I wondered if a man waited for Fatima somewhere in Gaza.

31

Giuseppe drove me to the Nice airport. London was drenched upon my arrival. In the limousine taking me to town, the fellow passengers spoke in strange tongues. In the hotel where I stayed the owner was Indian. I didn't talk to a Brit until the following morning when I hailed a taxi to take me to the gallery exhibiting Tonio's jewelry. The taxi deposited me outside a small shopping center. I placed the leather bag in which I had stored Tonio's jewelry under my injured arm and pulled out my bill folder with my right one. A dark-skinned youth in a soaked sweatshirt and a green baseball cap suddenly appeared running.

"Watch out," the taxi driver yelled too late. The youth grabbed the leather pouch and took off as if the devil was after him.

"Arab scum," the taxi driver said and asked me if I wanted a ride back to my hotel. I shook my head. He took off with a fast start, and the tires threw mud at a tall man in a black coat and a black fedora hat. I stepped into the unremarkable gallery selling Tonio's jewelry. His pieces lay in a small wooden case, all pieces identical, all shaped like serpents, all like the ones he had given me to place in my Santa Fe gallery.

That evening I called him from my hotel. "I've got bad news, Tornio."

"You are already in Santa Fe?"

"No, I'm in rainy London."

"So, what's the news?"

"I wish it hadn't happened, but an Arab—"

"A freedom fighter attacked the Israeli embassy? You called me to tell me that?"

No, Tonio. I called you to tell you that a freedom fighter snatched your jewelry bag as I was paying the taxi driver in front of the shopping center where your gallery is located.

"Say that again."

"Your jewelry was stolen by an Arab kid."

"How do you know it was an Arab?"

"He had dark skin, a Semitic nose, and thick black hair. He looked like one of the kids in the picture in your workshop throwing stones at Israeli soldiers."

"And you didn't go after him?"

"How could I, with my arm in a sling? But, even if my arm had been okay, what chance would I've had catching a youngster?"

Tonio hung up. Fate, I reflected, had sent an Arab to punish him for his intolerance and fanaticism. I secretly rejoiced at his misfortune. My pleasure was more than a reaction to his anti-Semitism. He had lorded over me from the day he had given me workspace in his atelier. I vowed that, upon my return to Biot, I would stand up to him, even if that meant ending my career of an artist in France. But I had made such vows before.

During the long journey from London to Santa Fe, I reflected on my two decades in the City Different. The Indian vendors under the portico of the Palace of the Governor, the arts and crafts fairs had filled me with joy. But over the years the joy faded. The New Age with its shamans, Tarot card readers, channelers, gurus, and astrologers, grew increasingly burdensome. The Anglos, people I mostly came in contact with, talked as casually about reincarnation as if commenting on the weather. My passive-solar home was livable enough with its wood stove, plenty of sun, and an unobstructed view of the Sangre de Cristo Mountains, but it was lost in suburbia. Yet, as the Delta plane approached the Albuquerque International Airport, I was glad to be back. It had happened before. I would go on a journey and return home with the eagerness of a horse returning to its barn.

I took the shuttle from the Albuquerque airport to the Eldorado Hotel, in Santa Fe. Oscar, my tenant, waved at me, helped me with my luggage, and we took off in his old Volvo.

"Your bed is all made up," he said.

"Shirley doesn't mind?"

"A few nights in the guest bedroom isn't going to inconvenience us too much."

"Keeping yourself busy?" I asked.

"Yeah, psychological testing and research keep me occupied."

"What's Shirley up to?"

"Repairing wicker chairs and baskets in your workshop." Shirley was watering outdoor flowers when we drove in. We chatted for a few minutes; then I excused myself and went to bed. I slept for twelve hours. In the morning, while dressing, I glanced outside the window, and saw the neighbor's white horse with black patches on its head chewing my wooden fence. I opened the window and screamed. The beast lifted its head and gave me a dumb stare.

"Are you okay?" Oscar asked from behind the closed door.

"I'm fine, thanks. Will be down in a minute."

Oscar and Shirley had placed whole-wheat bread, butter, marmalade, honey, orange juice, tea, and apples on the table.

"Are you enjoying your stay in my home?" I asked, lifting my cup of mint tea.

"Did Oscar tell you that I'm repairing wicker furniture in your workshop? I didn't move your things, though. They are as you left them," Shirley said.

"We replaced the house heater pump and fixed the leaking faucets in the basement bathroom," Oscar added.

"I got the bill. Oscar, are you still thinking of leaving at the end of June?"

"Yeah."

"And you Shirley?"

"I'll go to Albania as a Peace Corps volunteer in the fall. Our younger daughter is there."

"Will you stay in my home until then?"

"If you reduce your rent."

"By how much?"

"Sixty percent. That's all I can afford. Once Oscar is gone my income will be below the poverty level."

"I can't imagine anyone taking better care of the house than you, but I need the money."

"Suit yourself," she said.

"Oscar, what are your long-range plans?" I asked.

"First I'll go to Greece for a couple of months to pick grapes in a friend's vineyard, then on to Israel to start an orphanage with a group of acquaintances."

"Israel? Orphanage?" I said, buttering a toast.

"Being an orphan myself, I am the right person for it."

"What will you do with your car?" I asked.

"I'll sell it. My computer too. Everything I can't carry on my back, I'll get rid of."

Before getting married Oscar had been a Navy seal and had served as a Peace Corps volunteer in Nigeria. He had worked on plantations in South America. He had lived in various European countries. He had bicycled solo in India. He met Shirley in the graduate school which he had attended on a GI scholarship. After fathering two daughters, he left the family in order to join a little-known religious order, and thus dedicate himself to serving mankind. Shirley accepted his decision without bitterness. She believed it was his right to do with his life as he pleased.

They moved into my home at the urging of their college-age daughters. The young women hoped the experience would reunite the family. I wanted to ask if they shared the same bed, but decided that it wasn't any of my business.

Suddenly, the sight of the neighbor's horse chewing my fence sent blood to my head. I jumped, ran out, and threw a stone at the animal.

"What was that all about?" Oscar asked upon my return.

"Didn't you notice what he was doing to the fence?"

"But throwing a stone at a horse, isn't that a bit too much?"

"It's bad karma," Shirley concurred.

Ignoring her comment, I said, "Shirley, I would really love for you to continue living in my home."

"Make me your mistress and I will stay."

I glanced at Oscar. "Any problem with this arrangement?"

"It's a free country. Be my guest."

"Shirley, it wouldn't work. I'll be back in France in two weeks. Pay me two-thirds of the rent."

"I am staying here at Oscar's good grace. When he leaves, I must leave too."

Reluctantly, I agreed to her terms. I wanted peace of mind, a renter I could depend on to take good care of the house.

I called a mail-order computer company. The representative recommended a Toshiba notebook with a built-in CD-Rom. It was heavy at seven pounds, but I wasn't in a mood to invest more time in a search. It arrived with a defective screen. A few days later I received another one in fine working order. Two weeks later I opened my American Express statement and discovered, to my amazement, that I hadn't been charged for the computer. I called my attorney and added a clause to my will: I left four thousand dollars to the company, twice what I owed it. For months afterward I debated the pros and cons of my action, in the end arriving at the conclusion that I had acted dishonestly, even as I left a solid compensation in my will. In my dealings with fellow humans, I conducted myself honorably but my standards took a dive when dealing with corporations

Oscar drove me to Albuquerque airport. Three hours later I arrived in Atlanta, were I boarded a much larger plane for Nice. I reached out for the flimsy nylon blanket provided by the airline, covered my knees with it, placed a small pillow against the window, rested my head on the pillow, and closed my eyes. A blond stewardess stopped by and asked if I wanted something to drink.

"A cup of hot water, please. I carry my own teabags."

The woman to my right requested orange juice. In her late thirties, tall and thin, with long, blond, seemingly uncombed hair, and no breasts to speak of, she looked quite ordinary. But her black-rimmed glasses and lined forehead conveyed an appealing intellectual slant. Looks lose their luster over time; intelligence does not. An appealing and unfamiliar scent reached my nostrils. I took a better look at my travel companion. Her hair was combed, after all, just giving the appearance of neglect.

Out of a leather shoulder bag, she pulled out a paper-bound book. At the sight of the cover, I had the shock of my life.

"I don't believe it," I exclaimed.

"I beg your pardon?"

he Rebel. It's my favorite book."

She frowned, pulled at her skirt, and inched away. Feeling like a fool for responding impulsively, I extracted my portable, electronic chess set from my shoulder bag, and began arranging the pieces with an air of calculated nonchalance. I moved my queen pawn two spaces when she asked, "Did you really mean it?"

"Mean what?" I asked, as my electronic opponent requested that I move its king pawn one space.

"About *The Rebel*?"

"But of course. Why would I lie?"

"You could have said it to awaken my interest in you."

"I could have commented on the stuffy air, the narrow seats, the whining girl behind us just as well. But, I didn't. I was plainly startled to see you reading Camus."

She opened her mouth, but remained silent, as if unable to make up her mind whether or not to pursue the subject further. I moved my king pawn one space.

She cleared her throat and said, "On my last flight I was reading *Germinal* by Zola when the man to my right commented that he was passionate about French literature. I got excited. Someone to talk to and break the monotony of a long flight. It took only minutes to realize that he was quite ignorant of French literature."

"You must have been really disappointed," I said. "Having been brought up to think of myself as a human nonentity, I found in my adolescence Camus's notion that a slave, to earn the right to call himself a man must stand up before his master and cry, 'No More,' very appealing."

A few silent seconds later she mumbled, "So, you are for real?"

I laughed. "I sure hope so. And you? Are you for real?"

"I like to believe I am. Camus has taught me a lot, too. The thing that gets me," she said, "Is that the French read him as a school assignment. We Americans read him to grow wiser."

"You are the first American I've met, outside a university, who appreciates Camus. That's a ponderous event, deserving to be inscribed on a stone."

She laughed. "My, my, you like melodrama, don't you? Let me introduce myself. My name is Theodora."

"Theodora, did you say? You wouldn't be the reincarnation of—"

"You have met another Theodora?"

"Like a ghost, she appeared and disappeared in the blink of an eye. It was a formidable but short acquaintance." The stewardess appeared with a cup of hot water. I dropped my mint tea bag, and said, "I am Adam."

"Your Theodora sounds quite interesting. Tell me what she was like."

"She was English. I met her last New Year's Eve at Marina Piccola, a small port in Capri. The weather was atrocious. Piercing wind and cutting rain. To my immense shock, she told me that she had come to commit suicide."

"Suicide? Oh my God."

"She was deeply depressed because of personal compromises she had made with a man. Her loss of self-esteem was so overwhelming that she felt unable to go on living. Familiar with personal compromises, I empathized with her. After several hours of sharing our respective life stories, we became close friends, and she resolved to go on living. In the morning, the day after I met her, she vanished without as much as a note of explanation."

"It must have been quite a shock to you."

"It was, indeed. How about you? Is there a man in your life?"

She stared ahead, as if seeking a clue on the back of the seat in front of her, then glancing at her shoes, said, "I don't feel comfortable talking about it right now. Maybe later."

A bit embarrassed by my eagerness, I mumbled, "I think I will go back to my chess game, if you don't mind."

"Of course not. I will read my book."

From the corners of my eyes, I noticed that she was not reading. She was staring at her hands holding the book.

A kick in the back of my seat, followed by a girlish cry, "I want chocolate, now!" startled me. "We ran out of them," an adult female voice mumbled. A harder kick made me jump. I turned and said to the pale and haggard-looking woman, "Please, tell your daughter to stop kicking my seat." Moments after I finished my sentence, the girl did it again.

"Ignore her," Theodora said.

"I can't. It's like being in a motel and hearing one shoe fall in the adjacent room and not knowing when the other shoe is going to drop."

Tense, I waited for the next kick. It came sooner than I had expected. I jumped and screamed, "I'll give you a chocolate bar if you promise never again to hit my seat."

The girl wiped her nose with the back of her hand and said, "okay."

I passed her a Hershey bar with peanuts. "Don't forget you agreed not to–"

"I know what I agreed to. I am not stupid, you know."

"That was my last chocolate bar and I love chocolate," I said to Theodora.

"A mighty generous gesture," she said and broke into a sonorous laugh. I'll have to figure out more ways to make her laugh, I thought.

After recovering, she said, "I don't like to be nosy, but I'm really curious. Did you fall in love with your English friend?"

"By the time I did, she was gone. I felt sad, but I wasn't bitter." Glancing at the sky painted in vermillion, red, and orange hues, I continued awash in nostalgia, "She had enriched me in our short time together more than any other woman in my entire life."

"Would you rather I be quiet so you can reminisce undisturbed about her?"

"Oh, no. I enjoy conversing with you. But tell me, do you play chess?"

She smiled. "I am quite good at it."

"Richard Bach and Leslie Parish, his soul-mate, played too, and she beat him."

"Richard Bach of *Jonathan Seagull* fame?"

"The very one. In *A Bridge Across Forever,* he wrote that he and Leslie were so much in love that they encountered each other in their dreams."

Theodora pulled a mirror and a brush out of her purse, combed her hair, and said, "I find that hard to believe."

"I wrote to him, congratulating him on his good fortune."

The plane shook as if hit by an immense boulder. A female voice on the public address system advised the passengers to fasten their seat belts. Theodora's face turned pale.

"Just a bit of turbulence," I said. "In a few minutes, we'll be back to normal."

"Next time around, I'll take a boat," she said in a nervous voice.

The plane plunged. A woman across the aisle crossed herself. The kid behind me screamed. The ceiling lights went out. Theodora gasped for breath and dropped her head on my shoulder. The lights came back. The plane resumed a steady course. A female voice announced that the snack would be served shortly.

"God, that was terrible," Theodora said, freeing herself. "I am sure grateful for your help."

"I did no more than Richard Bach would have done for Leslie Parish."

"What was Leslie Parish like?"

"I've read the book many years ago. I think she was blond like you. At first, he did not want to get tied down. He believed in open dating. Hurt by his insensitivity to her, she told him to get lost. The rejection hurt him, and he gave up the notion of dating other women. She was a strong-willed, genuine, and innocent woman."

"Innocent, did you say? Children are before they succumb to adult programming."

"That's my view too. My parents had stolen my innocence in my early childhood, and I've been working hard on recapturing it ever since."

"Your Theodora was far from innocent, wasn't she? She compromised herself with her lover."

"You said it. Having lost her self-esteem, she was in so much pain that she wanted to die."

"Poor woman. I feel bad for her."

"She learned her lesson and redeemed herself. I still have to learn mine. I continue betraying myself with Tonio."

"Who's Tonio?"

"Tonio is a jeweler in Biot, the town where I live. Generous but intolerably vain, a year ago he offered me workspace in his atelier, thus making it possible for me to realize my dream of being an artist in France."

"Is he overbearing?" Theodora asked.

"Brutally so. Periodically he vanquishes me, then brings me back to life so that he can vanquish me again. He's my nemesis and my savior, if you can believe that."

Theodora became quiet. She lifted her book, seemed to turn pages at random, then frowned. "A penny for your thoughts?" I said.

"I was thinking of your failure to preserve your integrity with this Tonio. I used to tell myself that it was 'only' human to make personal compromises. Eventually, though, I realized that to live with myself, I had to preserve my integrity all the time."

She squashed her orange juice can, placed it in the mesh receptacle in the seat in front of her, and sighed. "In my freshman year in college, my roommate was raped by a student wrestler. She didn't report the incident out of fear that her reputation would suffer. When I confronted him, he barked that if I exposed him, he would rape me too. I did nothing. I probably wouldn't do any better today."

"You might and you might not," I said. "I considered myself a hopeless coward, then one day something snapped inside me. I was working behind the counter of the college cafeteria, when a football player barked, 'Get me that apple pie.' 'Get it yourself,' I said, knowing that he couldn't because it stood behind a glass enclosure. He pointed his calloused finger at me. 'You mother-fucker, git it!' 'I'll give it to you if you ask nicely,' I said. He jumped over the counter, grabbed me by the shoulders, shook me, and I wet my pants."

"What happened next?" Theodora asked, inching closer.

"Nothing."

"What do you mean nothing? You said that the guy grabbed you by the shoulders."

"He did that, but instead of hurting me, he broke into a laugh."

"And then?"

"He fixed me up with a cheerleader and we went out on a double date."

"Good for you. You stood up to the brute."

"Something inside compelled me to dare him. Do you detect such an impulse in yourself?"

"Are you asking because I am a woman? Perhaps, you think women don't mind being mistreated."

I stuttered. "I . . . I . . . don't know. I like to think that I'm open-minded, but I could be wrong."

"You need to work harder on outgrowing your prejudices," she said coldly.

"I couldn't agree more."

Giving me a piercing state, she went on, "You baffle me. I say something that I expect will irritate you, and you respond as if I had offered friendly advice."

"Could that be because of your own prejudice against men?"

"Me prejudiced? That's absurd. People who know me consider me fully liberated and open-minded."

"You assumed I wouldn't acknowledge my shortcomings, yet I gave you no reason to think that."

She bit her lips and mumbled. "Now, I feel cornered. My father called my mother a bitch whenever she found any faults with him. That gave me the idea that all men have tender egos."

"Don't be discouraged. That we're in the same boat might actually work to our advantage. Neither one of us will be able to feel superior to the other."

We stopped talking. Our knees met and I felt a tingling in my spine. My penis rose. How would she respond if she found out the effect she had on me? I shuddered at the thought of our age difference.

"I haven't been so open even with my best friend," Theodora said. "There is something about you that makes me want to reveal myself."

I smiled. "Could it because my features remind you of a Biblical sage?"

"Funny you said that. You do have a Semitic nose. And your salt and pepper beard bring to mind a prophet."

"People like to open their hearts to holy men."

She laughed. "Especially on an airline flight. Do you want to hear my story?"

"Need you ask? Everything you have said so far has interested me."

"My older sister, my protector, died when I was seven. I was a delicate, vulnerable child. In elementary school, because of my shyness, boys teased me mercilessly. The teasing continued into mid-high. It stopped in high school, largely because I became invisible. I didn't participate in school activities. I went on few dates. I spent my time studying and reading. A teacher suggested I consult the school psychologist. He said I needed to develop socialization skills. I learned to laugh at stupid jokes. I attended football games when I really wanted to remain in my room and read a good novel. In my freshman year at Yale, I put a stop to the charade. I made myself useful to the boys by writing term papers for them. Gradually, my intellectual skills came to be known." She smiled. "Before you pointed out that I was prejudiced against men, I thought of myself as a thoroughly emancipated and enlightened woman."

"I'm sorry I brought you down from your pedestal."

"Don't be silly. It's a good thing you did. 'When there is no character there is a method.' I want to shed all methods. I want to be totally real."

"Ah, my favorite saying by Camus."

We became quiet. It was as if periodically we needed to retreat into ourselves to savor the pleasure we obtained conversing with each other.

"How old are you?" I asked.

"Why . . . why are you asking? I'm thirty-seven. Does it matter?"

She was twenty-five years my junior. I felt paralyzed by desire and a fear that she would lose interest in me the moment she found out how old I was.

"Have you been married?" I asked.

She shook her head. "No right man has crossed my path. I am getting on in years, and would love to start a family. How old are you?"

"I'll tell you if you promise not to hold it against me."

"Hold it against you? Why would I? It never bothered me being asked my age."

"I . . . I . . .like you a lot, and I don't want to take a chance on alienating you."

"Alienating me by telling me your age?"

"You really want to know?"

"Just tell me, will you?" she asked in an impatient tone. "Sixty-two."

She laughed nervously. "I thought you were younger. You're old enough to be my father."

"I was afraid you were going to say that."

"Why? It's not a sin being—"

"An old man," I interrupted.

We became quiet. I fell in limbo. Longing for the unattainable. I thought of the first Theodora. She slipped, for reasons of her own, into thin air. The current Theodora was going to slip because of our age difference. A stewardess holding two plates in her hands interrupted my revelry. "You both ordered vegetarian dishes, didn't you?"

Theodora lifted the cover off her plate. "A cheese sandwich with pickles. At least they included a whole-wheat bun."

"An authentic life calls for sacrifices," I said. "Think of airplane food as an instance of a meaningful sacrifice."

"By the way, I make an excellent tofu stew."

"And I make excellent whole-wheat bread. We should prepare dinner together. I live in Biot, a medieval village between Nice and Antibes. Where do you live?"

"In Nice. I am working on my doctorate in European literature at the university. I'll complete my studies in two years."

"That ought to give us enough time to plan a meal together."

We passed our plates to the stewardess and left for the restrooms. When we returned a movie we both had seen was playing on the screen. "A good reason to take a nap," Theodora said.

"You're welcome to use my shoulder as a pillow," I said.

"That's very kind of you. It came in handy during the turbulence."

She tucked one foot under the her, rested her head on my shoulder, and soon assumed the quiet, regular breathing of someone in deep sleep. I closed my eyes and fell asleep too.

When I woke up, Theodora was away from me, her lips open in a smile. She moaned, moved closer, and put her head on my shoulder again. I felt as awed as when I saw a coyote peeking at me from the bushes in the Big Bend National Park. I stood still then, not wanting to break the magic, and I stood still now, not wanting to interrupt the flow of Theodora's vitality into my veins.

Theodora opened her eyes, stretched, and said, "Your shoulder makes a wonderful cushion. Thanks."

"It's at your disposal, day and night, here and anywhere else."

She laughed. "And you will offer it for free?"

"Gratitude. Pay me with gratitude."

"Never before did I sleep so well on a plane."

The pilot interrupted us with the announcement that we're flying over Greenland. Thousands of feet below two rivers of ice merged in a foaming sea. "Wow, look below," I cried.

Theodora leaned over, resting her breasts on my lap. "What a magical sight," she exclaimed, stretching further. The closeness intoxicated me. She was gazing at the scene below, and I was gazing at her hair, her neck, her back. She placed her hands on my knees, lifted herself up, and said, "Such beauty makes me want to cry."

I smiled. "I was on the verge of tears watching you."

"I've been known to induce depression in men."

"But what a depression! A depression to make angels sing. But tell me, do you remember what we talked about before we fell asleep?"

"We're talking about having a party."

"A party? My recollection is that we planned to have dinner, just for the two of us."

"It would be more fun if we invited other people."

"You wouldn't have a boyfriend now, would you?" I asked, fearful of what she might say.

"Is there anything wrong with having a male friend?"

"That was the last thing I wanted you to say."

"Why? You are old enough to be my father. A father wouldn't mind."

I shook my head. "Do you have fun with your male friend? Do you camp with him?"

"He likes the comfort of a hotel. Before I met him, I camped and backpacked with friends all over Europe."

"How about forgetting the dinner and going to Nordkapp instead?"

"That's on the top of Norway. It would take us many days getting there."

"During your break at the university."

"I don't think Tom would appreciate that."

"Tom, Tom. Does he have to know? Oh, my god, that is the stupidest thing I've said in a long time. I'm turning into an imbecile."

Her lips opened into a light smile. "It would be fun going camping with you, but–"

"But what?" I interrupted.

"Weeks on the road might lead to unwelcome intimacy. I wouldn't feel comfortable sleeping in a tent with you."

"You could have a tent of your own."

"Still, we would be close to each other for hours at end."

"I wouldn't force myself on you. I would respect your need for privacy."

She sighed. "You don't give up, do you? You're an interesting man. You look younger than your age, and you have plenty of energy, but that doesn't change the fact that I could pass for your daughter.'."

"Don't you find me even a bit physically attractive?"

"I do, very much so. But that doesn't mean I would want to get physically close to you."

"Okay," I said, "If to spend time with you, I must be your friend, I'll be your friend."

Her face opened up in a radiant smile. "I was hoping you would say that."

"Great, but why are you in a relationship with Tom?"

She frowned as if in deep thought. "Let me see. I, I'm not really sure. He's considerate and kind. I can say anything I want, and he never gets mad. He'll make an excellent father someday."

"Does he stimulate you? Does he excite you? Does he make you want to put your hiking boots on, and venture up a mountain?"

"He's more sedentary, more laid back, more serious than I."

"What about me? Do I stimulate you?"

"You want to know if I like your company better than his? Is that it?"

"Yes," I said in a low voice. "That's what I am wondering about."

"I've known him for a year. I've known you but a couple of hours. How can I form a reliable judgment?"

"Reliable judgment? You talk as if we were engaged in scientific pursuit. What does your heart tell you?"

"It's always a mystery to me what brings a man and a woman together."

Looking at her in disbelief, I cried, "I admitted that I was comparing myself with Tom, which wasn't easy. And you wonder about the nature of love. Can't you just for once say what's on your mind?"

"That's what was on my mind."

"I give up."

"My, my, aren't we touchy?"

"I hate to be left hanging in the air."

She took a deep breath, "You're right to feel annoyed. I was being evasive. I didn't want to acknowledge my growing feelings for you. I enjoy your company better than Tom's."

"Then, you don't love him?" I said relieved.

"I never did. Like I told you, he's kind and understanding. He'll make an excellent father, and I want to have a family someday."

A heavyset middle-aged woman stopped at the end of our aisle, her elbow resting on the top of Theodora's seat, only inches from her head. Theodora winced. I thought she was going to tell the woman to move away, but she turned toward me. "I want to tell you what crossed my mind before I fell asleep, but you must promise not to laugh."

I crossed myself. "So help me God."

"I wondered if the two of us got stranded on a deserted island, how would we get along. Would we argue? Would we have fun?"

"Tell you what. Let's do it and find out." A warm current washed over me. The current took the color of corn, of a lily, of a ripe tomato, of a golden apple, of a full moon, of the rising sun.

I took her hand in mine. "We would explore the sand dunes and the bush. We would catch fish which we would roast on the fire. We would collect birds' eggs. We would gaze at the stars and the moon."

"That's a sweet fantasy."

I sought her eyes. "We can turn it into reality."

She put the tips of her fingers on my lips. "Adam, I feel terrible. I've apparently misled you. You're a terrific guy. But when I ask myself what kind of a relationship I want to have with you, the invariable answer is friendship."

"But you imagined us being stranded on an island. Friends don't entertain such fantasies."

"We're getting along so well that I couldn't help thinking what it would be like if we were alone for a long period of time. She took my hand in hers and continued, "I'm truly fond of you. I would die of disappointment if our friendship should end because of my unwillingness to get intimate."

I withdrew my hand." I'll go along with your wish, but first I want to ask you a question."

"You are torturing yourself needlessly. Regardless of my answers, our age difference would continue to form an insuperable barrier." She sighed. "Let's listen to some music, what do you say?" She put her earphones on, fidgeted with the controls on the armrest, and closed her eyes.

33

I switched on the classical channel. Berlioz' Requiem, my favorite choral composition, burst into Te Deum. Spellbound, I listened for a few minutes, then thought of Paul Theroux, and decided to share with him my growing love for Theodora. I left the plane, and hitched a ride on a cloud to the hostelry at the foothills of Mount Olympus. He was stretched on the same recliner with a book in his hand, as I had seen him on my first visit.

"Welcome," he exclaimed and pointed at a nearby chair. "How is life in France?"

Watching a swarm of bees dancing over the bed of roses, I responded, "I've been making great jewelry in the workshop of a very abusive man. I hiked in the Maritime Alps and slept in a refuge. I visited museums, and spent hours exploring Biot, my village, and other villages and towns on the Riviera."

"And your search for a soulmate, how did that go?"

"I met a woman who would appeal to your Milroy. She's genuine, fully alive, and adventurous, but half my age. She wants a friendship, while I want love."

"It took Jill a long time to grow attached to Milroy. She was only sixteen and Milroy was . . . what would you say. . .? Close to a hundred. The age difference can present a problem, but it is not insurmountable. What's her name?"

"Theodora. I've been trying to persuade her that we belong together, with little success."

"Jill was turned off when Milroy performed miracles to impress her. The best policy is to be yourself and trust destiny, let that which is meant to happen happen."

At the thicket, on the other side of the lawn a deer—its antlers resplendent in the sun—stared at us with its melancholy oval eyes. "It looks like the one we saw on my first visit here," I said.

"Deer and other animals lead an uncomplicated life, bless them. We should learn from them."

"I love Theodora for who she is, but also for being very much like me."

"Narcissus enjoyed seeing his image in the well."

"Are you suggesting that my love for Theodora is egotistical?" I asked with poorly hidden irritation.

"All love is to a degree. We love the familiar and the—"

"Unique," I interrupted. "We love people in whose company we feel more than what we can feel alone. We want love to takes us to the outer reaches of the human realm, beyond set boundaries, beyond restrictions of any kind."

"That's what your Theodora offers you?"

"That and more. With her, I feel complete, true and immortal. I would give up all my possessions for the privilege of awakening in the morning with her by my side."

"Words of a true romantic. In this day and age, it isn't often that one hears such passionate proclamations."

"In *Milroy the Magician* you wrote about an all-consuming love. You must be well versed in romantic passion."

Paul Theroux broke into a laugh. "Do you really think that an author necessarily bases his writings on his personal experiences? The world of literature would be much poorer were that the case."

"But you do know the meaning of true love, don't you?" I persisted.

"It suffices to say that I can imagine it." Glancing at Mount Olympus' jagged peaks emerging from a cloud cover, Mr. Theroux continued, "May the Almighty bring you and Theodora together."

We embraced. I waved, hitched a ride on an air current, settled on a white cloud, and flew back to the airplane.

34

Theodora removed her earphones. "That was great. To think that Beethoven was deaf when he composed the Ninth Symphony is mindboggling. I've decided to answer your question because . . . because . . . I like you. But, please, don't take my willingness to cooperate as an invitation for intimacy."

"I'll keep that in mind," I said, feeling like a man walking on a high, tight rope, conscious that a wrong step could plunge him to the earth. "Have you . . . have you ever fully surrendered to a man while making love to him?"

She opened her mouth, but no words came out. Her eyes grew tiny as if trying to shut me off. Seconds later she said in a cold voice, "I wouldn't even tell that to my father confessor."

"A father confessor wouldn't care about it one way or another. I really must know. Our future depends on your answer."

"Our future? What future?" She removed *The Rebel* from her shoulder bag, stared at the cover briefly, then turned the pages seemingly at random.

"Theodora, I'm willing to be your friend, but I must make sure that friendship is the right thing for us."

"You don't give up, do you? I should have never agreed to participate in this abusive interrogation."

Feeling as if a fist had struck my belly, I mumbled. "I am sorry. I was just trying to clear the air, get to the bottom of things. I am willing to give up, if that's what you want."

"Now you are willing to give up, now that you have got my mind spinning out of control?" Shaking her head, she cried, "I am in a maze, and I have no idea how to get out of it." I wanted to take her in my arms but fearing that such a gesture would throw her into panic restrained myself. *Is this the path to love?* I wondered. *More likely, it is the path to insanity.* I vowed not to make additional inquiries.

"I wish now I had kept my mouth shut. Let's go back to Camus. I read his autobiography. He married a docile and passive woman. For someone who fought on the side of the French underground during the Second World War, and who published a resistance newspaper, you would think he would have chosen a partner of his intellectual and emotional strength."

"I am not a child, you know," Theodora exclaimed. "I can hold my ground. You challenged me. It is my choice to accept or reject your challenge. I will answer your questions under one condition, that you agree never again to get so personal."

"I agree to nothing," I blurted out. "I am a truth-seeker, and neither you nor anyone else will put a brake on my search for the Ultimate."

"You are crazy. You sure are," she cried and burst out into a hysterical laugh. Tears came streaming out of her eyes. She wiped her face with the back of her hand, and said, "One moment I feel like punching you in the face, and another like hugging you. Incredibly, now I feel like hugging you. My answer to your question is, 'No,' I have never truly surrendered to a man. My heart was never into it."

I took her hand, kissed it, and said, "There are no barriers separating us now. Never before did I feel like this."

"Neither did I," she said and rested her head on my shoulder.

I kissed her eyes, her cheek, brushed her lips with mine, and said, "That can mean only one thing. That we must continue on the path we have taken, grow ever more intimate, and find out if we are soulmates."

"Yes," she whispered in my ears. "The same thought crossed my mind. But, is it realistic? We have known each other such a short time."

"We have shared very personal details of our lives; we laughed; we joked; we rejoiced in each other's company. And above all, unintentionally, we had saved ourselves for each other. We're virgins."

"Virgins at our age?" she exclaimed. "When my friends boasted about their sexual escapades, I felt incomplete because I never attained fulfillment. I even considered going to see a therapist, but decided in the end that my inhibitions were too deep to be removed."

"Same with me," I said. "Sex was a release at the best. One-night stands depressed me. Hard as I tried, I just couldn't surrender to anyone. Then I had a dream. In the dream, I made gentle, absorbing love to an unfamiliar woman. With her I felt one. Upon awakening, I vowed to only make love to my soulmate."

"Did you cheat?"

"To my regret, I did. Driven by pent-up needs, I compromised and felt like a heel afterward."

We stopped talking. I visualized being with Theodora in a field carpeted with leaves, butterflies dancing, and birds singing. I imagined us leaning with our backs against a tree, holding hands, and inhaling the sweet scent of flowers. My reverie came to an end when she asked, "What's below? Anything worth seeing?"

"Just the wild ocean."

She leaned over and we embraced. "I'm floating in magic," she murmured. "But I'm afraid the magic will disappear the moment we hit the ground."

"We must find a place where our love can grow undisturbed."

"I have a good-sized apartment. Move-in with me. But I must warn you: I'm moody."

"I'll put up with your moods if you put up with mine. I'm painfully conscious of shortcomings in myself and others. I strive for perfection."

"I spill toothpaste on the bathroom sink, and don't clean up afterward."

"I snore."

"I'll put a pillow over your face. That will stop you."

"But I won't be able to breathe. I'll suffocate."

"I'll resuscitate you."

"Are you hard to get along with during your period?"

"Not if you feed me chocolates."

"You need to know that I've had an operation that prevents me from fathering children. I hate to bring the subject, but you've said that you desire a family. The day may come when you may want to leave me for another man."

"Soulmates don't split. They live together to the end of their lives. We can adopt. We can try artificial insemination."

I shook my head. "I'm a vagabond at heart. I need to travel, to camp, to hike, to feel that my life is complete. It's too late for me to raise a family."

"If you move in with me, won't that curtail your freedom?"

"It won't. You enjoy traveling and camping as much as I do. We'll do it together whenever time permits. My only concern is your wish for a family. Should your wish overpower you, we may have to split."

"Soulmates don't enter into a relationship expecting that it will end someday."

"We may have to settle for two years of bliss."

"Why two? Why not three? Why not four?"

"Because you'll want to regain your freedom while your body is still fit for motherhood. You'll want to outgrow your feelings for me. You'll want to find a man to have children with."

"What the hell are you talking about?"

"It wouldn't be a compromise if the sex is a means to a higher end."

"You sound like Tolstoy in his later years."

"Perhaps I do. I've transcended myself through my art and in nature, but never through love. Two years with you would make my life journey complete."

Theodora dug her nails into my hand, causing a trickle of blood to spill over my fingers, and said, "This is turning into a theater of the absurd! Right after I surrender to my feelings for you, you're informing me that we have to separate . . . for my own good."

"Camus—"

"Fuck Camus!"

"You can't have me and a family. You must choose between the two."

"Only God Almighty can predict the future," she said, her lips twisting in outrage, her eyes hard, icy.

I opened my mouth, but couldn't think of anything more to say. I felt dismayed, defeated by her inability to grasp the beauty of my generosity. Then, it hit me that I wasn't that much different from Tonio. He relished being a step ahead of people in their life. I was making decisions that would affect her years from now, without as much as asking what she thought about it.

"Theodora, please forgive me," I said. "I feel like a jerk for trying to impose my solutions on you. Let's put our trust in fate, and see what happens."

Theodora brushed my lips with the tips of her fingers, then kissed me. Our lips withdrew, and touched again, seeking the closest contact, the contact that would make us one. We left the plane. We flew over a sea of clouds. We skimmed their silky surface. We dove into their soft underbelly. Upon our return, the blonde stewardess said to straighten up our seats. Minutes later the plane shook and the wheels touched the ground. Theodora took a tissue from her leather bag, dried her eyes, and said, "I never thought I could be so happy and so sad at the same time."

Theodora's apartment overlooked Nice's horseshoe harbor, the pleasure boats, the ferries, the fishing vessels, the yachts with their multinational flags fluttering in the breeze. The nearby old town's twisting narrow streets dotted with bistros, pizzerias, patisseries, souvenir shops, art galleries, became our playground. We meandered through alleyways rendered dark by drying laundry; we inhaled garlic, onions, cabbage, and roasted lamb wafting out from laced curtains; we set the automatic timer on our camera, and snapped pictures of us embracing beneath weathered walls and pots with flowers resting on window sills. We watched seagulls pirouetting over milky waves crushing into swells. At home we read, played chess, drank wine on the couch to the tune of Vivaldi or Mozart, made love on the supple, queen-size bed, and fell asleep in each other's arms.

We lived in the moment, in the pleasure and joy of the here and now. During Theodora's long hours at the university, I read novels, strolled up and down the old town, and visited museums. My love for Theodora was deep, but not deep enough to assuage my yearning for creative self-expression. Watching jewelry displayed in stores and on women's wrists made my heart ache.

A month after moving in with Theodora, I finally willed myself to visit Tonio. I left the car in the village garage, elbowed my way through the morning shoppers, and wondered what kind of reception I would get.

"There you are," he said. "I thought I would never see you again."

"You mean you missed me?"

"But, of course, my boy. Half of the bench is yours for as long as you live in France."

"Ok, Tonio," I said. "But I won't take any more abuse from you. You treat me right, and I will treat you right. You throw shit at me, and I will throw shit back at you. Understand?"

"Calm down, my boy. You worry too much. Now, get down to work."

"I just came to say hello. I will return Monday morning. Will you be here?"

"Where the hell should I be?"

"You go fishing, don't you?"

"Yeah, I do that. Call me if you want to be sure."

That evening I shared with Theodora my conversation with Tonio.

"You did the right thing telling him that you wouldn't tolerate any more abuse," she said with eyes filled with love. "Give him one more chance. If he fails, forget about him. It's fine to examine one's motives, but introspection per se is not the answer. Standing up for oneself is."

Her words shamed me. Numerous times I had told myself the same thing, yet found excuses not to abide by the answer. With Theodora as my witness, I felt confident to finally act like a man."

"You are my guardian angel," I said.

"And you are mine," she responded and kissed me lightly on the mouth.

Nina and Giuseppe agreed to lower the rent by half. Theodora's apartment had adequate space for the two of us, but not for my camping and jewelry-making equipment. Theodora found Nina and Giuseppe agreeable company. Every so often we dined with them and, afterward, spent the night in my Biot apartment.

A fulfilling routine sat in. Theodora kept herself busy with her studies. I kept myself occupied with jewelry making. Tonio, perhaps sensing to my resolve not to tolerate further abuse, treated me with respect. On Theodora's breaks from university studies, we took short and long trips as time allowed. We particularly enjoyed vacationing in Corsica. Corsican nationalists periodically bombed unoccupied villas to send a message to the mainland folks that they were unwelcome. The act of terror effectively held in check real-estate development by outsiders, and helped preserve the island's authenticity.

Only a couple of hours by boat from the Cote d'Azur, the island was a pristine, unspoiled paradise. Huts dotted green, unfenced fields; sheep licked the salt off rocky rises alongside the highways; ancient fire towers rose out of deserted beaches. We bathed and picnicked in blessed solitude. At night we held each other and gazed at the stars.

Early in August, Nina invited Theodora and me for dinner. I decided to surprise her with a silver cross. Two days before our dinner date, I packed my silver wire into my backpack and drove to Biot.

"Good to see you, my boy," Tonio said. "It's been a while since you've been here."

"The wages of love," I said, smiling. "I've had too good a time with Theodora to want to make jewelry. Nina has invited us for dinner, and I thought of making a cross for her."

"Sure, get down to it." He rose. "I have an errand to do. I'll be back in a few minutes."

"Wait," I said. "I'll come back later, after your return."

"Don't be silly. I trust you." He was gone before I could make any further objections.

The responsibility troubled me. If someone wanted to purchase his jewelry, I wouldn't have known what to charge. Reluctantly, I pulled a thick silver wire from my backpack and cut it into two small segments. I was hammering them into the shape of a cross when Tonio returned. Frowning, he stared at the silver.

"What?" I asked.

"Where did you get that wire?"

"At home, in Santa Fe, where else?"

"Never before did you use that size gage."

"So what? I decided thick wire is best suited for a cross."

He eyed the spool of his wire of the same gage hanging on the wall, then at the wire in my hands, then back at the spool. Blood rushed to my head. "Are you accusing me of stealing your silver?" I yelled.

"The wire in your hands is identical to mine."

I jumped on my feet, threw the unfinished cross, the remaining silver, and my tools into my backpack, and screamed, "This time you went too far, you narcissistic, pompous asshole. You'll never see me again."

As if in a dream, I walked amidst adult shoppers, children with their small satchels, and constables regulating the traffic. Feeling free of all impurities, clean as a mountain brook, I reflected that my life of an artist in France had come to a bitter end, but that my self-esteem had grown as tall as Mt. Everest. My challenge now was to turn my life into a work of art.

Theodora was at her desk, bent over, taking notes from a thick book. The life of a student suited her. She brought to mind a Medieval nun exploring paths to God's realm. In the kitchen I cut a couple of slices from a banana bread I had made, brought her a slice and, unable to restrain myself any more, cried,

"It's all over. Tonio accused me of stealing his silver. I called him a narcissistic asshole, and told him he would never see me again."

"Good for you."

"I feel as if a pack of bricks has been taken off my shoulders."

The next morning, feeling particularly energetic, I headed for the Boulevard des Anglais to pick up my mail at the American Express. Nice's hustle and bustle, the ocean splashing against the rocky shore, the street performers, the exotic tongues on the streets filled me with joy. But something vital, something that only I could give myself, was beyond my reach: being creative.

I sat on a chair overlooking the sea and reflected on my predicament. I had come to France to be an artist. I loved making jewelry. After my breakup with Tonio, I thought my love for Theodora would compensate for my loss. It didn't. The inner void remained. *Was jewelry making the only way for me to feel whole*, I asked myself, or *would any creative endeavor do?* I enjoyed making bread. I enjoyed making strawberry jam. I enjoyed making energy bars. But there was a limit to how much cooking I could do. I rose with a heavy heart and headed home.

35

A stuffy evening in June, while Theodora was working on her dissertation, I put a CD of Berlioz's *Requiem* in the stereo, then removed it, thinking it might get in the way of her concentration. I tried to watch TV but found no program interesting. I then went to the kitchen to make energy bars. Afterward, when I took a plateful to her, she said, "You seem unusually restless. Is something bothering you?"

"I miss being creative. Making energy bars helps. Even washing—"

Theodora laughed. "You can't mean that washing our clothes gives you a high?"

"It doesn't give me a high, but it makes me forget for a while that I'm not being creative."

She nodded to the chair by her desk. "Sit down."

"But you have work to do."

"My work can wait. My life is complete. You only have me. That's not enough. We've got to find you a nourishing activity. You've been keeping a journal, haven't you?"

I nodded. "It's not as exciting as you might think."

"Turn the entries into a memoir. That would result in a creative enterprise."

"I've had some events worth writing about, but not enough for a book."

"What about our love? And your experience with Tonio? Giuseppe and Nina, your sister Carla, Olivier and Claire, the other Theodora—they are all worth recollecting about. And the realization of your dream to be an artist in France, your hiking, your reflections. There is enough material there for several books. And if you get stuck, make up scenes and people, create settings—let your mind soar."

"That would be cheating."

"Poetic license. Be open about it. Let the reader know that parts of the book are based on facts and parts on fantasy. Not one memoir I've read ever convinced me that the entire narrative corresponded to facts. Give it a shot. If it works, great. If it doesn't, you won't be any worse for it."

Her words struck a chord. Excitement rolled over me. The next day at dawn, I began composing my book. I used most of my free time writing the memoir.

The week of our second anniversary, Theodora completed her PhD requirements in European literature and I completed my yet-to-be-named memoir. We decided to celebrate the two events in a trattoria in San Remo. We left the car in a side street near the Casino, and minutes later stepped into the smoky, noisy Luigi's restaurant, decorated with posters of Capri, Sorento, Portofino, and other sites dear to the Italian heart. Checkered tablecloths and candles affixed in the necks of wine bottles added to the festive atmosphere. We ordered mushrooms filled with cheese and anchovies for antipasto, spaghetti alla marinara for the main dish, Zuppa Inglese for dessert, and half a bottle of Chianti. To our right, a dozen people occupied three tables end to end. A middle-aged gentleman lifted his glass and said in a bass voice that he wished the young, overweight woman by his side one hundred years of blissful birthdays. An accordionist came over and they all sang, "Happy birthday dear Francesca." The middle-aged man kissed Francesca to general applause.

"Let's turn ourselves into Italians," I said.

"But you are already Italian."

"I used to be. Then I became an American. Now I am a man in love. Does love give a man nationality?"

"It sure does. Trans-national, however. Love is a land without boundaries, without beginning and without end, stretching from one corner of the globe to the other. Indians, Pakistanis, Chinese, Bulgarians in love are our fellow compatriots."

"I'll drink to the good health of lovers in the world, then." I was pouring wine into our glasses when a young couple came in. The woman holding an infant wrapped in a beige blanket in a basket sat down, kissed the baby's head, lifted his tiny hand, and waved it at the man. The man smiled and waved back. Theodora held her glass of wine in midair transfixed.

An urge to snatch the baby and give it to Theodora almost overpowered me. Theodora took a paper napkin and wiped her eyes with it. I wanted to say something to ease her pain, but couldn't think of helpful words. It had happened before. The sight of a child invariably broke her heart. The words she had uttered as our plane was landing in Nice two years ago came back to me, "I never thought I could be so happy and so sad at the same time."

When I asked her if she thought that the answer to her dilemma might be that we split, so she could find a man to have children with, she protested. "Our love is strong enough to fill the void inside me." But I knew better than to believe her. In restaurants, on sidewalks, in supermarkets, the sight of a baby or a small child would make her sigh. She would stop and stare at the child as if at the source of life itself. It got so bad that I dreaded going out.

One evening I took her hand in mine and said softly, "Your longing for motherhood is killing both of us. We must do something about it."

"There isn't anything to be done. You don't want a family."

"That doesn't mean you can't have one."

"Without you? Are you crazy?"

"We both knew at the time we decided to live together that the day might come where we would have to go our separate ways."

"I can't bear the thought of living without you."

"And I can't bear the thought of not having you in my life. But what choice do we have? Your fertile years will end before you know it. You need time to find a man to have children with. The longer you wait, the harder it will get. Our two years together have enriched us beyond words. If we continue, I will flourish and you will wilt. We can't let that happen. You are too young to retire from life."

"But . . . but we are soulmates."

"Destiny has given us two years of engrossing fulfillment. That's more than most people get in their lifetimes."

"Adam, stop. I don't want to hear another word from you."

I said nothing. No words could sooth our pain. She dried her eyes with the back of her hands, then asked in a barely audible voice, "Should we split, will we see each other afterward?"

I shook my head. "No. You'll have to concentrate on your new life, on your husband and your children. You will have to think of our time together as a miraculous dream, a dream, you hear me, a dream," I yelled, then, froze. Self-contempt descended upon me. I felt despicable. I had been acting as if God Almighty had appointed me to shape Theodora's destiny. I had been as controlling as Tonio.

"Forgive me, Theodora," I cried. Forgive me for dictating how you should live. Do what you think is best. I will support you whatever you decide. I'll love you as much if you stay with me and if you decide to leave."

She embraced me, came close to my ear, and murmured, "I'll adopt a little boy and a little girl."

I am too old to raise a family, I wanted to say but kept my thought to myself.

EPILOGUE

On my first visit with Mr. Theroux, he asked that I come back to share with him the outcome of my quest. Believing that my quest has been completed, a sunny day in early September, I hitched a ride on a plump white cloud to Mr. Theroux' favorite resort at the foothills of Mt. Olympus. Moments after the mountain came into view, I left the cloud, arrived at the resort, and saw Mr. Theroux in the yard on a recliner, holding a book in his hand. He hadn't changed. He looked as fit as on my last visit.

"Well, look who's here," he cried. "I had been wondering about your French odyssey."

"I came to bring you up to date. And you, how have you been?"

"No complaints." He rose, embraced me warmly, and pointed at a chair. "Sit down. I'll order jasmine tea."

I smiled. "Ah, you remember my favorite drink."

"But of course. You look good. Life must have treated you well."

"It has indeed."

After placing the order, Mr. Theroux smiled, "So you prospered in France?"

"More than prospered. I realized my dreams. I made sculptured jewelry which I exhibited in a prestigious art gallery in Antibes, and I found my soulmate."

"Soulmate? Amazing. What's she like?"

"Theodora completed her Ph.D. in European Literature at the University of Nice a year ago, and got a job teaching."

"A brainy type, eh?"

"Among other things. But. . ."

"But what?"

"We split two years after living together".

"You don't split from your soulmate."

"You do, if children get in the way."

"Children at your age?"

I nodded. "She longed for motherhood. In restaurants at the sight of children tears would come to her eyes. I told her I was too old to raise a family. For weeks she pleaded for me to change my mind. I suggested she find another man. She couldn't do that, she responded. She was my soulmate. Then a month later, she informed me that she was adopting a little boy and a little girl. The day before their arrival, I moved out of her apartment."

"For good?"

"We continued seeing each other but the children oppressed me, and I kept away from her home. Theodora prospered. Motherhood suited her well. She exuded life energy even when displaying sadness at our separation."

"What a tragic scenario for soulmates."

"It was indeed but thankfully it didn't last. We reunited a few months later."

"How did you manage that?"

"Adventure travel had healed me in the past. Desperate for healing, I signed up with a touring company for a three-week visit to China and one week to Tibet."

"A wise decision," Mr. Theroux nodded. "Adventure travel has healed me as well on several occasions."

The waiter deposited the tea. I took a sip and continued. "In China I got inspired by the Terracotta Army, a panda sanctuary, the largest Buddha on earth, the Great Wall, Beijing with its awesome skyscrapers. and Shanghai graced with a mixture of modern and Baroque buildings. But the most remarkable occurrence of all was the treatment I received from the locals. Time and time again, they would ask me to pose with them for a photo. Why did they do that? Why they found me so appealing I never figured out."

"The Chinese venerate senior citizens, and you sport an impressive gray beard."

"Perhaps so. My journey fulfilled my expectations. All the pain related to Theodora disappeared."

"And then you went to Tibet?"

"Ever since reading Heinrich Harrer's *Seven Years in Tibet,* with its description of colorful religious ceremonies, chanting monks, people genuflecting on their way to religious shrines, men and women turning wheels with holy scripture inside I had been wanting to visit the country."

"Did it live up to your expectations?"

"Hardly. Lhasa, the capital, turned out to be as plain looking as any third-world city. The Potala Palace, the ancient residence of the Dalai Lamas, a handful of monasteries, and an occasional stupa awoke the glory of the old. On the whole, though, the city couldn't have been more ordinary."

"The Chinese conquerors destroyed the spiritual life but prolonged the physical one with hospitals, schools, and electricity in the remotest parts of the country," Mr. Theroux said.

"Yes, I know. Harrer returned after thirty years and was appalled by the sight of prostitutes, houses with metal roofs, and parlors playing loud music. Finding Lhasa uninspiring, I was relived to leave for the Base Camp. The road was atrocious. The potholes were so deep that we rode at a speed of ten, fifteen miles per hour. Upon our arrival, we obtained accommodations in an immense tent at an altitude of 17,000 feet."

"Did the thin air make you sick?"

"I was unsteady, fatigued, and disoriented. Mount Everest was hidden behind a cloud cover, so I stepped inside the tent to take a nap. Sometime later cries of, 'The clouds are gone. Mount Everest can be seen,' woke me up. I jumped, put my jacket on, ran outside, and saw an immense shoulder occupying the space between the earth and the sky. My body suddenly grew light, and I sat down on a bench trying to understand what was happening to me."

Leaning forward, Mr. Theroux asked, "What did you find out?"

"First that a mighty energy had seeped inside me. Second, that all consciousness of my body vanished. Third, that an invisible power enabled me to fly. I left my body on the bench and soared toward the mountain, higher and higher, until I reached the top. From there, I gazed in awe at waves of mountain peaks stretching into infinity. All sense of past, present, and future vanished. I felt as if at the center of the universe, united with the tallest mountain on earth, the sky, and the other celestial bodies. No thoughts of Theodora spoiled the magic. Then, a public announcement that dinner was being served broke the spell, and I found myself back on the bench. Thankfully, my sense of intense wellbeing remained. It continued even after my return to Biot, a week later."

"An impressive tale, Mr. Theroux said."

"The day after my arrival in Biot, I visited Theodora. Her two children trotting on their tiny legs came over and hugged me. We went to a park. The youngsters crawled over concrete obstacles with the agility of monkeys. With much pleasure I watched them perform acrobatics. The next day I distributed chocolate bars, sat on the floor, and joined them at their play. They started calling me 'Grandpa Adam.' The children I thought would lead me to an early grave filled me with merriment. I rose, joined Theodora on the sofa, and whispered into her ear, 'I'm ready for my comeback.'"

"She responded that before we settle down for good, we should take some time off to reflect on our feelings for each other."

"'You are having doubts about us?' I asked with a tightening in my stomach. 'After interminable hours of questioning each other, of struggling to transcend the obstacles getting in the way of our union, you still aren't sure?'"

"'We're planning a lasting journey. We must be certain that we are ready for it. Let's separate for two weeks. If at the end of that time our longings for each other are as strong as they are today, we'll know beyond doubt that we belong together to the end of our lives.'"

"It took only moments to see the merit of her suggestion, so I said, 'Ok, Theodora, let's plan a dinner at home Sunday, two weeks from today. Over spaghetti and wine, we'll share our feelings. I will come at six.'"

"'Adam, I can't tell you how happy I am that you agree with me. Goodbye my dear. Take care of yourself.'"

"We hugged and I left. I slept well that night. I woke up confident that if I lived according to the callings of my innermost nature, I would obtain all the answers I needed."

"The next two weeks, I alternated between reflecting about my feelings for Theodora and entertaining myself with visits to the coastal villages, Chagall, Picasso, and Leger museums, and the art scene at the Village of St. Paul-de-Vence. I did all that feeling as if Theodora were by my side."

"On second Sunday, at six, I rang the bell to her apartment. She led me to the living room sofa, filled two glasses with Cognac, and gazed at me wide-eyed."

"'After much soul-searching, I concluded that I need you as much as air,' I muttered."

"'What about the kids?'"

"'I need them as much.'"

"'Are you sure? Only a couple of months ago, you found them odious.'"

"'That was before they started calling me, 'Grandpa Adam,' before I saw them doing monkey acrobatics, before they warmed my heart with their innocence. I feel now as if they are mine. I want them in my life. You give me love. They give me mirth.'"

"Taking my hand into hers, Theodora uttered, 'Now I am complete. I have the kids and I have you. Come, I have made spaghetti and Zuppa Englese.'"

"'I love Zuppa Englese. It is my favorite Italian dessert.'"

"I opened a bottle of Chianti and we toasted to our future. The kids drank milk. I basked in warmth. I felt totally present. I felt at peace with myself and the world. Afterward we took the children to their bedroom, kissed them good night, and tucked them in. Passing the dining room, we glanced at the dishes we used on the table, shrugged, and continued to our bedroom. We held each other tight all night, allowing only our breaths to get in between us."

Mr. Theroux looked as if in deep thought. I smiled and said, "So you see, I realized my quest."

He rose, patted me on the back, and said, "You certainly did. You had a remarkable journey."